Paul J. Newell was born in Somerset, England, an unsettlingly long time ago. His first attempt at a novel was *The Turning*, which was considered almost unanimously as really not that bad. After running out of acquaintances to coerce into buying it, he decided it was time to write another. And, after a couple more years of procrastination, he immediately set the cognitive wheels in motion. *Altered States* was the product of that motion. His third novel, *Making a Mark*, was written almost exclusively on a train.

Claire,
    Hope you enjoy the
book.

Making a Mark

Paul J. Newell

Published by Appian Publishing

www.appianpublishing.com

First published in Great Britain by Appian Publishing 2017

Paul J. Newell asserts the moral right to
be identified as the author of this work

www.pauljnewell.com

1 3 5 7 9 0 8 6 4 2

ISBN 978-0-9552245-4-6 (paperback)
ISBN 978-0-9552245-5-3 (ebook)

For Mum

Acknowledgements

Specials thanks to Alan Newell (aka Dad), Sam Mills, Mark Garland, Lorna Mortimer, Reina Capus, Guy Slade and Ian Stoodley, without whose feedback and advice this book would only exist in a much poorer form.

Prologue

There was no natural light. Just the hazy glow of a city after dark.

But that was enough.

Enough to carry out his work. To create his final masterpiece.

The can of spray-paint resonated comfortingly in his hand as he shook it – an action more of reflex than necessity. He knew the sound would not betray him. Cities like this never fell silent. There was always a hum, a backing track to his clandestine endeavours, sufficient to shroud his every move.

With his free hand, he clung to a support on the outside of the bridge; his feet edging slowly along a narrow ledge. This was his office. The underworld office of an urban artist.

Precarious.

Solitary.

And exhilarating beyond compare.

The artist began to paint. Deftly. With natural sweeping movements. Like the master of an ancient martial art. And like those timeless disciplines, there was honour at stake in his works too. Not just from the mastery of the craft, but from the audacity of the canvas. Illicit, unreachable, perilous.

This would be his finest creation. It had to be. There

would be no more after this one.

No more art. No more days. Not even the coming sunrise.

Not for him.

He worked intensely, with the flair of a dancer but the precision of a machine. Until the last mark was made, and the work was complete.

When the end came, it was swift. To the observer, had there been any, it would have been over in a moment. But to the artist, as he fell, he was no longer bound by the rules of time. He felt a great relief – a release from all worldly pain. He sensed the Earth coming up to reclaim him, and he welcomed it. And then there was nothing. He was one with nature again.

For him, the event was the most significant of moments on his journey. The final moment. The end.

For most, it barely registered, on the day that followed. The merest flicker of firing neurons. A morsel of news that obscured the consciousness only long enough for it to be rapidly swiped from view to make way for the next.

For one unknowing individual, it was the beginning of a new chapter of their life.

One

Detective Inspector Harlyn Quaye arrived at the scene just before seven in the morning. Earlier than he'd like. He preferred to be at least partially acquainted with the new day before he started tiptoeing through body parts. But some dead people just aren't that considerate.

Despite the hour, traffic had already solidified to a parking lot in the vicinity, partly due to the burgeoning collection of blue-flashing emergency vehicles and partly due to the incident having closed a train line into the centre. The need to get commuters back on the move was paramount – so he'd been informed by his superiors. Whether this would influence his haste in assessing the scene was yet to be determined, but unlikely at best.

As a further contribution to the traffic chaos, Quaye haphazardly ditched his car half-way up onto the pavement by Parson Street train station, then got out and fetched his suit jacket from the back seat. The day was growing hot already. Over the last few weeks, the country had been experiencing one of those periods of weather that would once have seemed out of place before thirty-odd years of climate change. Now hurricanes and heatwaves were equally commonplace, and today it was the latter. In fact, already too warm for a suit jacket and tie, but detective inspectors were not yet permitted to adopt a smart-casual approach to workwear – not even on a Friday. There was a certain expectation to adhere to. The expectation that potential crime scenes were best surveyed by irritable detectives, Quaye assumed.

He approached Parson Street station. Although, identifying this particular stop on the line as an actual *station* was arguably overselling it. It was just two short platforms either side of two tracks. There was a set of steps leading down to each of the platforms and, on this occasion, at the top of each, a uniformed officer stood sentinel. Quaye badged one of them, who greeted him with a *good morning*.

The steps were steep and narrow, and each one seemed to slope forward in a disconcerting fashion. Quaye made his way down gingerly in his slick-soled shoes, reasonably determined not to add his name to the death toll at the station this morning.

A good few hundred yards along the line, some way beyond the end of the platform, he could see the site of the incident. To reach it he would have to make his way along the tracks. As he placed his foot on the rail, his mind cast back to his school days. He remembered how his class had been made to watch a video about railway safety that was so harrowing it would be classed as child abuse today. As with most moderate levels of so-called 'child abuse' that had since been banned, the approach served its purpose admirably, striking a lifelong fear of walking on train tracks into the souls of his classmates. In *his* case, not so much. No shivers of unease running down his spine; no nervous glances over his shoulder for oncoming locomotives. That's just the way he was.

Up ahead, the scene itself was cordoned off in standard

fashion. Though Quaye doubted a three-inch wide strip of blue-and-white tape was going to do much to protect anyone from the seven-fifteen to Bath Spa, should it not have gotten the memo about the track closure.

As he neared the cordon, a female officer approached to greet him. At least, he was obliged to assume she was an officer, based on the uniform she was wearing, even though she barely looked old enough to be on work-experience. He realised this assessment was in part just a reflection of how old he felt some mornings. Though, in truth, his own appearance was not as lacking in youth as it might be. He had to keep himself in shape for certain aspects of his life. Only a few specks of grey at his temples hinted at his admirable progress through his fourth decade.

'Morning, sir,' the officer said, thrusting out a hand. 'PC Katrina Wilcox.'

'Morning,' the detective responded absently, already surveying the scene. 'DI Quaye,' he added, though apparently no introduction was necessary. The constable had clearly been appraised of his attendance.

The area was littered with mounds of unpleasantness, concealed from the sensitive eyes of potential onlookers by blood-stained sheets. Fortunately, most of the gruesome remains were beneath the bridge, hidden from public view. Between them and beyond, both rails of the train track were slick with a red sheen.

'We've been expecting you,' Wilcox said, smiling. By 'we' she meant the British Transport Police. This was their territory, so the smile was reassuring. Quaye had been called in as the 'most available' senior detective in the area, just for oversight.

'What do we have here?' Quaye asked.

'The varied remains of a white male who seemingly fell from the bridge up there.' She pointed. 'And who was subsequently hit by a train.'

'When was this?'

'All we can be sure of is that the train came through here at six-fifteen. But on the assumption that the fall would have rendered the individual unconscious or dead, the body could have laid on the tracks for some time. The likelihood is that he was performing his handiwork in the small hours – any time after midnight I would say.'

The detective took a step back and looked up at the bridge above, adjusting his eyes to the bright sky behind. On the stonework were geometric and angular sweeps of blue, black and silver paint. He had the vague impression that the shapes formed letters, but not ones he could make out. The graffito looked fresh and unfinished.

'What does it say? Can you make it out?' Quaye asked.

Wilcox turned to get a proper look at the paintwork. After a moment she shrugged. 'No. It's a bit like any handwriting,' she reflected. 'If you knew what it said you could probably read it.'

Quaye acknowledged the observation and squinted at the markings some more, tilting his head one way, then the other. It didn't help.

'Do you think it's relevant?' Wilcox asked.

Quaye tried to gauge whether this was a polite way of her suggesting she thought it wasn't.

'Maybe,' he replied. 'Maybe not. But I don't like not

knowing things, all the same.' He flashed a quick smile at her then adjusted his stance, in line with his thought process.

The question was always the same in circumstances like these. Did he jump, did he fall, or was he pushed? Given the incomplete nature of his artwork, the first of these options seemed implausible. If Quaye knew one thing about the mind of a graffiti artist – and that was about all he did know – it was that the art was all about making a statement. If you knew it was going to be your last, you'd make sure it was finished.

'Can we be sure this was his handiwork?' he asked.

'He had a rucksack with a number of spray-cans in it. And one more was recovered from the track.'

The detective nodded. In all likelihood, this was a straightforward case of misadventure. But it was the coroner's place to make that call, with all pertinent evidence at his or her disposal.

'Identification?'

'Nothing on him.' She held up a clear plastic evidence bag. 'Except some cash and a Waitrose receipt for …' – she read it – '… a hummus and falafel flat-bread sandwich.'

Quaye raised an eyebrow. 'Hmm, the good-old Waitrose hummus and falafel flat-bread sandwich. The go-to pre-vandalism snack for all middle-class graffiti artists, so I hear.'

'Indeed,' agreed Wilcox, acknowledging his sarcasm. 'Bought with cash last night,' she added. 'So we might be able to source some CCTV. But in the meantime, we have nothing to ID him.'

The detective looked up at the bridge again.

'Nothing except his name daubed in six-foot high letters on the side of a bridge.'

Wilcox followed his gaze. 'Unfortunately, the whole point of graffiti, of this kind at least, is anonymity. His peers might recognise the work, but the authorities are less well placed.'

The detective accepted the statement contemplatively. 'Rather inconsiderate of them not to jot their LinkedIn details alongside. Could be missing some commissions.'

'It's almost like they're not business minded,' Wilcox concurred playfully.

Quaye returned his focus to the sheet-covered remains. 'Okay, well I don't know which pile his fingers are in, but get what you can of his prints. And dust all the spray-cans too. Wouldn't be surprised if we have him or one of his cohorts on file.'

Wilcox made a note in her book.

It was time for Quaye to take a closer look at what was left of the victim. Wilcox knew her way around the scene by then and lifted each sheet in turn. It didn't make for pleasant viewing, but Quaye had seen worse. He knelt down to inspect a left arm.

'TAG Heuer,' he announced indicating a smashed watch on the victim's wrist. 'Expensive.'

'Or fake,' pointed out Wilcox.

Quaye pulled himself up straight. 'But the rest of his clothes. Mostly designer brands too. Ralph Lauren polo shirt, Hugo Boss jeans.'

'What are you thinking?' Wilcox asked.

'Dunno.' Quaye shrugged. 'Just not what I was

expecting, I guess. But, then, clearly, I didn't know what to expect.'

'The dangers of stereotyping,' Wilcox pointed out.

'Guilty as charged,' Quaye admitted.

The detective turned back to face the platforms, to survey the wider scene. To his left, running down one side of the tracks was the high red-bricked wall of an industrial unit. On the other was a high viciously-spiked fence. Behind the fence was overgrown wasteland initially, but a bit further along the line was a row of terraced houses, whose gardens backed up to the fence. Due to the curve of the track, the houses were at a slight angle to the bridge making it unlikely anyone would have seen much from a window, but someone at the end of the garden might have.

Just as the detective's eyes landed on the gardens, he was briefly dazzled by a flash of light, as if the sun had been caught by a small mirror. But then it was gone. He peered more closely, but he could see nothing.

'Do a door-to-door,' Quaye requested of Wilcox. 'See if anyone saw anything. And gather what footage you can from any cameras in the area.'

'Sir,' she confirmed and turned away to instruct other officers.

Standing alone, the detective took a moment to absorb the scene. He had a sense that something wasn't quite as it seemed. But it was just a feeling that tickled at the edges of his mind; nothing he could get a grip on. Nothing he could justify an exhaustive investigation on if the evidence didn't allow. He snapped himself out of his reverie and pulled his phone out to take a few pictures, in particular of the graffito above. This was a subculture at the heart of this city, but not one he'd had cause to brush up against.

Now it was time.

Two

Lisa was late getting ready for school, which wasn't entirely unusual. It was not that she was a particularly girly girl. She didn't take an inordinate amount of time to get ready. She just found it hard to get out of bed some mornings. Burning the candle at both ends her dad might say, if he knew about both ends. But he only knew about one of them, and that was for the best.

She brushed the last of the knots out of her long hair – pale like her skin. She was used to it being fair again, now that her Goth phase had long since passed. The black had been washed away, cosmetically at least. Just as the dark ivy leaves around the doorframe had been replaced by colourful floral stencils. All making her out to be the normal well-adjusted schoolgirl she was expected to be. Despite … everything.

Lisa got down to the kitchen just too late to hear the story on the news. Her dad turned off the radio on her arrival. He was making them both sandwiches for lunch. To the best of her knowledge, Lisa's dad had had cheese-and-pickle sandwiches every working day for at least the seventeen years she'd been alive. It was a little joke she'd shared with her mum when she was still around.

Lisa sat down at the breakfast table and poured herself a bowl of Cheerios. Then stared at them blankly. A few moments later her dad sat down opposite.

'You planning on eating them or drowning them?' her dad enquired, nodding at the bowl.

She smirked wryly at him to acknowledge the sarcasm.

It wasn't that she was uncommunicative, as was the criticism often levelled at her peer group. Not anymore anyway. It was just that sometimes her mind operated in a different realm, and opted to stay there until something invited it back to the real world.

She looked down at her bowl. Then carefully lowered the underside of her spoon into the milk, until it spilled over the rim. This was a ritual of hers. *One* of them. She had to do this three times without a rogue 'O' breaching the defences. Usually, this was not a problem – she'd grown very adept. But today was different. On the third attempt, a honey-nut Cheerio came spinning into the spoon like a rubber ring at a water park. She paused, a sense of unease flooding through her veins.

At that exact moment, her phone buzzed beside her on the table.

She looked at her dad with wide eyes.

He looked back.

'No,' he said firmly. 'You know the rules. No screens at the table.'

'But this is a *bad* sign,' she said emphasising the 'bad' and raising her spoon slowly into view.

Her dad smiled and shook his head in amusement.

'Don't say it!' Lisa insisted.

Her dad refrained. He liked to refer to these such 'signs' of hers as *Cheeriomens*. Comedic gems like this are what dads are good for, it seemed.

'I'm serious,' protested Lisa.

'Then eat your breakfast quicker.'

She did. She inhaled the bowl of cereal and all its portents of doom with great haste, before launching from the table with her phone in hand. Unlocking the screen she saw that someone had sent her a private message on her blog. It was a guy called Luke. He'd commented on her blog before, a number of times, but they'd never communicated directly.

She opened the message. It just said, 'It's Gioco', followed by a link. She tapped on the link. It took her to a Breaking News article on the local news website. The headline read:

Graffiti Artist Dies in Bridge Fall.

She stood motionless, blood draining from her face until it was as pale as her shirt.

It couldn't be, she thought. It just couldn't.

Her dad noticed her frozen form.

'You okay?' he asked.

Her head snapped around at the sound.

'Err … yes,' she responded hesitantly. 'I'm fine.' She punched a response into her phone and hit send, then grabbed her bag from the back of the chair.

'Gotta go.'

'Don't forget your lunch,' her dad called after her.

Lisa turned and grabbed it from him. 'Thanks.'

She stuffed the lunchbox into her bag, then bundled herself into the hallway and out of the front door. After a few steps she cursed herself and turned back, shaking her head. Back inside she quickly checked the alignment of all the shoes in the hallway. Another of her vital rituals. She figured it might be especially important today; the fates needed all the guidance she could offer.

She walked at pace, and read the news report once again as she did so. It didn't have much detail – not even a specific location. But if Luke had known it was Gioco, he must know where – he must have seen it. Not the incident, the artwork. She'd asked him in her message for the location. In the meantime, she didn't know where she was heading – other than not to school. Not yet. She just needed to get out of sight of the house and off the route of the school run, while she waited for a reply.

This was bigger news than most people realised.

Three

Lisa arranged to meet Luke at the entrance to Parson Street station. Briefly, she'd questioned the wisdom of doing this, but he'd said he knew how to get a closer look. And she *wanted* a closer look.

When Lisa rounded the corner, she saw two cops at the entrance to the platform. She walked right past. Not that she was guilty of anything, other than skipping double Politics, but the mere presence of the uniforms made her feel like a serial killer regardless. As she passed, she naturally crowbarred an extra dose of *normal* into her stride, casually throwing a sideways glance down the track. She caught sight of a police cordon and a handful of busy folk within it – nothing else.

Safely out of sight around the next corner she texted Luke with her new coordinates. Five minutes later he arrived to find her super-casually leaning against a wall, phone in hand. He smiled at her.

'Hi,' Luke said with an upward nod of the head.

'Hi,' Lisa responded, feeling slightly awkward. They were of sufficient youth and opposing gender that shaking hands did not feel appropriate. Hugging, high-fiving, fist-bumping and nose-rubbing all seemed equally unfitting, leaving them with no satisfactory mode of physical contact to consummate their first meeting. But it was soon apparent that Luke was not someone in whose presence one could feel awkward for long.

'Police are still hanging round. What do we do now?' Lisa posed.

'Don't worry. This way.'

Luke led Lisa further along the street she'd been waiting on. There were houses on both sides. Those on the right would back onto the train track. Neighbourhoods in such proximity to railways are often less than salubrious, and this one was more than happy to conform. Most of the small yards in front of the properties lacked a certain level of basic care. They wouldn't be in contention for a Good Garden Award this year, for sure, and all they needed for that was a bedraggled pot plant and the absence of a burnt-out motorbike. Instead, these 'gardens' offered a varied display of tall withered grass growing up through mildewed paving slabs, busted recycling bins with the soggy rejects of refuse collectors, the rusting remains of long-abandoned bicycles and the general decaying detritus of unsavoury lives.

At least, that was how Lisa saw it. It made her feel unclean just passing by. But something else. It made her feel strangely melancholy too. Saddened that this represented the endpoint of humanity's physical and cultural evolution; that our success as a species had rendered laziness and uncleanliness as viable life choices. Whereas once, centuries or even decades ago, such a strategy would have led promptly to death.

'This one,' said Luke.

The house they stood outside was boarded up – or rather, locked down. Every window and door had a galvanised metal sheet riveted to its frame.

'Pretty sure no-one's in,' Luke added dryly. 'It's been this way for like a year. We just need to get round the back.'

Luke made his way down the side of the house, picking his way past piles of wood, stacks of breeze blocks and what looked like half a washing machine. Lisa followed in his path. Beyond the obstacles was a wooden gate. Luke rattled it. It didn't budge. Not that it was likely to. There was a hefty bolt on the outside.

'We'll have to go over,' Luke concluded.

'Hey, I'm pretty nimble, but…' Lisa pointed to the skirt she was wearing.

'Okay,' Luke accepted. 'Let me see how easy it is to get over. I can just take some pictures and come back.'

He looked around. First, he eyed up the washing machine as an ideal step up, but a quick tug revealed it to be pretty much immobile, wedged as it was into such a tight spot. Attempting to budge it would take too much time and attract too much attention. Instead, he dragged over a breeze block, sending a hundred woodlice that called it home scurrying for alternate cover. Once in place he upended it and stepped up.

'Wait,' said Lisa reaching out a hand to hold back his rising arm. 'Check the other side of the gate for razor wire.'

Luke looked back. 'You a *pro* cat burglar are you?' he asked, to which Lisa responded with only an enigmatic smile.

Luke proceeded with caution, resting his fingers on top of the fence to balance himself as he stepped up, then moving them gingerly over the edge, feeling the other side.

'S'okay,' he concluded. He brought his foot up onto the

bolted latch which gave him just enough purchase to pull himself up and swing his other leg over. Then he jumped down the other side.

As he surveyed the land in front of him, he did not expect to hear a clatter and a thud behind him. He turned just in time to see Lisa tugging her skirt back into position. He raised his eyebrows at her.

'Didn't think you were coming over.'

Lisa shrugged. 'Told you I was nimble.'

The crumbling concrete path led to a waist-high jungle of grass, weeds and stinging nettles, concealing any number of obstacles. They ventured into it cautiously, picking their way through. Past an old tyre, then an entire wheel and part of an axle, then the framework of a pram, and a steel oil drum that had been used as a cauldron. Finally, they found themselves at a wire mesh fence at the end of the garden, a few feet beyond which was a more industrial fence topped with lethal-looking spikes. The barriers obscured their view of the scene. Lisa adjusted her position, trying to get a clear sight of the image that adorned the bridge; a series of angular forms outlined in paint. Lisa studied it intently, narrowing her eyes against the brightness. After a moment she spoke with authority.

'It's not Gioco,' she said.

'What?'

'I mean, that's what it says – or is trying to – but Gioco didn't paint it.'

'How do you know?'

Lisa shook her head. 'It's just not good enough. Amateurish.' She turned to Luke, with a contemplative furrow of the brow. 'It's weird,' she declared.

'No shit,' Luke confirmed.

'I'm going to get a photo.'

Lisa looked around her feet and enlisted an old bucket into service, upturning it and stepping onto it. It buckled a little due to a split up its side, but held. The extra height was enough for her to reach up with her phone and get a clear shot of the bridge. She took a couple of pictures and then angled it to the scene beneath. There were half a dozen police officers. The one nearest to them was a man in a suit. Just as Lisa pressed the shutter button, the man turned around and seemingly looked right at her.

'Shit,' she exclaimed, performing a half-controlled dismount off the bucket and ducking down into the long grass.

'What?' asked Luke, following her lead without knowing why.

'Seemed like that cop looked right at me. Just made me jump.'

'Maybe it's time to make a move.'

Lisa agreed. They made their way back over to the gate, using the bucket this time for a leg up, then headed down the street. When they were comfortably far enough away, they slowed their pace.

'There must be a connection, don't you think?' Lisa postulated.

'Connection?'

Her favourite TV detective always insisted that there was no such thing as a coincidence. Lisa knew that the key was in seeing this incident not as a single event but as two events – and that neither was typical. Taken by itself, the art would be puzzling. Why would anyone go to so much trouble to paint someone else's name on a bridge? Similarly, the death by itself was unusual. Despite the risks artists take, it hardly ever happens.

'So, it makes me think there's a link,' Lisa concluded.

Luke shrugged non-committedly. He had a bigger question. 'So who *is* Gioco?'

Lisa's head snapped round to face Luke's.

'How should I know?'

'Come on, you know these guys.'

'I know *some*. But there are street artists and street artists. The ones I know are basically professionals. They get commissioned to do the fancy stuff. The shop-front shutters, the building site hoardings, people's living rooms. You can look them up online. But people like Gioco are different. They're subversive. They stick two fingers up at the establishment. That's their allure.'

'Well, whoever it is, I guess the cops don't realise the significance of finding out.'

No, thought Lisa, they really don't.

Four

'Do you recognise this graffiti?' Detective Quaye held up his phone in landscape orientation to the woman behind the counter. She looked at it suspiciously. Then she looked back at the detective suspiciously. It was a look she had nailed.

'No,' she said bluntly.

Quaye realised he was brushing up against the anti-establishment brick-wall, which was all the more solid when it was spray-painted with graffiti.

'I'm not looking to arrest the guy,' he pointed out politely but firmly. 'I'm trying to identify what's left of him on the tracks down at Parson Street station.'

Her eyes flickered a bit at this information.

'Well, the answer's still no, I'm afraid.' Her voice was softer this time.

Quaye accepted her response with a nod. He glanced around the premises – a street art gallery and supply shop. He knew of this place well by reputation but had never been inside. He figured the owner would be pretty clued up on the movers and can-shakers of the graffiti scene, so he'd decided to stop by on his way back to the office.

'Are you the owner of this gallery?' Quaye asked.

'Yes.'

'And can I take your name, Miss—'

'Alice.' She smirked mischievously.

Quaye smiled in acknowledgement. 'Do you mind if I take a look around, Miss Alice?'

'That's kind of the point,' she quipped.

He smiled again and then started to browse.

Hanging on the walls were large canvases offering an array of striking images. Some dark. Some vibrant. Some surreal. Some with an almost tangible realism. Some decidedly mediocre – even ugly – according to Quaye's tastes. Yet, some, surprisingly very good, he had to admit – though only to himself. He peered more closely at one; allowed himself to get lost in it.

After a while he grew self-conscious; sensed a pair of eyes observing his thoughts. He turned back to meet their owner.

'I didn't realise graffiti came on canvas,' he said. 'And for…' – he peered at the label underneath one of them – '…nine hundred pounds, no less.'

'Depends on your definition of graffiti,' came the response. 'Spray paint is just a medium. No reason why it can't be used on any surface.'

'I guess.' He took a step back toward the counter. 'Same goes for the emerging watercolour-on-brick-wall movement, I suppose,' he jested, trying to lift the tension.

Alice offered a sardonic smile in return. She sported a funky style; studded denim, loose chains, uneven haircut with blue highlights running through it. She stood casually at a counter that was a curved metallic affair – as if it had been panel-beaten out of an old Winnebago. Behind her, she was flanked by a wall of spray-cans, end-on in pigeon holes. Tools of the trade for a street artist. Weapon of choice in the fight against the establishment.

'It's a tightknit world though isn't it?' queried Quaye.

'It is,' she agreed.

'And Bristol is a small city. People in the scene would be familiar with the work of most artists?'

'On the street maybe. I'm not on the street. I'm in here.' She hardened again. 'Listen, Detective, we are a *legal* gallery dealing in *legal* artworks. As I'm sure you can appreciate, I am not at liberty to divulge the details of any of my artists; and I genuinely do not recognise the work in the photo. So I'm afraid I cannot really help.'

He nodded slowly, then reached into his wallet for a business card. 'Well, if any information comes to mind.' He placed the card on the counter, expecting it to make a short trip to the bin.

As he turned away, another question came to mind.

'What brand of jeans do graffiti artists wear?' he asked.

The question was met, unsurprisingly, by a look of complete bewilderment.

He shook his head. 'Sorry, ridiculous question.'

On his way out, Quaye paused briefly over the painting that had caught his eye before, then headed for the exit. A bell tinkled above the door to mark his departure.

'Widdles would have known,' came a voice from behind him. 'About the artist, that is, not the jeans.'

Quaye turned back, standing in the doorway. 'Come again?'

'PC Widdecombe. One of your lot. From a while back. An expert in the field.' Alice gave a thin smile. 'Ask around.'

Quaye indicated that he would by way of a thoughtful nod, and left.

As Quaye made his way back up North Street to his car, he began to pay more attention to the surfaces around him. And above him. There were marks everywhere. Not to the point of being a conscious eyesore. But on every building or so that he passed, there would be a name in pen or paint scrawled somewhere. Growing more elaborate the higher his gaze rose. On the gable end of some buildings that stood one floor taller than their neighbour, there was often quite a complex piece. Stylised interlocking and overlapping letters, multiple colours, highlights and shadows. He didn't know what they meant, or even what they said sometimes, but he saw them.

Now he saw them.

Five

Raymond made his way down Gloucester Road. Day three of his mission to visit every art gallery in the city. He knew there were over fifty *actual* galleries. Then there was the almost endless continuum of cafes, bars and restaurants adorning their walls with local artists' work. An impossible task maybe, visiting them all, but how else to identify an unknown artist in a city of this size? Traditionally, of course, an art gallery would be anathema to the kind of artist he was searching for – representing the very concept they stood against. But traditions change. Capitalism wins out. Even the anarchist has to fund his anarchy – however acute the irony. Bleeding the system to break the system – maybe that's the justification they would use.

On occasion, Raymond knew from the shopfronts alone that the proprietor was unlikely to be of any assistance. Windows filled with what some might call fine art: oil portraits of pets and watercolour seascapes. These were unlikely to sit alongside works from the artist he sought.

The gallery he stood before now was just such an example. In fact, one of the worst kind. One that seemed to specialise in realism. Raymond was not a fan of the abstract, but he saw even less point in realism. Didn't see its place in art. Art was about interpretation, not facsimile. But then, in truth, he wasn't really a fan of art, so what did he know?

He knew one thing only. He had to find this artist.

He stepped through the door; an electronic tone sounded toward the back of the shop. He knew there was no point in analysing the exhibits hanging on the walls. He would never recognise a hint of the style he was searching for in works of such different form. He headed straight for the lady behind the desk, who stood to greet him. She was elegantly presented in a short white dress.

Raymond already had the sketchbook in his hand. He opened it.

'I'm looking for this artist,' he said flatly.

The lady studied him, gave him a suspicious look.

'This is graffiti,' she said.

'I know.'

'We don't deal in graffiti.'

'Not all graffiti artists are exclusive.'

She gave a haughty snort. 'Well, I'm afraid, I am not acquainted with any.'

Raymond knew she wouldn't be at liberty to say any different, regardless of who she knew. But he also knew that in this case she wasn't lying. He had a sense for these things.

'Of course,' he said dispassionately and left the gallery.

His legs were tired, his feet were sore. He didn't have the right shoes for this task. But he kept on walking anyway, driven by an obsession unlike any he'd harboured before in his life.

With maybe the one exception.

A long time ago.

But he didn't allow himself to dwell on that. That was the past. He trudged on to the next gallery. It was called Wallz. It looked more promising.

The leather clad man behind the metal counter was more interested in the book this time, as Raymond turned the pages one by one. He stopped when he got to the name Gioco, crafted in overlapping block lettering.

'I've seen the name about,' the man said, but in a tone from which Raymond knew what was coming next. 'Don't know who it is.' The man shuffled his feet. 'Whoever it is, though, keeps a low profile. None of our artists write under that name. At least, as far as I'm aware. But, you never know do you?'

'You never know,' agreed Raymond solemnly.

'I'll ask around for you.'

Raymond nodded and left.

Walking down the street, he considered his predicament. He had to admit his approach wasn't working.

He needed another strategy.

Six

For the rest of the day, Quaye's mind had barely idled on the graffiti incident of the morning. That was how it was with his job; had its own special brand of normality. Dismembered body before breakfast and on with the day. If he'd had to make a bet, it would have been that his involvement in the incident would be no more. That the occurrence would be put to bed as the misadventures of a local scally; a sad but inevitable product of the urban grind.

That would've been Quaye's bet.

He'd have lost.

There was a half-knock at his open door.

'Called by on the off-chance you'd be here,' said PC Wilcox as she entered his office. 'The fingerprint analysis is in.'

'And what's the verdict?'

'Prints matching the victim were found on all recovered cans, unsurprisingly. But no matches on file, I'm afraid.'

Quaye shrugged, acceptingly.

Wilcox continued. 'A *second* set of unidentified prints were found on the one can we found on the track, but no other prints on any of the cans found in his bag.'

'None? Not even partials?'

'No.'

'That's kind of odd. *Somebody* must have handled the

cans before the victim.'

She shrugged. 'Could have been bought as a pack, cellophane-wrapped right off the production line.'

'I guess.'

'Oh, and one other little thing,' she announced.

'Yes?'

She paused for effect. 'It's all on camera.'

'What?' Quaye pulled himself up straight.

'Yeah, the industrial unit down the track has a camera. The bridge is just in its periphery.'

'Tease,' Quaye accused.

Wilcox smiled in acknowledgement and took a step into the room. 'Clips are on the network drive,' she said, coming to his side of the desk and taking control of his computer. She located the security footage clips and opened the first one. As it played, she talked him through what they were watching, changing the playback speed as necessary. The footage was distant and dark, but clear enough.

'Here he is, just after two a.m.,' Wilcox said. 'Climbing over the wall at the far end. Then edging along. Takes him a moment to get into position.' She steps the playback up to four-speed. 'Here he's painting the outline.' They watched the shadowy artist for a moment in fast-forward before Wilcox returned the playback to normal speed. 'Now, here, he switches colour. He looks to be wearing his rucksack on his front. Zips are a pain with one hand, maybe he has to let go, loses his footing a little. Anyway, he starts filling in with the new colour for a little while.' They watched in silence. 'Then … there we go. Bam. Just falls backwards.'

Quaye peered at the screen. It was hard to see the track

where the artist fell. But there seemed to be no movement thereafter.

Wilcox stood up straight, as if in conclusion. 'With a better idea of timings, we were able to look through CCTV in the area. There aren't many cameras around there, but we spotted him en route in three places. Always alone. The clips are in the same folder.'

'Good work,' Quaye acknowledged.

'So, I guess that's it. Hand it over to the coroner.'

He looked up at her, less than convinced. 'Something's not quite right.'

'What are you thinking?'

He shrugged. 'Not quite sure.'

He looked at the other clips. Then the one of the fall again. This time all the way through at normal speed. Then again. Wilcox stood silently beside him throughout. After the second time through all of them, he leant back in his chair, pondering what he'd seen. There was a tingling at the edge of his mind, but he couldn't get a handle on it. He knew there was no point trying to force it. If there was something, it would come in good time.

He made a dismissive hand wave and swung forward in his chair. 'Maybe you're right. Pretty much time to put it to bed. Apart from, of course, identifying the man.'

'That'll come soon enough,' Wilcox predicted. 'Haven't you seen the news?'

He hadn't. He pulled up a browser and hit a bookmark to the Bristol Post website. The incident was still the main story, but its gist had transitioned over the course of the day from tragedy to mystery. The news hounds were well aware of the public's tendency to be quickly jaded by straight-forward misfortune and knew that spicing it up with a pinch of intrigue would likely garner a few more hits. The typically pithy and borderline literate headline read: *Death Plunge Artist Identity Unknown.* It was followed by the statement: *Police are still trying to uncover the mystery identity of the graffiti artist who fell to his death early this morning.*

'I like the way they managed to throw in an element of police incompetency,' Quaye pointed out with dour irony. 'And now they have a photo of the artwork. Great.'

'Is that a problem?'

'Not per se. Other than we'll get bombarded with theories from amateur sleuths availing us of their theories over the enigmatic artist. Whereas without it, we'd just be getting his actual family calling in soon enough, when he doesn't turn up for Sunday lunch or whatever. That's the media for you. Making something out of nothing.'

'A shocking accusation,' Wilcox commented sarcastically.

Quaye rolled his eyes in resigned agreement. 'Well, until we have the answers, can't deny people the right to speculate.' He shut down his machine. 'Let's call it a day.'

As they walked out together, Quaye returned to another curiosity regarding the case. 'Who goes out without a wallet or a phone?'

Wilcox shook her head. 'Dunno,' she admitted. 'A tourist in Rio?'

'Ha, good answer.'

As they reached the car park, Wilcox invited Quaye to

join her and her colleagues. 'A few of us are heading out for a drink,' she said.

'Nah,' he said. 'Friday night. Date night.' He grinned.

It was apparent Wilcox did not know what to make of this, and Quaye was happy to leave it that way.

Quaye found himself thinking about the case later that evening, as he looked out over the city. His top floor apartment opened onto a roof terrace, of sorts. It wasn't one of those modern builds, with a designed-in 'rooftop experience'. His had more character. The building was well over a hundred years old, and it was as if this space had happened by accident, nestled as it was between jostling roof structures. He had enough space for a chair, a small table and a number of potted plants. The plants were not his idea, of course, but if he was going to have them then his rules were clear: no space could be taken up by anything he couldn't ultimately end up eating. Tomatoes seemed to grow particularly well up here, as did the French beans climbing up a trellis on the wall. He also had a blueberry bush. It had been small when it was given to him five years earlier, though still a fair weight in its ceramic pot to haul up three flights of stairs. Now it was so large it would never fit through the narrow spaces required to be returned to ground level. This would be its final resting place.

As he watched clouds gathering on the horizon, he thought idly about graffiti, though he wasn't entirely sure why. And as if his senses had been heightened to colour, when he brought his gaze to a nearer focal point, he spotted a patch of red nestling among the green leaves of his tomato plant. A ripened fruit he'd missed earlier, but which he could see clearly now from his new vantage point. That's how a lot of things worked, he'd learned.

He plucked the rogue fruit from its vine and placed it in a tub with the others of the day's crop. While still on his knees, his ears pricked to a sound, from over his left shoulder. Like the unlocking of a door. He made his way over to the edge of his terrace. Then, without hesitation, he scaled the slanting roof between his apartment and the adjacent, and jumped down the other side.

Mrs Granby was already in place, in one of a pair of low wicker chairs; between them a small table with a square tiled grid as its surface.

'Evening,' she said.

'Evening Silvia.' He sat down, the soft cushion on the chair welcoming him. 'Here,' he said handing over his tub of tomatoes and beans. 'Gonna be a good season,' he proclaimed.

'Very good,' she said with a wrinkled smile.

Soon enough the produce would be returned to him in the form of chutney, piccalilli or maybe soup – once combined with the onions and herbs from the chef's side of the roof. She had more space than him, but he didn't begrudge her that. She'd earned it.

What Quaye had come to understand very clearly since meeting Silvia Granby was that people today just didn't realise how tough it had been such a relatively short time ago; just basic day-to-day living. What people might class as an elementary human right now, was a luxury for our grandparents; or in some cases was not even comprehensible. From cold running water to hot running porn, in the space of two generations.

Progress.

Silvia was Quaye's touchstone. She helped him maintain perspective. That was important as a detective.

'Your turn to be black,' she announced.

Quaye plucked a black pebble from his tub and placed it on the board-cum-table.

He told her about his day as they played, and they glanced at the rooftops around them for signs of street artists.

'Superhero complex,' Silvia grumbled with more than a hint of disdain. 'Playing at being some comic-book crusader. Creeping about at night, with their secret names and logos. Acting like the whole establishment is against them; like they're fighting for the downtrodden underclasses. Pah.'

Silvia clearly had little time for graffiti artists.

And, as ever, she made a good argument.

But the word *superhero* put a thought into Quaye's mind. A thought about alternate identities. Maybe in the case of this individual, graffiti didn't *define* the man, but ran counter to him. An alter ego. Hence why he carried no identifying items on him; when he assumed the role of subversive street artist, he left his other identity behind.

So the question was, why did he assume this role?

Seven

It was Monday morning when Quaye got the call from Wilcox.

'Looks like we've got an ID for our artist,' Wilcox said. 'A friend of his contacted us when he didn't show for work.'

'What do we know about him?'

'Tobias Milner, thirty-four, local, works in finance.'

Quaye was silent for a moment. Before Friday, he'd had a pretty clear image of what he thought a graffiti artist was like. This man had not deigned to conform to it from the beginning, and was stubbornly continuing not to do so. The man had about fifteen years too many in age, and *one* too many careers in finance.

'Not what I was expecting. Again.'

'No.' Wilcox continued. 'He lived alone, but his parents are nearby. Officers are on their way round now to do the death notice.'

'Okay.' Quaye was glad this task didn't fall to him on this occasion. 'I'd like to speak to the friend who called it in.'

'Really? Do you think there's a need?'

'Just covering bases,' he added. 'Where did they work?'

'Trinoviant Finance.'

Quaye had heard of the company. Trinoviant. It sounded like they'd come up with the name by throwing a bunch of magnetic letters at a fridge.

'Can you send me the details?' Quaye requested.

'Will do,' Wilcox confirmed and signed off.

Quaye arranged to meet Milner's friend at a harbourside café that afternoon. Quaye arrived first and selected a seat outside. It was busy with passers-by, but the tables were sparsely populated enough now the lunchtime rush was over to allow some privacy.

A man approached shortly after and Quaye stood to meet him.

'Arrash Rahman?' Quaye queried.

'Yes,' the man replied, vacantly.

'Thanks for seeing me at such short notice. I know it's a difficult time.'

'No problem.'

The man pulled up a chair opposite Quaye. His movements were laboured and awkward, as if they had been outsourced to lower brain functions. Quaye recognised the look. He'd been there himself. A man dealing with death. A mind ill-equipped to digest the concept of existence transitioning to non-existence so suddenly and irrevocably. The realisation that a void had opened up in the world that would never be filled.

A waiter arrived and took orders for coffee. Then Quaye got down to business.

'Can you describe your relationship with Tobias Milner?' he asked.

Rahman shuffled a little, struggling to find comfort in his seat. 'Friends. We worked at the same place. Trinoviant.' He gestured toward the building where they worked, a little way down the harbourside. 'We didn't work together, as such. I'm in IT. And he's a … I don't know … does something to do with pensions.'

'And when were you first suspicious of Tobias's whereabouts?'

'Well, he didn't turn up for drinks, Friday after work. It's a regular thing, so I texted him to ask if he was coming. I didn't get a reply, but I didn't think much of it. He'd recently started seeing a new girlfriend, so I figured he had other priorities.' He smiled weakly. 'But then, when he didn't come into work today, and I learned that he hadn't done on Friday either, I thought it was a bit odd.'

There was silence for a moment whilst Quaye made notes in a small black book, before asking another question.

'Did you know he was a graffiti artist?'

Rahman looked away for a moment, gazing over the water, as if searching for something. As he did so, a waiter arrived with two coffees and placed them on the table gingerly. Rahman remained silent until the clattering of crockery had ceased. Then he spoke up.

'He wasn't a graffiti artist,' he snorted as if it was a ridiculous notion. 'He didn't come from that side of the tracks, if you know what I mean.' He leaned in to share the statement, as if it were sensitive information.

'I know what you mean,' Quaye reassured. 'But he was, on the night that he fell, painting graffiti on a bridge. You are aware of that?'

Rahman nodded with staring eyes. Then rubbed his face in his hands, frustration beginning to bubble through. 'I'm sorry,' he said with a cracking voice.

'That's okay,' reassured Quaye. 'Take your time.'

After a moment he readjusted himself to a more upright position, regaining a level of composure.

'It was the girl,' he announced flatly as he toyed with the saucer beneath his beverage. 'The one I mentioned.'

'His new girlfriend, you mean? What about her?'

'She was into *that* scene.' He referred to it with a note of disdain. 'He must have done it for *her*.' Then he looked at Quaye square in the eye. 'She drove him crazy, to be honest. You know, like some women can. Not necessarily in a bad way, but he was pretty besotted. I'd not seen him this way before. He was normally pretty casual with girls. Bit of a player, you know? This was different.'

'What was this girl's name?'

'Cynthia – that's all I know. Some foreign chick. Eastern European, I think. Guess that was part of the fascination for a straight-laced banker. A touch of the exotic.'

'Did you meet her?'

'Oh yes, I was there when they met. Remember it well.'

'When was that?'

'Couple of months back. Las Iguanas, just round the corner. We were there for happy hour, Friday after work, as we always were. Sitting outside. Her and a friend came and sat at the table next to us. There was some banter, yada yada. Toby worked his magic. Or rather he didn't.' There was the trace of a smile at the memory.

'He didn't?'

'Well, Toby usually went for the young blonde bimbo types, where his *magic* basically emanated from his wallet. He was no Brad Pitt shall we say, but these girls generally fawned over him because he had a job and a positive bank balance and a BMW. He liked the attention. But this Cynthia girl was different. She was smart, witty and attractive. And she wasn't having any of his big talk. He'd met his match with that one.'

'But obviously, he won her over.'

'Yeah, somehow I guess. Gotta hand it to him for his perseverance. The knock backs just made him more determined.'

Quaye paused for a moment to catch up with his notes.

'So, how does the graffiti thing come into this?'

'Well, I never saw her again. But I got the full story, that's for certain. It was pretty much all I heard about. Like I say, Toby got a bit infatuated. Got pretty wound up at times too. And he always came to me to chew it over.'

'What sort of things did you chew over?'

Rahman took a moment to re-group. 'The thing is, this was a super-hot girl and quite a bit younger than Toby. To be fair, probably a bit out of his league. And her previous long-term ex was some really big graffiti artist. Some real grungy cool dude I guess. Maybe she was curious for a bit of normality with Toby. Fancied a convertible over a skateboard, I don't know. But anyway, she was really into the whole art scene as you might imagine. The whole *this guy's great* and *that guy's great.* And it got to Toby, big time. He'd always been judged by his status in *his* world. His grade at work, his money, what-have-you. Suddenly, that wasn't even part of the equation. It was all about the art. It was all about writing your name on a wall. And he just didn't get it. Just couldn't compete.'

'So, you think that's why he did it?'

Rahman shrugged one shoulder in response.

'Did he say anything about it?' Quaye added.

'No.' Rahman answered firmly. 'I didn't think he was even entertaining the idea. If I did, I would have told him he was being a prick. But, people have done crazier things for love right?' He shrugged. 'Now that I know what's happened, I can totally believe he did.' His eyes drifted for a moment, as if it had triggered a thought.

'What is it?' enquired Quaye.

'Just remembered a story he'd told me. Something Cynthia told him about her ex.'

'What was that?'

'That this guy who ultimately became quite a big shot in the graffiti world, only got into it in the first place because of her … to *woe* her. Back at school. Writing her name all over stuff just to get her attention.'

'And Cynthia told Toby this?'

'Yeah.'

'About this big romantic gesture her ex had made back at school?'

'Exactly. Insensitive huh? What can I say? Some girls like to play mind games.' He drew circles with his index finger at his temple.

Quaye frantically scrawled all the details in his notebook. 'Don't suppose you have a name for the ex?' he asked.

Rahman shook his head. He allowed himself a long breath as he slumped back in his chair, reflecting on recent events. 'Fucking waste,' he exclaimed. 'Sorry,' he added quickly.

'That's okay,' Quaye reassured. 'I can't say I disagree.' He closed up his notebook with a definitive slap. 'I think that's enough for now. Thank you once again for seeing me at such a difficult time.' Quaye presented a business card. 'I would really like to talk to this Cynthia individual. If you think of anything that can help identify her, however insignificant it may seem, then do not hesitate to contact me.'

The two men stood and shook hands.

'Take the rest of the day off,' Quaye advised.

Rahman indicated that he'd consider it, and they parted company.

Quaye only got as far as the railing overlooking the harbour, standing in deep contemplation, assimilating his thoughts. This would be the point he'd choose to light up a cigarette, if, that is, he'd ever had the inclination to smoke – which he hadn't. So instead he just casually failed to conform to the brooding detective stereotype, as he contemplated the facts.

A few things troubled him, but most significantly now was why Milner's girlfriend had not reported his disappearance? He'd been missing for three days, and if she'd seen the news she'd be sure to know who the mysterious bridge faller was. She may even have known about the plan beforehand. Maybe she felt guilty; felt responsible for driving him to this act.

The rate of Quaye's thoughts slowed as his gaze swept from left to right. It was time to go; time to move. But not yet, not right now. He was in the right place; this was where he needed to be. He knew this at some deep level – that's why his feet weren't moving. His consciousness just hadn't been availed of the reason yet. His eyes moved back across the vista. Something was holding him in this spot; something was poking at his mind. And then he realised. It wasn't something in his *mind*, it was something in his *vision*. He'd glimpsed an image. During his moments of introspection, his idling visual circuits had processed a relevant form, triaged it for later examination. But the fuzzy filing system of the brain being what it is, he could not retrieve the details. He began to study his surroundings more carefully; breaking down the components of every frame. His gaze was no longer vacant. His eyes no longer swept smoothly, they moved in discrete steps. From structure to structure. From building to boat to body.

To building.

Finally, his eyes snapped into a groove; locked on and zoomed in. It had been there forever, he was sure. Across the water from where he was standing. Right next to his favourite café on the harbourside, just along from the museum. There was a storage unit, with large doors, barn-like doors only twice the height, decorated with harbour-themed murals – aged and flaking, but aesthetically pleasing. He was familiar with these; he'd stared at them over a coffee and a book many times. What he *hadn't* noticed was above them. Fitted so perfectly into the square structure on top of the building, it was like it had always belonged in this space. But it did not. Not according to the strict word of the law. Illegitimate lettering. It was different in style, certainly. Different shape and colour and finish.

But it read the same. He was sure of that. Now that he saw it in a different form it was obvious.

'Gioco.' That was it. That was what this word read here; and what it read at Parson Street station too. But what did that mean?

Quaye swung around. His recent interviewee was out of sight. Rahman had been pretty sure that the world of graffiti had been only a recent influence on his friend's life. But this looked to have been here for some time. He pulled out his phone and was soon flicking through tourist snaps of the area – some tagged right to the spot he was standing. It didn't take long to confirm that the graffiti had been on the building at least a couple of years.

This fact added a new dimension to the puzzle; at least in his mind. Why had Milner risked his safety painting another artist's name? Surely promoting one's own reputation was what it was all about?

He started the walk back to his car at a quick pace. He was more intrigued than ever now, as to what this was all about. But was all too aware he may never be allowed to find out.

Not officially, at least.

Eight

Back at the police station, he didn't make it to his desk without being pulled into the Superintendent's office.

'Please tell me you have the tiniest slither of evidence to suggest this little investigation is anything more than a mere personal curiosity of yours?' the Super challenged, continuing without a chance for Quaye to respond. 'Because as I understand it, we have in fact got video evidence of what amounts to – ' he looked at his notes for maximum effect '– a man falling off something.'

Quaye listed his reasons for suspicion – or was it just intrigue? The spray-cans with only one set of prints, the absent girlfriend, the profile of the dead man. Quaye was painfully aware of how weak his argument sounded even as he was making it.

'It's not good enough,' his boss concluded. 'Mere oddities and intuition do not make a crime. You know better than that.' The Super walked around to the other side of his desk and sat down. His tough guy demeanour faded. He had borne witness to Quaye's intuition on more than one occasion before. It had afforded some leeway in the past. But not today. It was too much of a leap. 'Write it up. And file it. We can't justify any more time on this.'

Quaye didn't protest. He knew it was futile. He had no ammunition; had to walk away. Back at his office, he twiddled the blinds shut and slumped himself at his desk.

He was frustrated. But more than that, he was unfulfilled, unsatisfied. He knew the very qualities that made him a good detective in the general sense, had the potential to make him a very poor one professionally. He harboured a natural curiosity in people's behaviour. Whether or not that behaviour was deemed to be legal felt somewhat inconsequential at times. To him, this particular incident was a riddle, and so regardless of criminal activity, he wanted to solve it. He wanted to know what kind of love drove a banker to graffiti. He knew that meant he was perversely questioning the motives of a victim, rather than a perpetrator – even if the man was only a victim of his own misjudgements – but he wanted to know all the same.

He buckled down and achieved three hours of paperwork with the aid of only four cups of coffee.

Then it was time to leave it behind.

Just as Quaye was exiting the station, as he swung the door open, he recalled the tinkle of a bell, from a few days earlier, when he was leaving the street art gallery. In turn, he remembered the reference that the owner, Alice, had made. Initially, he'd figured that all of his colleagues were too recently appointed to know anyone from way back. But he'd forgotten someone. He'd forgotten Harry, desk constable since Brunel got busted for disorderly engineering.

Harry looked up from his crossword at Quaye's enquiry, peering over the top of his reading spectacles.

'Widdecombe? Old Widdles, you say? Of course. He must have left here, I don't know...' He whistled as he calculated. 'Must be fifteen years ago now.'

'He dealt with graffiti?' Quaye asked.

'That's right. They brought him in from the Transport Police to crack down on it. That was back in the nineties, when it was really rife. He knew them all, and they knew him too.' Harry leant back in his chair, removing his spectacles and folding them up. 'There was no love lost between 'em either, I can tell you.'

'No?'

Harry shook his head. 'Nah, Widdles was pretty relentless in his pursuit. Didn't give 'em any second chances. And they were more than keen to retaliate when they got a chance.' Harry grew momentarily wistful, a smile falling on his lips. 'Tell you a funny story about Widdles. He was in a band, you see. Not like a rock band. Some kind of folk thing. Anyway, he had this gig up London one time. But one of those graffiti lads found out. They all got a coach up there, didn't they, and totally blasted the place round where he was playing with his name. Painted 'Widdles' all over the walls, cars, urinals. Everything.'

'I should imagine he was not amused.'

'Ha, I should say not.' Harry smiled as he returned from his reverie and focussed on Quaye. 'Graffiti's not your thing, though, is it? Bit petty. Aren't you murders and all that?'

'Yeah, murders and all that,' Quaye confirmed with a thin smile, then mused for a moment on the old cop. 'That was all a long time ago, though. This Widdecombe is not going to know the scene now. Who's the equivalent?'

'There isn't one as far as I know. Not like him.'

Quaye shrugged. 'Never mind. Not relevant now I

guess.'

But even as he said that out loud, a part of him still wanted to find someone who knew the scene: well enough to be able to help, but not so well they wouldn't.

Someone who *knew* the scene, but wasn't *in* it.

Nine

It was one minute to closing when Quaye arrived at the gallery. This time, the owner was not present at the counter. Alerted to his arrival by the bell over the door she emerged from the back room. Her swift pace slowed on seeing who it was.

'I have no more information, I'm afraid.' Her tone was pleasant this time, maybe mellowed by seeing the news report.

'That's okay,' Quaye said. 'I want to buy this painting.'

She looked at him as if she didn't believe him, or didn't trust his intentions.

'Genuinely,' he added. 'I like it.'

'Then you have good taste.'

'That's good to know.' He smiled.

'Do you want to take it now?' she enquired as she approached. 'I'll need to package it up for you.'

'Umm, I don't really know what the protocol is. I've not done this before. I don't want to keep you if you need to shut up.'

'No, that's fine.' She reached up and carefully plucked the canvas from the wall, then carried it to the counter where she began to deftly wrap it. Every movement careful and precise, as if she were handling a dinosaur egg.

'I guess it's unusual,' Quaye said as he studied her actions. 'A cop buying graffiti.'

She shrugged. 'You are my first. But that doesn't mean a lot of cops don't appreciate what they see. It's hard not to when you notice it. Don't you think?'

'Well, I can hardly counter that point,' he said, nodding to his purchase. 'Are you going to get in trouble, fraternising with the enemy?'

'You jest, but some writers are quite … militant … in their views on police.'

'Writers?'

'Graff artists who focus on letters; on writing names. The street art spectrum is wide. From kids that scrawl their tags on road signs with marker pens to pro illustrators who do murals on walls. Don't try to make sense of it. You can't pigeon hole a movement that's influenced by anarchism. You can't pin a label on it.'

Quaye watched in silence as Alice wrapped a second layer of bubble wrap around his purchase.

She continued. 'Some of the crews round here think that it's not graff unless you're defacing public property. They think anything else is selling out. Those kind hate even the slightest hint of officialdom – and they *really* hate the police. But then, those guys don't hang their work in galleries.'

'So they hate you too?'

She shrugged. 'Some of them, I guess.'

Alice fell quiet as she focussed on her task. Quaye filled the silence with a question.

'So how did you get into it?' he enquired.

She looked up at him as she reached out for the tape dispenser. 'What is this, an interview?' She tore a piece of tape from the device. 'Am I a suspect?' She didn't sound like she was being serious.

Quaye laughed. 'No, sorry. Just … just curious.'

'My brother,' Alice said flatly after a moment, but didn't elaborate.

Quaye didn't press. Glancing up he saw row upon row of spray-cans behind the counter. They reminded him of another question Alice could help with. 'Those cans. Are they usually bought like that, individually? Or do they come as multipacks?'

'Multipacks?' she mimicked. 'Asda's two streets that way,' she hooked her thumb over her left shoulder and delivered a wry smile.

'Point taken.'

Alice put the final touches to the wrapping before announcing she was done.

After paying up, Quaye left the shop with his purchase tucked under his arm. Alice followed behind him to lock up for the night. She secured the door then pulled the shutters down over the shop-front to reveal a muralled façade.

Quaye regarded it idly. Then, as he was about to walk away, he stopped himself.

'Listen,' he said. 'Can I drop you somewhere? I feel guilty for delaying you.'

'No, it's okay. I'm heading to the station. The traffic will be a bitch this time of day.'

'Not with a siren,' he said playfully.

'Do you have a siren?'

'Yes,' he beamed. 'Not really allowed to use it though,' he admitted glumly. 'Come on, you can walk two paces behind if you like. Don't want to ruin your street cred.'

She gave a what-the-hell kind of shrug and walked with him to his car. It took them fifteen minutes to get to the train station, filled mostly with idle chatter, Quaye making the conscious effort to not get to questiony. But then it was Alice who returned to the subject.

'You really interested?' she asked, as they pulled in over the cobbles of Temple Meads station.

'I am,' he confirmed.

'Then get yourself a ticket.'

He was surprised by the invitation, but didn't hesitate in accepting it. He left his car at the Transport Police car park and followed her into the train station, getting himself a return ticket to Bath.

'Platform 15 is where we start your education,' she announced.

They made their way to the far end of the station via the underground concourse, bathed in warm air laced with the unmistakable odours of coffee and Cornish pasties. On emerging onto the platform, they were greeted by the vast husk of what was once a postal sorting office. Now derelict and gutted it stood as a decaying icon. Or eyesore. Opinions were divided on the topic.

'The history of the graff culture is intimately entwined with two things,' Alice declared.

'Skateboards and cider?' Quaye suggested.

'Ha,' she laughed. 'Well, maybe in some respects. But more fundamentally, the movement's beginnings are linked with hip-hop and…' – she raised her arms – '…trains.'

They took a seat on a bench overlooking the decaying

building, and Alice began her story.

'The rolling stock of New York and Philadelphia were the moving canvases of where it all began. Not just the outside either. Before the mayor got serious, the interior of every subway train in New York was plastered with ink. So too in Bristol, the train lines are where the serious writers cut their teeth. Even now. For some, throwing up some letters at a skatepark, where it's actually *allowed*, doesn't quite have the same buzz to it.'

They remained in silence as Alice seemed distant for a while. Then she opened up.

'This is where it began for my brother and his mates. They got up to some crazy shit back then. Used to come home and regale me of their antics. One night they bombed the shit out of a *moving* train, I kid you not. When it was rolling into the station, passengers inside banging on the windows, going like: *what-the-fuck*? Nuts, when you think about it now.' She turned to face Quaye, an earnest look in her eye. 'You have to understand that it's about the act as much as the outcome. It's not so much about making a mark on the *walls*; it's about making a mark on *history*. It's the *stories* that will last forever. Look up at this building: a washed-out roll-call of writers past. I know at least three of them are dead – died young. But long after the paint has faded and the building's been pulled down, their stories will live on. Their name will be cemented in graff history.'

'And those who don't die young? When they grow up, what do they become?'

She shrugged. 'Whatever. Some never stop; never really get a foothold in society; in and out of jail all their lives.

Most get themselves sorted. Some go professional. Some get a nine-to-five and leave it all behind.'

'And your brother? Does he still paint?'

She shook her head. 'No. He got too involved in one of the other facets of the graff scene.'

'Drugs?' Quaye guessed.

Alice nodded solemnly. 'Lost his mind, literally. He'd arranged to go down to Newquay one bank holiday weekend. Packed enough drugs for five people for three days and did the whole stash in one night on his own. He was on a secure psyche ward for seven months after that. The paranoia has never left him. He can't paint now.'

'I'm sorry,' Quaye offered.

Alice dismissed it and looked at her watch. 'Come on, Platform 9 for my train.'

They stood up from the bench and made their way to Platform 9, picking up coffees and pastries as they did so. When the train arrived, they embarked and found themselves a seat.

'You'll get a flavour for the roots of the movement on this journey,' Alice said.

Quaye had been on a train pulling out of this station hundreds of times before. On each of those occasions, any examples of graffiti had washed by him unnoticed. The grimy examples of a broken society. This time, he paid them greater heed – and respect. On walls, junction boxes, carriages. Alice described what they saw. Tags, burners, throw-ups, pieces.

While Alice carefully dissected a cinnamon whirl, she also dissected the anatomy of the graffiti world.

Quaye posed a question. A pertinent one. 'Do graffiti artists ever write each other's tags?'

She considered this for a moment. 'Well, most of them are in a crew. Sometimes they'll write their crew name, sometimes their own. And often they learn to write each other's tags.'

'Why?'

'Well, it's all too easy to get nicked if you leave your name at the crime scene. Mixing it up a bit makes it harder for a conviction to stick. The *it-wasn't-me-it-was-my-mate* defence.'

This made sense to Quaye. 'So if someone were to write another's name, that would more likely be a sign of respect than disrespect?'

'Yes, I'd say so. Why's that?'

Quaye remained pensive for a moment, thinking about the name Milner was in the process of painting, and the fact that it was that of another artist. In the end, he decided to discard the thought and shook his head. 'Don't worry,' he said.

'Talking about writing another's name, that's kind of where it all began; depending on how much you want to romanticise the history.'

'How do you mean?'

'Not that you can really pinpoint the beginnings of the movement. Like a river, it has many contributing sources. But remember how I was saying that it's the stories that live on; growing stronger with every retelling. One enduring story maintains it all began with a guy called Cornbread in Philly. It's true he was a key player. And where did his motivation arise? The strongest motivation of all, of course. Love. Trying to capture the attention of a girl at his school. He wrote her name all over the halls and her locker and when that didn't work, along her bus route to school. Finally, he broke into the bus garage and wrote all over the bus.' She noticed Quaye's expression, staring at her with a quizzical brow. 'What?' she asked.

'I've heard this story before,' he announced.

This time, it was her turn for the quizzical brow.

'How does the story end?' he probed.

'He got his girl. Then the girl got to compete with his *other* passion. Writing.' Alice looked a Quaye with a stony expression. 'She lost.'

Quaye considered this; drifted into thought.

A story. Make-believe. Was that all it was? The tale about Milner's girlfriend, Cynthia, and her ex? If so, whose story was it? Was it Cynthia's, inciting jealousy over a previous boyfriend that never existed? Or was it Milner's story? Did Cynthia not really exist – beyond the night that Milner and his friend met her?

Or *was* it real, after all? Was it a copycat act of a graffiti legend? The ultimate street way to woo a girl.

He pondered this as the scenery flashed by. Though, he didn't have much time to ponder; it was only a short trip to Bath.

'This is me,' Alice announced as they approached the station.

'Guess, I'll get the next train back then.'

They made their way off the train and toward the platform exit.

'Just one last thing,' Quaye said as they negotiated the steps down from Platform 2. 'I promise.'

Alice rolled her eyes playfully.

'How do they get into it, in the first place? Assuming it's not always for the attention of a girl.'

'Back in the day, in Bristol, a lot of it centred on the boys' clubs. Now?' she shrugged. 'More varied I guess. Considering how it spans the class divide. Maybe they just wake up one day and fancy painting on their walls.' She smiled.

They were standing by the exit barriers through which Alice would leave the station. Quaye waited as she fetched her ticket from her purse.

'Usually more prepared than this,' she muttered, half to herself, before triumphantly holding her ticket aloft and bringing her eyes up to meet Quaye's.

'Thanks again for your time,' Quaye said with a polite nod.

'Pleasure,' Alice assured.

There was a moment of pause, before Quaye turned to walk away.

'It's Ellingsworth,' came Alice's voice.

Quaye turned back. 'Sorry?'

'My name.'

'Ah, I see.' Quaye already knew. He'd looked her up. But remembered she'd refrained from telling him on their first meeting.

'And this is where you tell me yours, DI Quaye.' Alice made a back-and-forth gesture with her hand. 'It's kind of a thing people do.'

Quaye laughed. She had a way with words. A way he liked. 'People just call me Quaye.'

'And I'm just people am I?' she teased.

Quaye took a deep breath and shuffled uncomfortably on his feet. 'Okay, fair enough. It's Harlyn. With a Y. My parents thought it would be fun to name me after a village in Cornwall.'

'Then your parents sound kinda cool.'

Quaye shrugged, non-committedly.

Alice offered a hand. 'Well, Harlyn Withawhy, nice to formally meet you.'

'Likewise.'

Their hands remained locked for a moment as they exchanged a smile, then Alice left. Quaye stood and watched as she walked away. Watched as she crossed the road. Watched until she had disappeared from sight. With the void that was left in her place, Quaye's mind turned back to the subject they had been discussing, and to the case it was related. His curiosity was piqued. He couldn't banish the mystery from his mind, however much he ought to. He felt that just one more detail could open the whole thing up. He wasn't sure what it was. Had no clue in fact. But there was only one place he could think to look for it.

The apartment of the fallen artist.

Ten

The man sat in contented silence on a trackside bench at Temple Meads station, until a train rolled in and clattered to a halt. After a pregnant pause, the locomotive spilt its human cargo onto the platform, right in front of the man. People skittered past him without affording him even a glance, all keen to be elsewhere as a matter of urgency. Much the same as when he sat on the streets of the city centre, or sheltered in a doorway on Park Street, or simply existed just about anywhere. The vague notion of his kind meant something to these people, in a peripheral kind of way. The homeless guy, the tramp, the beggar, the vagrant. But he did not belong in their sphere of existence. The sphere of existence where people got trains and commuted and busy-busied themselves across platforms.

This time, though, he didn't mind. Didn't dwell on his insignificance to them.

This time, he was asking for nothing.

Today, he had what he needed – had found what he'd been looking for.

He flicked through the pages of the sketchbook in his hands, as he had done so a thousand times before; every sheet full to the edges with drawings – some elaborate and detailed, some just the seminal outline of an idea that might one day be born.

He stopped at a particular page near the middle of the

book and turned it to sit landscape in his hands. Not that he needed to – he knew intimately what it looked like. He knew it was the same as on the wall in front of him. He looked up again at the derelict postal sorting office standing adjacent to the station; an open canvas for local artists, yet relatively untouched – presumably due to the robustness of the security. But there, right at the top, was the image he'd been searching for. Just like the one on the page before him.

The mere presence was not that significant. He'd found the same tag in a dozen places about the city. The significance of this particular example though was not to be overlooked. And the significance was simple.

It wasn't there yesterday.

The artist was still active.

The artist was still in town.

That's what was important; that the man's search had finally been validated.

Satisfied with his find, the homeless guy returned his sketchbook to its plastic carrier bag and wrapped it up tight, before packing it into his duffle bag. Then he headed to Platform 4. He didn't have a ticket to get out through the barriers at Temple Meads. From Platform 4 he could get a train along a branch line, get off at the first stop, where there would be no barriers, and walk back to town. The train would consist of only two or three carriages, but he knew that as long as he got on at the right end, he'd be off before the ticket inspector reached him. These were the tricks you learned as a homeless guy in Bristol. Not that most would recognise him as such today. Just a man with a beard, scruffy clothes and a duffle bag. He'd stashed his other belongings in the doorway of a disused building in town.

His train plan came off smoothly. When he'd made it back to the centre, he found a friend of his sitting on one of the giant steps at the amphitheatre. He was glad to find him. Because to his friend he was not just the homeless guy. To him, he was a person.

He was Raymond.

'What are you doing here, Eric?' Raymond asked.

'Watchin' the skateboarders,' Eric stated like it should have been obvious. 'You knows how I like the noise. Kach-ch-ch kach-ch-ch-ch.' He tried to imitate it. 'Likes a train.' He grinned a toothless grin.

Raymond sat down next to him. 'Here,' he said, offering a can of beer from his bag, which was eagerly accepted and opened.

'Where's you bin, anyways?' Eric asked.

'Station.'

'Not looking for that artist again?' His own words prompted a thought. 'Oh, you knows Valerie.'

'Valerie?'

'Yeah, we saw her couple weeks back. Going round and round the roundabout with her trolley.' Eric swirled his finger in the air.

'Oh yes.' Raymond remembered the trolley, so laden with bags, mounded inside and hanging around the edges, that virtually no sign of a trolley was actually visible. 'What about her?'

'Spoke to her, 'bout your artist. She says she knows a guy who knows a guy that might know.'

'Great.' Raymond wasn't optimistic.

'Let me 'ave a page of that book and I'll show it her.' Eric reached for the sketchbook poking out the top of Raymond's duffle bag. His attempt was rapidly thwarted.

'No! Don't touch that.' Raymond grabbed the bag to his chest. 'You don't need to have a sketch. There's plenty on the walls. You just need the name. Gioco. Yeah? Can you remember that? Gioco.'

Eric looked confused.

'I'll write it down.' Raymond tore a scrap of paper from a copy of the Metro he'd picked up at the station and wrote the name on it in clear capital letters. 'There,' he said. 'Gioco. Tell that to your friend. Any of your friends. Ask if anyone knows who it is.'

Raymond studied Eric for a moment. He had little faith in his companion's ability to assist in this quest, and even littler patience. He had to follow this up himself. He had nothing better to do.

'Where would I find this Valerie?' he asked.

Eric seemed to delve deeply into his thoughts for a moment before slowly responding with a number of suggestions.

With another lead in hand, Raymond left. As he trudged along, he found himself harbouring a sense of frustration that he just couldn't shake. And he began to reflect on his place in the world.

His life hadn't always been this way. He used to have a wife and a job and a home. But he'd learned the hard way that nothing was constant. Not even one's state of mind.

Especially one's state of mind.

Sometimes an event can occur that will make you switch

track. Consciously or otherwise. The life he used to lead was no longer his – no longer even felt real to him. A life he kept locked in a box.

Eleven

'What's this all about?' Wilcox asked of Quaye. He'd invited her to meet at a bar near her place of work.

Quaye slid a photo across the table, protected by a clear cellophane bag. Wilcox looked at it.

'It's a photograph of the bridge at Parson Street station,' she stated matter-of-factly. 'Before the incident occurred.' This was an easily discernible fact from the absent artwork of recent interest.

Quaye turned the photo over. On the back were the words:

GIOCO. SHOW ME WHAT YOU CAN DO. CX

Wilcox's eyes widened. 'Where did you get this?' she hissed in a stern but hushed voice.

'His apartment.'

'*His apartment*?'

'Tobias Milner's.'

'I know who you mean. It was your judgment I was questioning. What were you doing in his apartment?'

'Looking for this, it turns out.'

'You know what I mean. How did you get in?'

'I badged the porter. Not difficult.'

'Not difficult, maybe. Not *allowed*, certainly. What were you thinking?'

'I was thinking that it was never going to happen otherwise.'

'There's a reason for that. There was no justification.'

'Well, now there is.'

'Justification can't be applied retroactively.'

The tone of Wilcox's reaction amused Quaye a little, although he chose not to show it. He was her senior in profession by several ranks, and her senior in age by *more than* several years. They were not in the same force, but all the same, Quaye was pleased that Wilcox was willing to raise objections where she had them.

'What does this tell you?' Quaye asked, nodding to the photo.

Wilcox thought for a moment. 'Exactly what we knew already,' she concluded. 'That Tobias Milner's girlfriend, Cynthia, goaded him into doing this deed at which he met his unfortunate demise.'

'But she wrote the note in block capitals. What does *that* tell you?'

Wilcox shrugged. 'They had bad handwriting?'

'Or whoever wrote it wanted to hide their identity,' Quaye suggested.

'Or … they had bad handwriting,' Wilcox repeated.

'Okay, okay. Forget the photo.'

'I'm finding it hard to forget the photo. Are you going to *unsteal* it at any point?'

'Don't worry about it.'

Wilcox carried a distinct look of still worrying about it. She wasn't familiar with Quaye's way of working. Yet.

'You know, you remind me of my neighbour,' Quaye said.

Wilcox raised an eyebrow at the sudden tangent.

Quaye caveated his statement. 'I mean, I didn't know my neighbour – Silvia's her name – when she was your age, but I imagine she'd have been a lot like you.'

Wilcox regarded him suspiciously. 'Is that good?'

Quaye smirked. 'It's good,' he confirmed, but didn't elaborate. In Wilcox he recognised a sharp enquiring mind, fuelled by unfettered tenacity – qualities his neighbour would have needed in her youth in spades, and indeed were still evident today.

'Anyway,' he said, returning to the matter in hand. 'There's something else.'

'Oh no, please don't tell me there is something else,' she half-mocked.

'Something intriguing,' Quaye added, with wide eyes.

Wilcox rolled hers. 'Can't wait.'

Quaye leaned in, undeterred. 'Cynthia told Milner that her ex was this big-time artist and that he'd only gotten into graffiti to woo her.'

'Okay, so?'

'So this was inspired by a *real* story about a guy called Cornbread. He was one of the founding fathers of the movement from Philadelphia back in the seventies. And do you know what the name of the damsel was in *this* story?'

'I think I can guess.'

'*Cynthia*.' Quaye marked the name with a tap on the table. 'Before I discovered this, I was trying to figure out whether the story she'd told about her school-day suitor was one she'd made up, or even one that *Milner* had made up for some reason.'

'Or even, his friend who you spoke to.'

'Right, Arrash Rahman. But now it turns out that even the girl herself was made up.'

Wilcox tried to process what this meant. 'Hold on, but she's real to some degree because Rahman met her.' She thought this through for a moment. 'Well, unless Rahman made the whole thing up. But that doesn't make sense. *He* approached *us*. Why would he volunteer all this made up information? What would he gain?'

'I agree. So on the premise that Milner and Rahman *did* meet a woman called Cynthia on a night out, for some reason she was using a pseudonym. Right from the get go. And one with distinct poignancy.'

'Poignancy in the world of graffiti,' Wilcox pointed out.

'Yes.'

'Okay, so, reality check. That still doesn't mean anything other than this girl was just playing around and didn't want to get caught. And I agree it looks like she was a bad influence on him, considering his ultimate demise, but that's still not a crime.'

Wilcox looked Quaye in the eye earnestly. What she didn't realise, was that it didn't matter to him whether there was a crime here or not. It was still a worthy puzzle, and that's what drove him.

'You need to move past this, Quaye,' she urged.

Quaye gave pause, as if he was reflecting on this suggestion. Though, in truth, he was not. He knew, one way or another, he'd pursue this. But his contemplation gave Wilcox a window to ask a pointed question.

'Why is this so important to you? Why's it got under your skin?'

He thought about the question for a moment. Eventually, he spoke again in a vague tone. 'Keyser Söze.'

'Keyser what-now?

Quaye's eyes snapped back to Wilcox's.

'*Who,* not what!' he exclaimed.

She shrugged.

'Seriously?' he questioned unbelievingly, then stated firmly: 'You're not old enough to be a detective.'

'I'm not a detective.'

'Yeah, it's cos you're not old enough.'

'Whatever. So who's this Keyser chap?'

'Someone who's a myth and yet real at the same time. In fact, someone whose influence is *enhanced* by not being real; because he's someone who can't be touched.'

Wilcox looked puzzled. 'I'm not sure that makes a lot of sense.'

'Well, this Gioco character. That's exactly what it is, a character. It's not a real person. It doesn't have an address and a National Insurance number. It's just fiction; just a *reputation*. We don't know who is behind it. Whether they are alive or dead; male or female; one person or many. That's what makes it so powerful. You can't harm what you can't see.'

'Hmm.' Wilcox considered this for a moment. 'So who was this Keyser Söze?'

'Ha, oh, well he was just a character from a movie. Usual Suspects. You should watch it.'

'Have you got it on vinyl?' she teased with a laugh.

'Ha, funny.' Quaye gave a sardonic smile. Then seriousness returned to his face. 'I came close to someone similar once,' he said in a much graver tone. Quaye's thoughts rested on this for a moment, slipping back to the place. It was not a pleasant place to linger.

Wilcox sensed his hesitation. 'Go on,' she urged.

'My first job in the city. Myco, that's what they called him.' Quaye looked at Wilcox with a darkness in his eyes that hadn't been there before. 'His name cropped up in connection with a number of serious crimes. But we could never identify him. No-one seemed to know exactly who he was. People had met him, but their descriptions never tallied. There were theories that he masqueraded as many different people.' Quaye grew silently distant for a moment then shook his head to dismiss the line of thought.

'That's a story for another time,' he said. 'Right now, I need you to do something for me.'

'What's that?'

'I need you to get those spray-cans you found at the scene to forensics.'

'Why? They've already been analysed. There's nothing on them.'

'It's not what's *on* them that interests me,' Quaye affirmed. 'It's what's *in* them.'

'What are you expecting to find?'

'The only thing that can make sense of any of this.'

Twelve

Raymond found Valerie in the doorway of a disused office block. She sat crossed legged on a folded up duvet reading a paperback novel. He sat down beside her and handed over a coffee. She smiled a semi-toothless grin.

One thing Raymond had learned in his time on the street, which hadn't been as long as most, was how unassuming most homeless people were; how accepting they were.

'I hear you might be able to help me,' Raymond asked.

'Might I?' she stated, upturning her book on the ground to keep its page, then taking a sip of her coffee.

'You know about the art, on the walls?' Raymond said.

'Maybe.'

'I need to find an artist.' He opened up his rucksack, pulled out a plastic bag from within, and from that produced his sketchbook. He leafed through the pages, each one a collage of line drawings jostling for position. Some just of letters, words. Some more complex: people, animals, buildings. There was no pattern, no theme. Just an endless stream of images. Like the manic outpourings of a cluttered mind.

Raymond stopped at a page, on a sketch he knew was duplicated in grander form on a wall nearby.

'You recognise this artist right?'

'Of course. But I ain't never be seenin' 'im.' She spoke with a thick accent. Local but not from the city. Rural.

Drawn to the bright lights.

'But you know he's dead?'

'Aye.'

'I know who killed him,' Raymond announced. He turned pages of the sketchbook rapidly but carefully, before coming to rest on the page he was looking for. It was covered from corner to corner with a single word, written over and over. Each one in a different style. Different colours, different effects. Some with emoticon-inspired faces in the 'O's or as the dot over the 'I'. This was graffiti of the internet age.

Raymond turned the page once more to reveal still further of the same word. Then another. Finally, he stopped and turned the book on its side to show Valerie a full landscape version. The final design.

'Gioco,' he said softly. 'That's who killed him.'

For the first time, the old woman looked at him.

'Story was he killed himself. Jumped, didn't 'e.'

Raymond shook his head. 'Never that simple. Someone's always responsible.' He grew distant.

There was silence for a moment, until Valerie prodded her finger at the page.

'Well, I don't know who that be,' she said. 'Don't know anyone who does.'

Raymond sighed deeply. It was a story he was getting used to hearing. He knew one other thing about the person behind Gioco, which could help jog Valarie's memory on the subject.

He shared this detail with her.

It didn't help.

Raymond packed up the sketchbook dejectedly and stood, not knowing where he was going next.

Valerie spoke up. 'Could try the galleries,' she offered.

'Tried them,' he said with a tired voice. 'Tried them all.'

He chose a direction at random and walked off, scuffing his well-worn shoes as he made his way to nowhere in particular. After walking for twenty minutes, the heat got to him. Being homeless, Raymond realised, was a case of extremes, as far as body temperature was concerned. He was bundled under far too many layers for the current conditions, but he needed them all for colder times, and this was the easiest way of carrying them.

When Raymond found himself in Castle Park, he slumped down in the shade of a tree. It was busy with students laying out in the sun, and tourists strolling by the river. He watched them idly. He saw two pushchair-wielding mums coming from opposite directions perform an elaborate and superficial act of wonderment at their chance meeting: '*hi's* and '*how are you?*'s with elongated vowels. It seemed sickeningly insincere to Raymond, but maybe he was just a cranky old cynic. In fact, no maybe. He was *definitely* a cranky old cynic. But he felt he had a right to be. And being a cynic didn't make him wrong.

He couldn't hear what the mums were saying, but he knew what their topic of discussion would be: the fine art of child-rearing in the minutest of detail.

One of the mums had a second child in tow, a toddler. The boy was swinging on his mum's arm, vying unsuccessfully for attention. Eventually, he seemed to realise he wasn't going to win this battle. He let go of his mum and started wandering around studying blades of grass, which appeared to provide endless fascination.

The boy was gradually edging towards where Raymond was sitting and when he got to about ten feet away the boy stopped and looked up. The dishevelled looking man seemed to present almost the same degree of intrigue as the grass. Raymond made eye contact with the child. The boy reminded Raymond of his own son at that age. Although the memory of that time, of that world, was so distant as to not even feel like his own anymore.

'Hello,' Raymond said, softly.

The boy didn't say anything for a moment, just cocked his head to one side as if to study his subject from a different angle. Eventually, the boy offered a 'Hi' in return.

'What's your name?' Raymond asked.

'Aaron,' the boy said, more immediately this time. 'Two 'A's'. He held up two fingers, in a victory V.

Raymond smiled. It was at this point that Aaron's mother noticed the utterly perilous situation her child was in.

'Aaron,' she called to the boy in a shrill tone as she rushed over and dragged her son away by the arm. 'Don't talk to that man!' she admonished forcefully. And they were gone.

Raymond had to choke back a tear.

That was what he'd become.

The monster.

Thirteen

Quaye tapped his pen habitually on the edge of his desk. When his phone rang, his Pavlovian response was nothing more than a kind of detached unease. As a kid, he couldn't understand why his parents dreaded the telephone so much. But now he understood. It's what comes of growing up. Not every incursion into one's life is welcome.

This particular one could go either way.

Wilcox had protested, of course, when Quaye had asked her to re-test the spray-cans. He had to reassure her that he would take the rap, should there be one. And there probably *would* be, either way. But the intensity would be mollified should his theory prove to be accurate.

Quaye answered the phone tentatively.

'You were right,' Wilcox announced. 'I don't know how, but you were right.'

Quaye released the tense breath he'd been holding. He was relieved to hear her say it. Though he wasn't sure whether he was more relieved his actions had proven justified or that his mind had proven sound.

Wilcox continued. 'The paint in the can was laced with…' – she paused as she quoted from a toxicology report – '…a derivative of something called Sevoflurane, an inhalation anaesthetic used in the medical industry, usually administered directly in a mixture of nitrous oxide. Has a very fast onset time. The geeks at the lab say that in close quarters, inhaling a few lungfuls of the fumes from the can would have rendered the user disorientated and potentially unconscious in seconds. It wouldn't last long, but then the fall saw to the rest.'

'And then the train,' Quaye added.

'Indeed, then the train,' Wilcox concurred. 'How did you know?' she asked. 'Especially considering the video evidence to the contrary.'

'It was the fall, initially.'

'The fall?'

'He didn't fall right. Not like he'd slipped or lost his grip. There was no sudden movement, no flailing. That was what was bugging me when I first watched the video, though I didn't know it at the time. After that, there seemed to be too many oddities to be as straightforward as it appeared.'

'So do we have a murder on our hands?' Wilcox enquired.

'If it were just the asphyxiate in the cans, maybe not. But the location was chosen with maximum effect in mind.'

'Over a train line?'

'Yes, that combined with the butter-side-down effect.'

'Come again?'

'The toast always lands butter-side-down.'

'What of it?'

'It's just physics. If you slide an average-sized slice of bread off of an average-sized table, it will do one rotation before it hits the floor.'

'And our man is the toast?'

'Indeed. In more than one sense of the word. If a man of his height falls passively backwards from where he was standing, pivoting at his feet, he's going to land on his head.'

'Rendering him further debilitated.'

'Right. To be honest, whether this was intentional or just luck, I don't know. But the fact is that the gas, the height of the bridge and the train-line were a combination that was almost certain to end fatally for our artist.'

'And from the photo, we know he was cajoled into doing it.'

'Right, so that's justification enough for an investigation.' There was silence for a moment from both parties. Finally, Quaye asked, 'How do you fancy getting out of uniform?' Adding quickly: 'That didn't come out right.'

Fourteen

Quaye arrived at the police station to find Wilcox arranging her security pass at the front desk. It was her first day on secondment. She looked even younger in plain clothes, he noted, absent of the tone of authority cast upon her by uniform. He tried *not* to note that this made him feel even *older*, regardless of personal attire.

'Welcome to the madhouse,' he said, lamely. He didn't do wit this early in the morning.

'Thanks,' Wilcox replied, looking up from the form she was filling in.

Quaye waited for Wilcox to complete her admin, before walking her through to his department's corner of the building. There were no free desks in the open-plan area, so he'd organised a space for Wilcox in the corner of his office. Suddenly, he found himself questioning his motivations behind this arrangement. Was it purely logistical, or the result of some subconscious and misplaced paternal instinct? He gauged their age gap to be around fifteen years, so he was not strictly old enough to be her father, or not *legally* old enough at least. But he could certainly fulfil the uncle role. Not that he should be attempting to. He wasn't sure whether this uncle-ing instinct was some vestigial kernel of gender bias left over from a million years of evolution or simply the outcome of his earlier career experiences. Either way he cursed himself. Wilcox was a strong character, who clearly had her shit together better than he did, by some margin. And so was probably far better equipped to handle the modern world than he was right now.

'I thought you could park yourself here whilst you were working on the case,' Quaye said, indicating the small table in the corner of his office, and then set about justifying it. 'We don't have any desks free right now.'

As if to offer his mind an entirely different sentiment to be profoundly resentful over, he suddenly found himself wondering whether the arrangement could even be considered inappropriate. He knew he wouldn't be suffering this inner turmoil if Wilcox had been a male officer, or indeed an older female one. The legacy of misogynistic bosses and general female exploitation throughout the ages. He pre-emptively leapt into an apology and an offer to rectify the situation.

'But if you prefer, we can sort something else out. I think Malia is on leave this week, or –'

'It's fine,' Wilcox interjected as she dumped her black rucksack on the table.

Quaye filled Wilcox in on some of the housekeeping details of his department. It was familiar patter to him; from timesheets to fire escapes to security protocols. After the induction, he offered some advice.

'As far as being a detective goes,' he said, 'just remember one thing and you won't go far wrong.' He paused. 'Everyone is an actor.'

'Okay,' Wilcox acknowledged, quizzically.

'The little old lady, the caring neighbour, the innocent

child – none of them are who they seem. They are all playing a part. And you must be able to project on to them the role of bad guy, imagine every word they utter as deceit – and see where it leads you. Only when you can truly detach yourself, see the world as a theatre, can you begin to judge a situation impartially, on the merits of the facts alone. When you can honestly say you've cracked *that* … you will be a great detective…' – he paused – '…and a really lousy dinner party guest.'

Wilcox looked at him, questioningly, seemingly in hope of the last part being in jest. Quaye disappointed her.

'That's the sacrifice, you see. Never being able to trust another human being. Not even those closest to you. If you can live with that … you'll do okay.'

Quaye saw Wilcox consider this for a moment. Consider whether this was really what she could expect or whether it was just the views of man jaded by a mediocre life and unfulfilling relationships. Maybe it was.

Finally, Wilcox shrugged. 'I'll take whatever comes.'

'Fine. Let's get to work.' Quaye's expression softened. He stood up, stretched his back and paced for a moment behind his desk, shifting his mindset back to the specifics of the case.

'Our budget is limited on this one,' he began. 'Until we get better evidence. It's just you and me. The first element to focus on is the two key players we need to identify. The candidate femme-fatale Cynthia and the mystery artist Gioco. Helpfully, we know that neither of these are real names, and the latter may not even be a real person.'

'So good start there.'

'Indeed. There's only one person we know who met Cynthia in the flesh, and that's Tobias Milner's friend from work, Arrash Rahman. Have another word with him. In particular, get a date for that meeting and scout out the CCTV in the region. You seem to have a knack for that.'

'Sir.' Wilcox nodded purposefully. 'Any ideas on Gioco?'

'Well, if we had the funds, I'd start by getting an army of officers hitting the streets to identify every last scrawling associated with this name. But we haven't. And if I could track down our last resident graffiti expert, PC Widdecombe, I'd be tapping his knowledge on how to uncover this artist. But I can't. He got involved in a big crime and had to take witness protection.'

'So?'

'So, in lieu of these lines of inquiry, I shall be seeking the counsel of a seventeen-year-old schoolgirl.' He stated it dryly.

Wilcox looked at him questioningly. 'Makes sense,' she played along. 'Any particular girl in mind, or just going to hang around the school gates?'

'A particular one,' he reassured. 'Lisa Peake'.

'And she would be?'

'She would be, apparently, the leading expert on Bristol street art. At least if the number of followers of her blog is anything to go by.' He slid his phone in her direction, watched as she scrolled past images of graffiti-laden walls.

Wilcox read out the title of the blog pensively: 'Street Shapes, Bristol Fashion.'

'A play on the old expression,' Quaye pointed out.

'Mmm, clever.'

Quaye was pleased at his new partner's keenness. She seemed to have the right attitude. And attitude was the most important thing. His reasons for requesting her secondment were partially selfish in nature. Making this case a collaboration was the best way of keeping it on his desk. Otherwise, it would likely have been returned to his transport counterparts. But from what he'd witnessed so far, he had a sense Wilcox would do okay. Not that he should be too trusting of his senses as a detective, where cold hard evidence should be his ultimate concern. But sometimes that has to wait. Until all the facts become available, the gut has to be the arbiter. A call has to be made. And with Wilcox, he'd made that call.

Time would tell.

Fifteen

Quaye knocked on the door of Lisa Peake's house. After a moment it was answered by a middle-aged man.

'Mr Peake?'

'Yes.'

'DI Quaye.' He showed his badge. 'I wonder if I could have a word with your daughter, Lisa.'

'She's not in any trouble is she?'

'Not at all. Quite the opposite. I was wondering if she might be able to help in an inquiry, regarding the death of a graffiti artist nearby. You are aware of her website?'

'Yes, of course, come in.'

Lisa's dad showed Quaye through to the living room and offered him a seat, before calling up the stairs to his daughter.

'Can I get you a drink?' Mr Peake offered while they were waiting.

'Tea would be good, thank you. White, none.'

Mr Peake smiled and headed for the kitchen as Lisa appeared at the bottom of the stairs.

'A detective is here to talk to you about the death at Parson Street,' Mr Peake informed his daughter.

Lisa looked uneasily at Quaye, as he stood to shake her hand.

'Pleased to meet you,' he said.

Lisa looked uneasy.

'No cause to be nervous,' he reassured her as he returned to his seat. Lisa sat down opposite. 'You are a bit of an expert in the street art of Bristol, judging from your website.'

She shrugged. 'I wouldn't say expert.'

Quaye assessed her as best he could in a moment's pause. Updating his mental model with new details. Her hair was immaculate and fair; her skin even fairer. She was smartly dressed, well turned out; as was the house she lived in. Not an obvious candidate for graffiti expert, but as he'd recently discovered, it wasn't prudent to pay heed to stereotypes in this domain.

'You heard about the incident?' Quaye asked.

'Of course.'

'And are you familiar with Gioco's work?'

She shook her head. 'No.'

'Why is that? Your site seems quite comprehensive.'

'My site features only legitimate art.'

'Why is that? Do you not consider illegitimate art of merit?'

'On the contrary. I appreciate it. But at arm's length only. My website is part of a school project, and so you'll understand why I don't feature illegal work. As part of the project, I get to know the artists. I do profiles on them and capture work-in-progress shots. As you might imagine, my teachers and my dad might not be best pleased with me hanging around railway sidings at two in the morning with a bunch of drunken vandals.'

'You see them as vandals?'

'Some of them, not all. Case-by-case.'

Lisa's dad returned to the room with tea. He placed a mug on the coffee table which Quaye thanked him for, and then took a seat silently. This was a polite family, Quaye observed. Manners were one attribute very hard to fake.

'So you *are* familiar with illegitimate art?'

'Yes. I take more notice than most. Of course.'

It struck Quaye how the girl spoke in a manner beyond her years. As if she had matured well ahead of her time.

'But you are not aware of the identity of these artists?' Quaye asked.

'In general, no.'

'But the lines are blurred, as I understand it.'

'Yes. That's why I say, in general. Some who are muralists by day, throw tags up at night. But I don't pry into that side of their life.'

'And you don't know the identity of Gioco?'

'No.' Lisa looked confused. 'But *you* do. They gave the name out on the news of the person who was killed.'

'Of the person who died yes. But sometimes it's not that straightforward. Sometimes artists write each other's names, isn't that right?'

'I guess,' Lisa agreed. 'So you don't think the person who died was Gioco?'

'We are considering that option.' Quaye tried to decipher Lisa's thought process, wondering why it mattered. He decided it was time to reveal the final detail. The crucial one. 'We are also considering that it was not an accident.'

Lisa's expression didn't change much. Her eyes maybe widened a little, perhaps conveying just the right level of shock and interest. Not so little to suggest this was not news to her. Not so much as to convey it was of any concern to her. But everyone wore their masks differently. Everyone's mask was of different construction – some latex, some steel.

'If so,' Quaye continued, 'this would be a substantially more significant matter than mere vandalism. And as such, if you did happen to know anyone who might be involved, or know anyone who might know, then I would urge you not to keep that information to yourself.'

The silence hung in the room like a fourth presence. Lisa's dad did not speak. In Quaye's experience, parents react to police interrogating their children in one of two ways. Some are concerned about any potential wrong-doing on the part of their offspring. They are just as keen to get to the truth and are readily apologetic should any misdemeanour come to light. These are the good parents. At the other end of the spectrum are the parents who will jump to the defence of their child, attacking the accuser and/or victim, and being entirely unreceptive to the possibility of their child being anything other than the personification of virtue. Lisa's father was fortunately of the first kind.

'So you think Gioco had something to do with this?' Lisa queried.

'It's the only line of inquiry we have to go on at the moment,' Quaye suggested, though not entirely true. 'So you understand how important it is that we find out anything we can about who is behind this name.'

Lisa's dad looked at her sternly. She looked back at him and then at the floor, before finally connecting with Quaye's eyes again.

'I promise,' she said. 'I absolutely swear I know nothing about this incident. I'm sorry, I wish I could help more.'

Lisa's dad chose this moment to speak up. He turned to Quaye. 'For what it's worth, I think she's telling the truth.'

Quaye smiled. For what it was worth, he thought so too. He also thought there were other truths she was hiding. But then, she was a teenage girl, of course she had secrets. He wasn't here for her secrets. He was here for her help.

'How would one find out who Gioco is?'

Lisa shrugged. 'Head down the skateparks? But in all honesty, you're a cop. You're not going to find out anything.'

Quaye sighed. 'I figured as much. That's why I gave you a shot first.' He smiled at her.

'Sorry I couldn't help.' She appeared to have genuine sadness in her eyes.

'Not a problem. If anything else comes to mind, just let me know.' He slid a card onto the coffee table before standing up. 'Good to meet you, Lisa.'

Lisa nodded and her dad offered to show Quaye out.

On the doorstep, Lisa's dad spoke to Quaye in a hushed voice.

'She's a good kid, you know. Her mum died four years back. I'm ashamed to say I wasn't a very good father during that time. That's when she got into the street art thing. She went off the rails a bit, it's true. Dyed her hair black. Well, blue *then* black. Got her tongue pierced. There wasn't anything behind it. Just a cry for attention. Attention she wasn't getting enough of from me.'

Quaye nodded solemnly. 'You seem okay now,' he

observed.

    'Yes.' He smiled. 'We're okay now.'

    Quaye thanked Mr Peake for his time and left.

Sixteen

Lisa watched out of the window as the detective walked away from her house; drove away in his car. It left her feeling anxious. There was a time when she might expect to be the object of suspicion, a few years back. Her trauma-fuelled adolescence. Playing truant, hanging around with so-called unsavoury characters, dysfunctional relationship with her father, rebellious fashion statements. It was expected, almost *designed*, to attract the attention of authority figures, be it parents, teachers or, yes, maybe even the police.

But now? She'd turned it around. The epitome of innocence. The model daughter. Yet, she still felt uneasy in the presence of a cop. Felt his enquiring eyes burrowing into her soul. She needed a distraction. Needed to get away.

She picked up her phone, searched for Luke's name. She'd only met him once, when they went spying on the scene of the unfortunate faller. But that was a good thing. Someone who didn't know her, didn't know her history. Besides, he seemed funny. And funny was good right now.

She sent him a message and they arranged to meet in the centre of town.

As she waited, Lisa sat on a bench by the dancing fountains. She allowed herself to be mesmerised by the jets of water, jumping through the air like cartoon snakes. When

Luke arrived, he greeted her with a 'hey'. She looked up and reciprocated.

Luke sat down beside her and didn't speak for a moment, joined her in her reverie. Then finally he asked:

'What's up?'

Lisa didn't turn, just spoke, distantly. 'Why should something be up?'

She sensed his shrug beside her.

'Just a hunch,' he replied.

Her eyes remained fixed on the water in front of her.

'A cop came to talk to me,' she said, scuffing her feet back and forth on the slabs.

'Why?'

'About the death of the artist. Because of my website. Thought I might know something.'

'But you don't.'

Lisa couldn't tell whether it was a question. She turned to Luke. 'I don't. I really don't know anything about that incident.' She paused and looked away. 'I wish I did.' She shook the thoughts from her mind. 'Anyway, I don't want to talk about it.'

'Okay.'

She knew what he was thinking. Their only connection was the incident. Why had she come to him as the person not to talk to about it? In truth, it was not so much the incident she wanted to avoid but what it represented, what it reminded her of. Her mum, her friends.

Ryan.

Luke didn't know about any of that. And that was the way it would stay.

'Come on,' she announced eventually, in a more upbeat tone. 'Let's go do something fun.'

Lisa led the way, trying to cast dark thoughts of her past from her mind.

But they were always there.

Lurking.

Seventeen

Three years earlier…

Lisa didn't want to go home today. She hadn't wanted to for a while. Not since it had happened. Too many memories. They said she shouldn't really be at school. But she preferred it there. Marginally. Her dad obviously felt the same about being out of the house. He was not handling things well. And at this time, when being together, being *there for each other*, ought to help, it did not. It was just a stark reminder of who was absent; of not being whole.

So today, she didn't go home. Didn't get on the bus with her schoolmates. Just started walking. She wasn't looking for anything in particular – other than herself. If that didn't seem too cliché. She ended up on Park Street, browsing around in little shops and boutiques – figuring that was what a fourteen-year-old girl should want to do. But she didn't. Not really. She found no solace in it. Moreover, it meant being social. Putting on a face to parry the nauseating hospitality.

Hello, can I help you?

No! Fuck off.

She realised she was most comfortable just being on the streets. As long as she walked, as long as she kept moving, she didn't feel out of place, didn't feel lost.

She *did* feel alone. But it was a loneliness that wouldn't

be remedied by the presence of others. In fact, the more people that surrounded her, the lonelier she felt. At this realisation, she trudged away from the centre of town, sought out new streets and alleyways. And in those dark places, she found new friends. Flat and two-dimensional maybe, but vibrant and colourful too. Sometimes. Not always. Sometimes just grungy and ugly. And that became the challenge, the quest to occupy her mind. To heal her soul.

She wasn't an expert in graffiti. Living in Bristol, she couldn't help but be aware of it. It was part of the fabric of the city. Most of it was just vandalism. To counter this, its destructive nature, the city authorities had welcomed it in its legitimate form. Whole sides of buildings overtaken by masterpieces – sometimes four or five stories high. These were captivating. She'd never really appreciated them before. Now she did. With nowhere else to be, she just stood and studied them. Though it was not these grand works that gave her most comfort. It was the more subtle pieces that attracted her attention.

Low down on one wall, Lisa found a stylised image of a horse smoking a pipe. It had crazy eyes and goofy teeth. It was playful. But more importantly, it was surreal, and this pleased her; spoke to her need for escape.

Nearby, Lisa was surprised to find a character that stirred fond memories of her childhood. A simple stencilled image of Paddington Bear, with his duffle coat and his suitcase. Lisa's mum used to read her stories about the little bear when she was small. Seeing him again now, she recalled how excited she had been when she'd first visited London as a young girl, arriving at Paddington station, which seemed vast beyond compare.

The character, with his deepest darkest homeland in mind, had been chosen by the artist to make a point. *Migration is Not a Crime* were the words stamped in ink underneath the little bear on the wall. It made Lisa smile. She hadn't smiled for a while.

The smile faded quickly when her phone rang. It was her dad.

'Where are you?' he demanded.

'Out.'

'It's late.'

'So?'

'So you should be home.'

Where you can treat me like I don't exist some more? she thought, but didn't say it out loud. She just hung up and turned off her phone.

That's how it started for Lisa. Her first steps into the world of graffiti. From that point forward she spent a lot of time scouring the streets. After a while, the quest became more focused, more systematic. Street-by-street she mapped out her findings. Taking pictures on her phone and making notes. At first just for herself, but then she posted them to a blog too. In truth, this didn't expand her reach beyond a total of one either. Not for a while anyway.

A few months after her task had begun, Lisa started to feel she needed a way into the scene, if she were to truly understand it. She'd read books, but now she needed to meet people. In *this* world, this *under*world, she was ready to meet people. She likened her occupation to that of an investigative journalist, like the ones she saw on the news in far-flung war-torn corners of the world. And she knew that if she wanted to report on *this* particular corner, she would need to make contact – with someone. But there were two problems. One, she was fourteen, and, two, she was a girl. The natural homelands of the graffiti artists, in this town at least, were raves and skateparks. Neither readily accessible territory to a middle-class schoolgirl. Ultimately, she had to resign herself to the fact that this was a world she would always be at a distance from.

But then, she saw him.

Just along the path ahead of her.

Eighteen

Ryan awoke with the sun beating through the thin vale that masqueraded as a curtain. It made him uncomfortable, but not enough to motivate any movement. There was little point. Yesterday he'd had a job, which at least posed as some kind of purpose. Today he had nothing worthy of his engagement. The yesterday in which he'd had a job was a metaphorical *yesterday*, a biblical *yesterday*, in that it existed in some period of time prior to this. He wasn't sure exactly how many days ago it was. He wasn't sure exactly how many days he hadn't even got out of bed – or whether he would today. What he did know was that the rent on the tiny damp bedsit he inhabited was due in a week; the Value box of cornflakes in the cupboard was down to dust; and his overdraft was less than a hundred pounds from maxing out. Yet it was none of these facts that ultimately spurred him into action. It was instead … the ceiling.

The ceiling was white, save for the damp patch that started in the corner of the room and snaked along a crack in the plaster to almost the centre. Besides this, it was blank and had served as a canvas for his mind as he'd laid on his back hour after hour. Even at night – especially at night. The bright streetlight outside his window kept total darkness at bay, and in the half-light his creative mind was all the more active. Images of fantasy dancing across the surfaces.

He'd always dreamed of being an artist. But then,

everyone dreamed of being an artist – in one way or another. At least, that's what his father had told him. That's what his father had told him when he was choosing his A-levels – when the compromise had been Economics, Maths and Art History. That's what his father had told him when he was choosing his degree – when there had been no compromise and he'd had to trudge his way through three years of accountancy. Well, *this* is where that little experiment had ended up, figured Ryan. This was his castle: four damp-stained walls that weren't even his.

His dad was right in one respect, though. Everyone wanted to *create* something. Not necessarily in an artistic sense; just to *produce* rather than *consume*. Just sometimes. Few could hope to bear fruit sufficient to feed themselves. But that didn't mean the urge should be entirely stifled; didn't mean the creative juices should be choked off with a tourniquet around the mind. That's what it had felt like at home. Just the sight of him sketching would send his dad into a frenzy of fear at him turning into some kind of hippy.

Ryan shook thoughts of his father from his mind and returned to the now; to his incapacitated state. And a flicker of inspiration sparked within him.

Sometimes the transition to vertical, both literally and figuratively, was a gradual process. This time, it was quite immediate. He had a plan. He knew what he was going to do with his last few borrowed pounds.

His progression to normality was so rapid he even managed a shower, before pulling on some clothes that were barely laundered and *entirely* un-ironed.

The stairs down to the street were covered in an ever-growing pile of unwanted mail, the walls were covered in an ever-growing life-form of some kind, and the front door was now so warped it wouldn't close despite his best efforts. But his mood would not be subdued. Not this morning. He walked with the stride of a man who had a destination. And that destination was, excitingly enough, an auto-parts store.

He made two detours on his way. First was via number thirty-seven, Avonleigh Road. A ginger Tom lived there who was usually in the vicinity, lazily staking out his territory. Today the feline was curled up on top of a high wall in a patch of sunlight sneaking between the houses opposite. Ryan stopped underneath the cat's basking spot and said *hello* to attract his attention. The cat idly raised his eyelids halfway and decided any further movement would be way too much trouble.

Suit yourself, thought Ryan.

Ryan's other detour was via an ATM. He stood nervously before it, summoning the courage to ask of it one last favour. He checked his balance: £906 overdrawn. Apprehensively, he requested the machine to spot him ninety quid, praying that some algorithm hadn't prophetically divined him to be an unwise risk. The machine came good for him, and the irony of this unfettered faith in his intentions struck him. After his family, his employer and a sleepy feline had cast him aside as unnecessary, it was a *bank*, of all things, that still believed in him – albeit completely unknowingly.

That was it. He was on his way.

He fetched the required supplies from the auto store and

set off back to his flat, detouring via number thirty-seven again. This time the ginger Tom was inside, basking on the window sill. Its eyes followed him past.

Back at his place, he wasted no time in setting to task. He'd never done this before, but figured that the inside of his squalid abode was the most deserving canvas on which to cut his teeth. He shook the can of spray paint vigorously, aimed it at the centre of the wall, and fired.

He painted for fourteen hours straight. When he'd finished, every surface had been covered. A night-time cityscape in some futuristic world engulfed him. Vibrant lights reflecting off of a wet street, tall glistening buildings, a funky girl with red spiky hair. Above him, a dark scarlet sky with rain-laden clouds. To his side, the moon rising over distant rolling hills. And at the bottom … a sleepy ginger cat.

Ryan flopped back onto his bed, now smattered with fine coloured speckles, and admired his new view, before falling asleep.

The next day he awoke quite differently than the previous. A man with a vocation. It was time to hit the streets.

Two weeks later Ryan was homeless. And happier than he could remember being in a long while. He didn't really consider himself as homeless; more … alfresco. The country was experiencing another exceptional summer. There had been so many consecutive now that he wondered how many more there would need to be before it was just considered summer. Even at night the temperature barely dipped below eighteen degrees. He was wild-camping more than he was rough-sleeping. Not that it was all that easy. He had to learn the ropes in order to eat. But he was in such a frantic phase of creation, food seemed like an incidental matter. The raw material which certainly wasn't incidental was paint. And this was becoming more and more problematic.

It was when he was down to his last can, embarking on an enforced monochrome creation, that he realised he had an observer. Across the road behind him was a green telephone exchange box, and sat on top of it was a girl.

Watching.

Nineteen

Lisa watched the artist for some time. It was unusual to see one working alone, in daylight. When he finally spotted her, he seemed unsure how to react initially. Then he clearly decided it was time to go. He stepped backwards from the wall, catching his foot in the handle of his bag, almost losing his balance. Then in a slicker motion he collected his belongings from the ground and started to walk away.

Lisa hopped down from her vantage point and chased after him with a fast walk.

'Hey,' she said when she was close enough.

The artist turned his head but kept walking.

'You should be careful,' Lisa continued. 'I've seen images just like these recently, in less legitimate places.' She smiled.

'Right,' was the only response.

Lisa stopped and watched him for a moment. She had assumed he would be some hard-arsed *don't-give-a-fuck* type, but he was clearly more retiring. She followed with a quick step to catch up before calling after him.

'I was only kidding, you know. The council ain't that smart.' She had a bigger smile for him this time when he turned to her.

He gave an upward nod of the head.

'What's your name?' she asked.

'Umm, Ryan,' he said, almost timidly.

Lisa laughed. It was obvious this guy was new to the game. 'No, what's your *name*?' she asked again, this time pointing over her shoulder toward his recent artwork.

After a pause, Ryan admitted, 'Oh, dunno yet.'

'Fair enough,' Lisa acknowledged, and after a pause introduced herself.

Finally, the artist stopped moving. The two stood looking at each other for a moment, both wondering what the next move was, for different reasons. They had different motivations. When the move was finally made by Lisa, it was clearly not one anticipated by her new acquaintance.

'Wanna get a coffee?' she asked.

'Umm.' Ryan processed the suggestion quickly. 'I haven't got any money,' he said, quickly adding, 'On me.'

Lisa smiled. 'S'okay, I'll buy you a coffee. Come on.'

They walked into town and took up a seat on the harbourside.

'So how come there's a new graff artist in town and he doesn't have a handle?' Lisa asked.

Ryan shrugged. 'It wasn't really a pre-meditated career choice,' he admitted. 'I just woke up one morning and started painting.'

'So, you not interested in getting up?'

'Getting up?'

Lisa smiled quizzically. 'You really aren't in the scene are you?'

'No, I'm really not,' Ryan confirmed.

'Getting up means gaining reputation.'

'Okay.' He sounded hesitant.

'So what makes a guy just wake up and start painting?'

'That's kinda complicated.' He moved on quickly before he was pressed. 'What about you? What's a girl like you doing in this scene? You an artist?'

'Ha no. I'm a … collector, shall we say.' She held up her phone, then grew pensive for a moment. 'I guess my story is complicated too,' she admitted, but didn't elaborate.

The two sat in silence for a moment. Comfortable. Lisa studied her companion with a sideways glance. When she'd first spotted him painting, she saw it as an opportunity to get deeper into the subculture of graffiti writing. But on discovering he was far more distant from it than even she was, it was almost more exciting. There was a vulnerability about him that she couldn't place, but that she found attractive – appropriately or otherwise. He was a lot older than her, relatively anyway.

'Come on, follow me,' she announced with wide eyes and a smile. 'You need some lessons in graff.'

The two strangers headed toward the centre at a casual pace. Neither had anywhere they needed to be.

'So, Bristol's not really typical when it comes to graffiti,' Lisa explained to Ryan. 'It's much more of a commercial street art thing. Pretty far removed from where the movement began in American in the seventies. Back then it was all underground; basically turf warfare. There were gangs – there were even murders. And it was *all* about getting up. It was like a massive multiplayer platform game on a city-wide scale. Like, Super Mario Art or something.' She imitated a computer game character with jumping movements and sound effects. She made like she was spraying a can into the air. 'Pssst pssst.' Then added points-scoring sound effects. 'Bee-beep bing!' She whirled on the spot and sprayed some more.

Ryan laughed at her as she played up.

'So what were the rules?' he asked eventually.

Lisa stopped, looked at him, beaming with a glint in her eye, revelling at the opportunity to actually *talk* about her passion for once.

And so she talked.

She talked for the next two hours, animatedly detailing every aspect of the graffiti scene. Its roots, history, styles, culture. And, most importantly, the rules for getting up.

When the time came to part company, she didn't want it to be permanent, but writing was a personal thing – she could hardly expect her new acquaintance to let her tag along, so to speak. She decided to delay the moment of leaving once more.

'Can I see your black book?'

'Black book?'

'Your sketchbook.'

Ryan looked up at her solemnly. 'I don't have a sketchbook,' he admitted.

'How does an artist not have a sketchbook?'

He sighed deeply. Then rubbed his tired-looking eyes for a moment, as if to hide them from interrogation, before clearly coming to a conclusion.

'Thanks for the coffee,' he said, without making eye contact. Then he grabbed his bag and left.

Lisa rushed after him.

'Hey, what's up?' she asked. He didn't stop. Lisa had to skip alongside him to keep pace.

Ryan didn't talk for a while, not out loud. But there was clearly a silent dialogue thrashing about within him – some kind of anguished debate. Eventually, a verdict was reached.

'I'd like to buy you a coffee in return,' he said without breaking stride. 'But I'm not sure I'll be able to.'

'Why's that?' Lisa asked.

'Because…' Finally, he stopped. But he didn't turn to Lisa. He turned away, resting both hands on the harbourside railing and looking out over the water. 'Because, I don't have any money. None.' He paused. 'I'm homeless.'

'Homeless?' Lisa echoed enquiringly. He didn't look like the homeless guys she usually saw around the streets. And she'd seen a few.

He nodded almost imperceptibly. 'I spent my last few pounds on cans of paint and now they're almost dry. So after today I won't even be an artist. I'll be nothing.'

'Hey,' she admonished. 'I can see you're not nothing.'

They stood silently for a while.

Lisa didn't want this to be the end. She'd met a stranger, yet found an ally. Someone she could talk to about her secret world without the baggage of her past. But she knew about men and their pride. He wouldn't accept charity, even in the form of coffee.

Eventually, something occurred to her, and she just allowed herself to vocalise it.

'Can you design me a tattoo?'

Ryan turned to her with a look of mild concern.

'You don't need a tattoo,' he stated.

Lisa noticed Ryan's reflexive glance to the bare skin of

her upper arm, before almost immediately catching himself and pulling his eyes away with an air of awkwardness.

'Why not?' she asked. For her it was the obvious progression of her adolescent rebellion. The escalation of tactics in her war of recognition. After the hair, the piercings, the truancy, the drinking. This was the ultimate act, the *irreversible* act.

'Because skin isn't the right canvas for art. It's … pure. Sacred.' He was looking for the right words.

'You don't strike me as religious.'

'I'm not. But I wouldn't paint on a cathedral either.'

'Some would.'

'Not me.'

Lisa shuffled her feet.

'It wouldn't be an ugly tattoo,' she said. 'Just a discreet one.'

Ryan shrugged. 'Either way.'

'It's your first commission. You can't turn it down.' She smiled. 'Call it a hypothetical tattoo.'

He turned to look at her. 'And my payment?'

'One cup of coffee, and … six cans of paint. Colours of your choosing.'

He tipped his head to one side in consideration, before replying.

'Deal,' he said, offering a hand.

Twenty

Although it was getting late when Quaye finished his interview with Lisa Peake, he decided to swing by Alice's gallery, as he was in the vicinity. He wondered whether her memory would have improved now this was a murder inquiry. Or at least, maybe that would pass as a good enough reason to return. On rounding the corner of the street he was not expecting to see a cop car already parked outside, lights flashing. He pulled up and saw that both the large plate windows of the shopfront had been smashed in. He jumped out of his car and ran inside.

Alice was sitting on a chair, her hands cupped around a mug of tea. Opposite her sat a police officer. Quaye flashed his badge at the officer. 'Can you give us a moment?'

The officer departed silently and Quaye turned to Alice. 'Are you okay?' he asked.

She nodded. 'Take more than a couple of masked scumbags to shake me.'

'Anything else damaged, or just the windows?'

'No, thankfully, nothing else,' Alice confirmed.

'What happened?' Quaye took the seat that had been vacated opposite her and pulled it in closer.

'I was in here late to do some hanging. Fortunately, I'd locked the door, else I'd have been a damn sight more terrified. It was just an intimidation thing. Two guys, baseball bats, freaky masks. They just rocked up and stood there, staring. Told 'em to fuck off, of course, but they didn't budge. Seemed like an age but I guess it was only minutes. Soon as I picked up my phone they gave the windows a good smashing. And then they ran.' She looked Quaye in the eye. 'Teach me to fraternise with cops.'

Quaye was taken aback. Not because this might be the reason, but that Alice *thought* it was. He had a suspicion as to the real meaning behind the attack, but it was nothing she could've been aware of. He played along with her theory. 'You think that's what this was all about?'

'I guess.' She shrugged. 'Some of the more hardcore graffiti artists are pretty anti police. Like *violently* so.'

'You got any idea who?'

Alice shrugged in response.

Quaye didn't say anything for a while. 'You're pretty shaken. You got someone to be with tonight?'

'I might head to my sisters.'

'Good plan. Do that. I'll get an officer to drive you there,' he offered, throwing a thumb over his shoulder.

She didn't protest. 'Thanks.'

'I gotta go, sorry. You be okay?'

'Sure.'

'Good.' Quaye turned to leave, his mind being invaded by destructive thoughts.

'Hey,' Alice stopped him with a hand on his arm. 'Did you come here for another reason?'

'Doesn't matter right now,' he insisted.

'Okay.' She looked vulnerable for the first time. Not a look she was used to wearing, he figured. 'I mean it, though,' she added. 'It'll take more than this to shake me.'

Quaye understood. It was an invitation to return. He didn't respond. Just smiled thinly and left.

On the street, frustration finally consumed him. He had to fight just to keep it locked down. Alice was almost right about the motive behind this attack. It *was* about fraternising with cops. But not just any cop. A particular one.

This one.

He knew what he had to do.

He had to go play poker.

Twenty-one

Quaye approached the imposing Victorian structure; descended to its base down steps worn slick by a century of heavy soles, and even heavier souls. The tradesman's entrance. He pounded on the solid door. When the sound of movement came from behind it shortly after, Quaye announced his name loudly.

There was a moment of silence before a bolt scraped and a lock tumbled. The door swung inwards under the power of a man of inhuman proportions. Quaye stepped in and spread his arms. He knew the drill. The man patted him down for concealed artefacts, but not just the usual stabby and shooty ones. Digital recording devices were the weapons of real concern in a place like this, with people like these.

He got the all clear, in the form of indignant inaction, which was significantly preferable to the form of indignant violence that was the alternative.

Quaye walked through the small anteroom into the main one beyond. It was dim. The décor managed to pull off a unique combination of seedy yet opulent. There were a dozen or so gaming tables, populated by men of varying descriptions, yet staffed by female croupiers of cookie-cutter regularity – all as immaculately presented as they were proportioned. Beyond the gaming tables there were clusters of deep leather armchairs and a small bar in the far corner.

This was an exclusive club, if that was what it could be called. Membership, such as it was, was strictly invitation only. In Quaye's case it was an invitation he couldn't refuse – but not in a good way. It was *literally* an invitation that he could not refuse. In the same way that you can't refuse to be mugged, if someone else is intent on the idea.

There was a top table, raised on a dais on the far side of the room, currently occupied by half a dozen men. Quaye made his way over to this exalted platform and pulled up a seat. There were no introductions, no nods of greeting, just a bank of steely expressions. There are few colder welcomes than from a bunch of hard-nosed criminals, mid-hand of a high-stakes poker game.

This was a cash game. Quaye knew the drill; threw a stack of twenties on the table when the hand was over. The croupier deftly scooped up his notes and piled neat stacks of chips in their place, pushing them over to him.

He smiled at her.

She smiled in return.

And his heart sank.

He knew her smile was as hollow as they came. She didn't want to be here. Any more than he did. He felt for her. His mind relapsed to a previous time, a previous girl.

One that wasn't here anymore.

He shook his mind back into the present. No time to wallow. He had to focus.

The next hand was dealt with a flurry of cards. Two arrived neatly in front of Quaye. He slid them closer, peeled up the corner of both to take a peek and laid them flat again.

When his turn came around, he slid them away unceremoniously. And that was pretty much how poker went, for a tight-style player like him; a player who may play only one hand in ten. There was a reason for that. There were two games of poker being played at this table, and the important one had nothing to do with cards. A folded hand for him meant a chance to weigh up the characters around him; commit their faces to memory.

He didn't recognise any of them. But he knew who one of them was, by virtue of the signature brown hat.

They called him Myco.

Quaye remained stoic. Resisted making eye contact. Not yet. It wasn't time.

The next hand came round. He peeked. He folded.

Poker is a game so often misrepresented; the prowess of the movie hero perversely demonstrated by the good hands he is dealt. But the hand you are dealt is *luck*. It's what you do with it that requires skill. Winning with a good hand is easy. How you play the bad hands is what separates the strong from the weak.

In this respect, it's just like life.

A waitress appeared to take orders. Quaye requested a whisky. It arrived shortly on a silver platter and was placed on a small table beside him.

After an hour of play, some of the faces around the table had changed. Some joined, injecting fresh cash into play. Of those who had departed, some had sloped off empty-handed – all-out. Some had left with a small profit. *No-one* won big. Or if they had, they'd had the good sense to stick around as a target for a while at least. Such was the posturing etiquette at the top table. The table where Myco played. Like a courtship ritual of the animal kingdom.

Quaye's stack had grown incrementally, courtesy of the odd blind steal and small pot win. Nothing too brash. No showdowns.

The next hand came around. He peeked. He flinched. Pocket rockets. Two aces. Worst. Hand. Ever. Well, not strictly, according to the math, but to a Hold'em player those two stones were the devious eyes of Eve herself, tempting him to taste the forbidden fruit. Today, though, the fruit might just be sweet. He played it big, pushing in a quarter of his chips. Those who'd observed him playing tight all evening had a choice of thinking either that Quaye had something good to shout about or was bluffing for the first time. Four dropped out, leaving Myco and one other – a thick-set man with a tattoo over his ear. The next three hole cards hit the deck. Nothing to help Quaye, very little could, but the tantalising prospect of a flush or a straight was there for the others. There was only one right move for him now: both in the poker game and the wider game he was playing.

All-in.

The neatly stacked chips toppled as he slid them forward over the green baize. Tattoo man contemplated for a moment, but it was easy to tell he was out of this hand.

Fold.

Just Myco left.

This was it, the moment Quaye had been waiting to orchestrate all evening. All that was left was to pray it went the right way.

For the first time, the pair locked eyes. Myco's cards were face down on the table. With his right hand, he deftly played with a stack of chips, cutting them in two and then rifling them back together. He stared Quaye down like a predator. Quaye was banking on him being the kind of predator who would never consider showing weakness at a moment like this – even if he wasn't all that hungry for a lone detective.

After letting the moment condense in the air, Myco made his move, an almost imperceptible nod followed by the pushing forward of a symbolic number of chips.

Quaye nodded in return, then flipped over his aces.

Myco made no reaction and turned over his. Nine/ten suited. Nothing yet but fishing for a flush or a straight. Both were on. The odds were well in his favour. The dealer cast the turn card onto the table. No use to either man.

This was it.

The showdown. All resting on that last card.

The croupier allowed a moment of tension to build before revealing it.

Seven of hearts. Together with the eight and Jack on the table and the cards in Myco's hand, he made his straight.

Myco smiled broadly as he reached forward to claim his chips. Quaye's smile was on the inside.

It had played out well.

He stood. Made eye contact with Myco.

'I got the message,' he said, then left the table.

The attack on Alice's shop was just a warning from Myco. A warning that he was still being watched. Quaye had to signify he'd heeded the message; had to come here and play the dutiful subordinate. That was the deal.

As Quaye picked his way across the room, he clocked as many faces as he could. Everyone here was a crook – or in debt to one.

Including him.

The latter.

And every crook knew Quaye was a cop.

That's why they came here. For the cops, the judges, the councillors, the doctors. For some kind of privileged immunity. All they needed was leverage.

Quaye had managed to remain relatively uncompromised so far. But it was only a matter of time. It was not a situation he could allow to perpetuate, but also not one he could end. Not right now.

He stepped out onto the street. It was dark, but warm.

He walked. Put distance between himself and that world as quickly as he could. He knew it was only temporary.

It would catch up with him again.

And next time it would be worse.

Twenty-two

Lisa had good intentions of going to school today, and she made it through to lunchtime, which she classed as a success. But her mind was filled with thoughts other than education, and in the afternoon she headed home. Her urge to escape her world had intensified.

As she ambled back, she wished she'd arranged to meet Ryan earlier. But he didn't have a phone so she was forced to stick to the plan. A rare glimpse at what life was like before everyone was connected; before gratification was instant. Before Generation-Now.

Lisa endeavoured to make use of the time productively. Firstly, she would re-dye her hair. The blonde roots were starting to peek through, and that was not who she was anymore. And maybe would not be again.

Her other task was more creative. Another attempt to elicit her father's disapproval. Ryan had told her about his first foray into graffiti – on the interior walls of his own abode. She was not so brave, or talented, to do likewise. She would just end up destroying the aesthetics of her own sanctuary. What she had in mind was more subtle – yet just as Gothically influenced as the rest of her appearance.

Her plan was for a trail of ivy leaves to descend down the wall beside the doorframe. Dark but tasteful. After many discarded attempts at cutting out stencils with a craft knife she finally arrived at an assortment of leaves of varying sizes. Then she set to work.

She patiently stencilled leaf after leaf after leaf, and then inked in spindly tendrils between them with a thin brush. All in black, a stark contrast to the pale vinyl finish of her bedroom walls. She finished each tendril with a spiral, thinning towards nothingness – she found the intricacy difficult, but immensely satisfying.

Lisa was still at work when her dad arrived home, but she didn't stop; didn't make an appearance until he called for her. Then she made her way down to the living room begrudgingly. Her dad was sat in front of the news, watching blankly as he ate fish-and-chips from a polystyrene container. On the coffee table was a portion for Lisa.

She sat silently, unenthusiastically pushing food into her mouth, not really having any appetite for it. In parallel she semi-consciously consumed the sensationalised offerings of the TV news, filling her with content equally as wholesome as the greasy food of her dinner. More wars, more terror, more intolerance. A tirade of never-ending inhumanity. She often felt there should be a law that every negative story must be balanced with a positive one. She knew there were positive stories, plenty of them, just smaller scale. Mass peace rarely breaks out, but none-the-less, anecdotes of selflessness are just as powerful. Heart-warming tales make you want to do good. Tragic ones make you want to give up.

They all seemed tragic.

Lisa observed her dad. He was sad. She found it hard to deal with. Her strategy was not to try. Not to be present. Not to wallow in his stagnant air of self-pity.

She finished her dinner as quickly as she could. Or at least, got as far through it as she felt necessary. Then she left. Her dad did not question her destination. Just let her go.

Forty minutes later she was in town.

'Here,' Lisa said handing over a bag. 'Got you something.'

Ryan looked inside and pulled out a black spiral-bound sketchbook. He opened it and smoothed the crisp white pages with his hand, like he'd discovered a rare and precious artefact.

'Thanks,' he said, smiling meekly.

'I wasn't sure what you like to sketch with so I brought you a variety of pens and pencils.'

He beamed at the implements in his hands. 'Thanks, Lisa. I … I really appreciate it. But…' He paused. Lisa could see he was not comfortable receiving gifts from almost-strangers.

'Look, before you say anything else, it's really nothing. They're just sourced from my dad's office at home. Not like he ever goes in there anymore. Too busy serial watching American TV shows.' She rolled her eyes glumly. 'Besides, I'm selfishly motivated. Want to see some more of your work.' She smiled softly.

Ryan nodded in humble acceptance. 'Funny, I never thought of getting myself an actual sketchbook. Most of my art has been doodled in the margins all my life. Ha, that's kind of a good euphemism.'

Lisa frowned questioningly.

'My dad,' Ryan continued. 'He had some kind of obsession about it. Well, an obsession about *stopping* me doing it. So I suppressed any kind of formal expression.'

'As formal as buying a sketchbook?'

'Right, sounds crazy now, huh?'

'So how did you end up suddenly painting the town?'

Ryan didn't say anything. Lisa sensed the heaviness that lay beneath the answer.

'That's kind of hard to talk about,' he said eventually. 'Well, no, I don't have a problem talking about it. Just people have a problem listening to it.'

'Trust me, I'm tougher than I look,' Lisa assured.

'I can sense that,' Ryan said, but he remained silent.

Lisa let the subject lie and decided to lift the mood by setting off to explore the various funky side-streets Bristol had to offer. She was familiar with almost all of them. At least, those in the centre and on her side of the city. She had done *the knowledge*, and then some. Ryan was less well acquainted and Lisa was happy to play tourist guide. She knew that a walking tour in the area was not complete without a trip to Castle Park. When they got there it was heaving with evening sun-worshippers – mostly youths drinking beer from cans. Lisa said she knew of a quieter spot and marched Ryan off to a small area of tranquillity known as Temple Gardens – a patch of grass and trees around the ruins of a church.

'I've got a thing for old buildings,' Lisa said as they sat on a bench facing the church's grand façade.

The two new friends sat in silence for a while. The sound

of nearby traffic muffled enough for serenity to reign. And that's when Ryan chose to talk. He took in a deep breath and just said it:

'I'm bipolar.' He stated it matter-of-factly, as if he were commenting on the weather. Then continued, 'That's the official term, anyway. But, in some ways, I prefer the old one, manic-depressive. It describes it better.'

Lisa thought about this for a moment, then looked at him. 'I'm not really sure what that means,' she admitted.

'It means different things for different people. For me, it means that for three months each year I'm suicidal, twenty-four-seven. For the rest, I'm pretty much normal, with the bouts of hyper-motivation. *Mania*, as they say.'

'Like when you started painting this time?'

'Yeah, that was when I came out of my annual downer. Usually, during my down periods, I manage to function. It's not fun, but I function.'

'But this time?'

'This time, it was different. Worse. New job, new city, no support network. And a complete asshole of a boss. HR were made well aware of my condition, and I don't expect any special treatment. Just during this point in the year, I may have the odd day off or late morning in, that's all. Just a bit of tolerance. But the finance industry is pretty full on, and my boss was a complete arrogant twat. Liked to make smart quips about me being a girl, PMS-ing. You know, really clever things like that. Took pleasure in piling it on to see if he could break me.' Ryan reflected for a moment. 'Guess he succeeded,' he added with a shrug. 'One day I didn't turn up to work, and that was that. It wasn't a conscious choice. I just physically couldn't get out of bed. That's how bad it gets. That lasted for weeks after; perpetually contemplating the point of my own existence.'

'Shit, that doesn't sound fun.'

'Nope. But on the upside – literally – the deeper I fall into the abyss, the higher I climb into the euphoria that follows. That was when I covered the town in paint in my rather haphazard fashion.'

Lisa smiled. 'Yeah, we need to work on that. If you're serious about getting up, you're going to need a style, a theme. And a name.'

'And a boat load of paint,' he pointed out.

'Don't worry. We'll sort that out.'

Lisa stood up and Ryan followed. They continued their exploration of the city.

Reflecting on what Ryan had revealed about himself, Lisa wondered whether she should reciprocate. She'd not spoken to anyone about it before. She'd not felt ready. Or not found the right person. Maybe this was the moment, the person. A stranger. But one in her new world. The world she'd adopted to escape from the other one.

Eventually, the words just came out.

'My mum died,' she said. 'Last year.'

'I'm sorry,' Ryan said.

He looked at her, but her focus remained in front.

'It hit my dad pretty bad,' she continued. 'He's still in pieces, to be honest. Our relationship broke down. We didn't argue or anything. We just stopped existing on the same plane. I guess that's why I started to rebel. Just to be noticed again. That's why I did this.' She pointed to her dyed black hair. 'And this.' She indicated the row of studs along the top of her ear and then the one through her tongue. 'Started playing up at school too. I would have been damn well expelled by now if it wasn't for the *extenuating circumstances*. Not that it made any difference. He still hasn't noticed me. And my friends ... well, fourteen-year-old girls just aren't equipped to deal with things like this – life tragedy. I kind of feel guilty in their presence; guilty about putting them in that situation; about bringing an elephant into the classroom; a big dark elephant, sapping the energy from everything, bringing down the mood.' She paused. 'Anyway, that's why I started walking the streets. It was the pieces that interested me initially – that's what they call big murals. As with most people on the outside, I just thought the rest was an eyesore, vandalism. But then I read some books about the history, where it all started. It began to fascinate me.' She looked up at Ryan. 'Sorry, I'm babbling. Maudlin, as my mum used to say.' Her mood lifted, a spark returned. 'Let's get back to you. Thoughts on a name?'

Ryan slowed his walk and looked around for inspiration. 'It's like getting a tattoo, isn't it? It'll stay with you forever, how can you possibly choose?'

It was getting dark now as they walked along beside the river near Temple Meads station. Ryan spun around as if looking for inspiration, then stopped, facing away from Lisa.

'NDA,' he said.

'What?' She followed his gaze. Across the other side of the river there was a motorcycle showroom, with large neon signs illuminated along its storefront. One in particular had obviously caught Ryan's eye. It was supposed to read 'Honda' but the bulbs behind the first two letters were out.

'If ever I needed a flash of inspiration, I couldn't do much better than a red neon sign,' Ryan stated as he turned to Lisa.

She contemplated the name for a moment. 'Lots of writers use abbreviations,' she mused. 'Does it mean anything to you?'

'Non-Disclosure Agreement is what it refers to commonly. Kind of apt for us, right?'

'I guess.' Lisa smiled. 'Now you need to work on some sketches.'

'I will.' He tapped his new sketchbook.

The tide was high as they walked along beside the river; the water still rushing relentlessly in the wrong direction. It was a sight that still fascinated Lisa; how dramatic the change could be in just a few hours.

'Sometimes it floods,' Lisa announced to Ryan. 'When the tides and the weather align. I quite like it. A reminder that we are not so in control as we might think.'

Ryan studied the surface they were walking on. 'I like this path,' he said, looking at its surface made up of small brown tiles. 'It's kind of rustic.'

'They call it the Chocolate Path,' Lisa informed. 'Cos it looks like a Dairy Milk.' She smiled and Ryan reciprocated.

The path was nestled between a river on one side and a single rail track on the other, abandoned all but for the tourist steam engine that pulls a couple of open trailers half a mile from the docks and back in the summer.

'So, where are you staying?' Lisa asked.

'Well, between you and me – in accordance with our NDA – I've got a tent in Leigh Woods. Well off the beaten trails of course. It's not so bad; this time of year at least.'

'But how come you're so...'

'Clean?' He laughed. 'Well, due to my non-standard mode of departure from work, it took them a month to disable my pass. HR get a bit confused if you don't do things the right way. They have a gym and showers in there. Very few people knew me well, and those that recognised me by face didn't know I'd left. So I could just stroll in there every day for a work-out and a wash.' He held out is arms as if to demonstrate his cleanliness. 'During that time, I developed a few other tricks.'

'Such as?'

Ryan flashed a wry grin. 'Meet me for breakfast tomorrow and I'll show you.'

Twenty-three

Quaye arrived at work mid-morning – he'd had other matters to attend to first.

'Any luck with the CCTV?' he asked as he walked in to his office.

Wilcox looked up from her laptop with a weary expression and inhaled a deep breath.

'I bloody well hope so,' she said, followed by a long puff to emphasise her efforts. 'Las Iguanas doesn't have their own camera, but there are plenty in Millennium Square and around that area. I've been through them all from the night in question. From the description we have I've narrowed down a dozen or so potential Cynthias. Our friend Arrash Rahman is due in later to see if he recognises any of them. Fingers crossed.'

'Good,' Quaye said, detached, setting himself up at his desk.

'Any luck with the schoolgirl?' Wilcox asked in return, swinging around in her chair.

He shook his head, dumped himself in his chair and stared as distantly as he could manage in a four-by-four metre office.

'What are you thinking?' Wilcox probed.

He turned to her. 'You heard of geographical profiling?' he enquired.

She shook her head.

Quaye wheeled himself around to her desk.

'Works like this. Criminals act on instinct. Just like any human or indeed any creature. So patterns emerge from their behaviour. In particular, in the case of their movements, the pattern criminals follow happens to be one that is ubiquitous throughout the natural world.'

'And what pattern is that?'

Quaye picked up a pen-pot and placed it in the middle of the table.

'This is your beehive,' he announced.

'It is,' Wilcox confirmed.

'You buzz off foraging.' He plucked out a pen and circled it around the pot. 'You're keen not to give away the location of your hive, so you don't hang around in the vicinity.' He fluttered the pen through the air. 'But also you don't want to expend too much energy. So you stop here.' He dropped the pen on the desk. 'You follow this process every time you come out looking for nectar.' He scattered other pens about the desk. 'If an observer were to profile all of these incidences, then they could work out the location of the hive.'

Wilcox nodded to convey her understanding. 'It's kind of a doughnut distribution.'

'Right, in a perfect world it might be yes. A ring doughnut. But that's only if you have enough data points. Serial killers don't tend to be as busy as bees. But it can still help in locating them. Probability distributions are generated around each point and aggregated together. The result is a map of varying probability densities. It doesn't pinpoint a single location, but it highlights a number of areas to focus a search.'

'Interesting. But what are you saying? How does it help us?'

'Well, serial killers may not be so prolific with their acts, but graffiti artists are. If we could map out all the tags of a single artist and profile them, we'd have a good idea of where to find them. Either where they live, or where they base themselves.'

'You're thinking of tracking down the elusive Gioco?'

'Right. The only problem is, we don't have a definitive list of Gioco's work. It's not featured on Lisa-the-schoolgirl's website because it's not legit. And if we went looking for it, by definition we'd only find it where we looked. To get a meaningful distribution, we'd have to walk down virtually every street in Bristol.'

Wilcox leant back in her chair, toying with her hair. 'Use the power of the crowd?' she mused. 'Put it out on social media?'

Quaye wasn't comfortable with this idea. 'Not yet. Don't want this artist going to ground. Besides, the demographic we'd be appealing to on social media would be the demographic least willing to help the police track down a graffiti artist.'

'Guess you're right,' Wilcox acknowledged. She grew pensive for a moment. 'Let me think about it,' she said eventually.

'I was intending to,' Quaye quipped with a smile. 'I've got some jobs to attend to on other cases.' He stood to leave. 'Good luck with Rahman. Let me know.'

'Thanks. I will.'

It was evening by the time Quaye got back to his apartment. When he crossed over the threshold, it was with a heavy step. The images didn't often come back to him. On this occasion they did. A vivid recollection of the very first time he'd stepped inside this place. His very first day in this city. The memories were still raw. The blood on the walls, the body-parts on the table.

He passed through the apartment out onto the terrace, to suck in some of the summer evening air – not as fresh as he'd like it to be but good enough.

Then he heard something he wasn't expecting to hear.

Laughter. Female laughter.

Then voices.

One was Silvia. The other seemed familiar. He tried to place it but couldn't. His curiosity was piqued. Not that it was entitled to be, but he was a detective after all. And he knew exactly how to crack this riddle: he had to harvest some blueberries.

After doing so, he scaled the section of roof straddling the two terraces and peered over the top.

'I've brought some blueberries,' he said holding the tub aloft in one hand. Then, 'Oh, hi,' directed at his neighbour's companion.

'Err, hi,' was the equally bemused response from Alice.

'Oh, do you know each other?' said Silvia with convincing surprise.

Quaye knew better and shot her a suspicious look. She was one of those characters he'd warned Wilcox about. Not quite what she seems. In a good way, in this instance.

Usually. The frail exterior masked a smart, sly and well-connected woman. A woman who could make things happen, should she want to.

'Join us,' Silvia directed.

Quaye dropped down the other side of the roof. He fetched a chair and a wine glass from the kitchen. He and Silvia had an understanding.

'What brings you here, Alice?' he asked.

'Mrs Granby called me asking for advice on artwork for her apartment.'

Quaye turned to the old lady. 'Oh, I didn't know you had an interest in street art,' he quipped flatly.

Silvia smiled. 'I have an interest in everything.'

'And you?' Alice asked of Quaye. 'Do you spend most evenings clambering over rooftops delivering berries?'

Quaye smiled. 'Only this one.' He poured himself a glass of wine and took a sip. 'How's your shop, all patched up?'

'Yes, thanks.'

'Any more trouble?'

'Not so far.'

'Good.'

Quaye fell silent on the subject. Alice noticed. 'Don't feel responsible,' she reassured. 'You didn't force me to speak to you.'

All Quaye could do was nod. She was right, but she didn't know what she was dealing with.

'I have a confession to make dear,' Silvia said leaning forward and touching Alice gently on the arm. 'Harlyn told me about your little incident. So sorry to hear about that. He also showed me the picture he bought. That's why I asked you over, to see if you could assist in brightening up my walls.'

Closer to the truth, Quaye thought. Though he suspected another motive. Always suspect another motive – that was one of his rules.

The conversation meandered congenially though a number of topics, from art to local politics to the exceptional weather, of course, which ultimately got them back to the topic of berries and other such produce included in the neighbours' exchange programme.

'Oh, you must see Harlyn's terrace,' suggested Silvia. 'Quite the green fingers he has.'

Quaye's subtle protests about Alice not wanting to clamber over rooftops were overruled by Alice's simultaneous noises of excitement at the idea.

'I'd love to,' she beamed with a mischievousness behind her eyes.

'Go on,' encouraged Silvia. 'It's almost time for my tele programme anyway.'

Quaye resigned himself to the inevitable. He showed Alice the technique for scaling the roof, and they dropped down onto his terrace.

'Wow, quite the oasis you have here,' Alice noted, as she made her way to the nearest crop and gently smoothed a leaf between thumb and finger. 'This is the blueberry,' she declared with the mischievous grin Quaye was becoming used too. 'I can tell by the berries.'

'The blue ones?' he suggested playfully. 'Good spot.'

He identified each of the other plants in turn. There were tomatoes growing up a wigwam of bean poles, French beans winding their way up a trellis on a wall, onions in a tub, strawberries in a hanging basket. The list went on.

'Amazing what you can grow on a rooftop,' Alice remarked, genuinely.

'Urban farming,' Quaye stated. 'It's the future.'

'I don't doubt it.'

'I admit to not being the architect.' He turned at this point, heading for his chair, and Alice chose not to follow up the statement. When he turned back, she was admiring the flora with delicate touches, silhouetted against the setting sun.

Suddenly a vivid image was projected into Quaye's mind, a memory of who had stood there before. The sensation was so powerful it caused him to freeze for a moment before stepping back and dropping himself into the chair. As he watched the figure gliding across his vision, he allowed himself to regress, to be drawn back to another time. He swam in a misty sea of reminiscence, enjoying the waves that enveloped him. It lasted only a moment, but felt much longer.

When the silhouetted figure turned and took a step toward him, it eclipsed the fading sun. A face became clear, but it wasn't the face in his mind.

It wasn't *her* face.

Quaye snapped back to the present, to reality, violently, yet not unpleasantly.

'Don't get many guests?' Alice questioned, observing the lone chair Quaye was sitting in.

He jumped to his feet. 'Not so many,' he confirmed. 'I'll grab another seat.'

Moments later they were reclined, furnished with a bottle and two glasses, watching the last rays of sun disappear over the horizon.

'What's this?' Alice asked regarding the bottle, which had no label and a swing top. 'Something of your own making?'

'Sloe Gin,' he confirmed. 'Locally sourced sloes. Have you tried it before?'

She shook her head.

'You'll like it.' He poured two measures over granite cubes and raised his glass. 'Cheers.'

'Cheers.' Alice clinked her glass against his, then took a sip. Her eyes widened. 'It *is* good.'

Quaye smiled. They sat in comfortable silence for a moment, until Alice made a playful observation.

'So, I didn't realise cops were so well paid,' she commented, referring to the penthouse apartment. 'You realise that's just another reason for people to hate you.'

Quaye laughed. 'I got a good deal on this place.'

'Dodgy backhanders, huh?' she joked. 'Even worse.'

'Not quite. It was somewhat devalued by the previous owner.'

'How so? The décor?'

'Well, it certainly needed a lick of paint. But I'd say the primary issue was the way he'd left his severed body parts scattered around the kitchen.'

'What? You're kidding me?' Her eyes were wide. 'His *own* body parts?'

'Yes. You are supping spirit at the scene of a brutal murder.' He took a sip of his own drink. 'So this place was never going to sell quickly. Plus the guy owned five more flats in that building over there.' He pointed. 'So when his elderly mother, his only relative, inherited the lot, she wasn't too concerned about hanging around a few years to get top dollar for this place. It was my first case in the city, I was looking for a place to live so…'

'So what would make more sense than snapping up your first crime scene to settle down in?'

'Exactly.' He smiled. 'Unexpected perk of the job.'

'And I assume you set up a website for flogging your subsequent crime scenes. Homes-under-the-dagger dot com.'

Quaye laughed. He liked her wit. 'Tell you what, you might be on to something there. Target the right clientele, and a murder or two probably would increase the house price. Some strange folk out there.'

'You're not wrong,' she confirmed, raising her empty glass and rattling the granite cubes in it.

Quaye poured her another measure and then topped up his own.

'So, what brought you here?' Alice asked, after taking a sip.

'Here, this city?' Quaye queried.

'Here in *life*,' she clarified. 'What's your backstory?'

Quaye shook his head firmly. 'I don't do backstory.'

'Hmm.'

Alice stood up to stretch her legs, paced over to the edge of the roof, sipping from her glass. After a moment she turned, leant back against the wall. 'I think you *owe* me a backstory,' she said, her eyes teasing yet piercing.

'*Owe* you?'

'You bugged me for mine, remember? Then I obliged. *Then* I got my shop smashed in.'

Quaye contemplated this for a moment, looking down at the floor, ashamed that he'd brought this upon her. Scared even.

'They got the little toe rags by the way – I guess you know.'

'What?' His eyes snapped to hers. He didn't know – petty vandalism wasn't his department. But moreover, he hadn't even considered that they might be petty vandals.

'Don't be so shocked. Your lot aren't so useless all the time,' she beamed. 'Some wannabe local graff artists. Known to the cops. Caught one of them on camera down the street taking off his mask. Idiot.'

Quaye's mind quickly assessed this new information. He'd thought this was the work of local crime-lord Myco. Thought it was a warning that he was still being watched. A not-so-subtle threat toward someone he … someone he what? Suddenly it was so obvious. Myco might have eyes everywhere, but how could he possibly have made any connection between him and Alice, over and above the professional capacity that it was. If there was any other connection, it was only in his mind. His mind getting ahead of itself, without him even knowing. Foreseeing the potential?

In light of this revelation Quaye considered that maybe Alice was right. He *did* owe her. A backstory. But that would mean … *talking*.

Maybe he could manage that, he figured.

Maybe it was time.

He looked up at Alice who was studying his silence. 'Okay,' he said, patting the seat beside him. 'Backstory.'

Her eyes widened. 'Goodie,' she said gleefully, rubbing her hands together as she returned to her seat.

Disarming, that's what she was, Quaye decided. It made things easier.

'Before this,' he began. 'I was involved in missing persons. Kids mainly, of course. You know the stories. On the news about once every couple of months. "Police are growing increasingly concerned for nine-year-old Matilda, missing since yesterday evening". And you know how they turn out.' It wasn't a question, everyone knew. 'A body is usually found within a week,' Quaye continued. 'Usually in connection with a relative or family friend. Or no body is ever found. Fortunately, a lot of stories don't make it to the news. There's a window of only hours, twenty-four at the outside, where there's hope of getting the kid back alive. Otherwise…' He made a shrug. 'If it gets to the news, it's too late. And often, one of the sobbing relatives appealing for information at the press conference *knows* it's too late.'

Alice curled herself up in her chair to face Quaye as he told his story.

'There are two cases I know of in this country where a child went missing for more than a couple of months, but who ultimately turned up alive. One was my very first case as a detective. Sweet looking nine-year-old girl from a middle-class suburban family. There was a media storm, of course. Normally, it would die down – but the family did well to keep it in the spotlight.'

'And you found her? Alive.'

He nodded solemnly. 'In a disused cow shed ten miles from home. Abducted by a neighbour. Locked up and abused.' Quaye paused as he looked out into the distance. 'Some people would say we found her in time.'

Alice looked confused. 'But you did.'

'In time for her to recover physically, yes. But mentally? Will she ever be the same? Should we have got to her sooner?' He shrugged.

There was silence for a moment, before Alice asked the question he'd prompted her to, subconsciously. Like he'd tossed a coin to fate to decide whether he'd reveal the next bit.

'And who was the other child who went missing and was found?'

That was the question.

'The other kid to come back alive?' Quaye clarified. He took a long swig of his drink before looking her deep in the eye. 'The other one was me.'

Alice's eyes grew wide, but she said nothing for a moment. What could you say to such a revelation? Finally, she knew.

'Shit!' It was a slow, considered exclamation. 'How old were you?'

'I was five. And I was gone for six months.'

'Shit!' She repeated, more reactive this time.

Quaye retained an emotionless exterior. 'I don't remember much,' he lied, closing off that line of enquiry before it began.

'So that's why you joined the police?'

'Not really. Not consciously anyway. It just happened, as these things do. But when I found that missing girl, and someone found out about my history, it made a great story. People assumed I had some *special insight*.'

'And did you?'

'I don't know, maybe I did. But I got tired of being *that* guy. Got tired of finding bodies instead of children. Usually – sadly – it's too late before we even start looking. There's only so many little Millies you can find in the stepfamily's attic before it gets to you. Before you become a different person.'

'So you became a murder detective. Where you *know* they're already dead.'

'Ha,' he laughed. '*Serious crime* detective actually', he corrected. 'Not *always* murder.' He smiled at Alice then suddenly looked at his watch. 'Shit, what time is it?'

'Is it past your bedtime?' Alice mocked.

'No, my neighbour's!' He looked over at the adjoining roof, couldn't see any light pooling onto the wall from the kitchen window.

'What's up?' Alice asked.

Quaye locked concerned eyes with hers, as he considered the situation. Myco may not be aware of her yet, and he wanted it to stay that way.

'This may sound odd,' he put to her, 'but I wanted you to leave the same way you came in.' He gestured toward the adjoining building.

'You embarrassed about having a guest?' she toyed.

'No,' he replied flatly.

'You're not married are you?'

'No,' he snorted as if that were a ludicrous suggestion. 'It's just, as we've discovered, it's not safe for you to be associated with me.'

'Oh come on, they were local scallies. And they've been nabbed. Who do you think is camping outside your door exactly?'

He sucked in a deep breath. 'Cops have a *lot* of enemies.'

'Well then, I fear we're already too late,' she said in a conspiratorial whisper, as she pointed to the sky. 'You've forgotten the spy satellites. Any moment now masked terrorists are going to be rappelling from a helicopter to abduct me.' She looked nervously to the heavens for a moment before cracking into a smile.

Quaye couldn't stop himself from laughing. He knew his caution sounded over-dramatic, and in truth he was approaching this situation with disproportionate concern. But something echoed within him – echoes of a previous time. Like an overpowering sense of déjà vu. Only *real*. Real memories.

Knowing it was too late to change the situation, Quaye cast the concerns from his mind as best he could.

They stayed outside chatting until they grew cool, before moving indoors and watching the end of an old movie on TV they both had fond memories of from childhood. After that, Quaye taught Alice the basics of Go, the game she had learned of earlier from his playing partner on the neighbouring roof.

It was one of those evenings when time seemed meaningless, and tiredness never came. Quaye remembered such times from his younger days. But as an adult they were rare and to be cherished. All the more so because they cannot be planned. They can only be wished for.

Twenty-four

Lisa waited for Ryan by St. Mary Redcliff church. He had promised her breakfast, and this was where they'd agreed to meet. She sat on a low wall admiring the grand building before her. She had always appreciated its ostentatious architecture; its tall Gothic spire reaching up to the heavens. She knew a structure such as this wasn't just *built*. It *grew*. Evolved over centuries. A million lives and stories wrapped up in its stones and mortar. She knew some of those stories – she'd studied the building for a project a while ago. She knew it was maybe the fourth or fifth church at this location, and that the site was a place of worship for centuries even before that. She knew it had lost its original spire to an act of God, ironically, and had lived without one for over four centuries.

And yet it stood strong.

It felt a shameful fact to Lisa that the church was now sandwiched between a roundabout and block of council flats. Not the merest hints of the red cliff whence it got its name, just concrete and tarmac. Its beauty was muted, its majesty extinguished, its history disregarded. All for the sake of so-called progress. Just a building for commuters to ignore on the way to their lives.

It may just as well be graffiti, Lisa thought.

A faint voice scratched at the back of her mind, but didn't make it into her consciousness as her thoughts wandered. Then it came again, a little louder.

'Hey, Lisa.'

The voice came from behind her. She snapped out of her reverie and turned to see Ryan. He was smiling. This was the first time she'd seen him smile unprovoked.

'Hey,' Lisa responded. She smiled in return and hopped down off the wall. 'I'm hungry,' she jested with wide eyes.

'Follow me,' invited Ryan.

They walked just a short way down the road to the Mecure hotel, then in through the main entrance.

'What are we doing here?' Lisa asked.

'Just act natural,' Ryan said. 'Act like you belong.'

Lisa followed Ryan's lead. As they passed reception, Ryan smiled casually at the man sitting behind the desk. This was a side of Ryan she hadn't seen. He'd come across as timid and shy when she'd met him. Now he was different. Now he was in control.

They took the stairs up to the first floor and followed the long corridor, past room after room.

'What are you looking for?' Lisa asked.

'You'll see.'

After lapping the first floor they took the stairs up to the next and proceeded to do the same. Eventually, Ryan pulled up outside room 207.

'Here we go,' he said in a hushed voice. 'This morning's newspaper, remnants of last night's room service and a Do Not Disturb sign. These two aren't getting up for breakfast today.' He turned. 'Come on.'

Ryan ran playfully back along the corridor, goading Lisa to chase him. She did so, suppressing laughter so as not to break the silence. They raced down two flights of stairs, before Ryan pulled up abruptly at the bottom, putting an arm out to ensure Lisa did likewise. He made a gesture with both his palms face down, indicating the need to compose themselves.

After a moment to catch their breath and dispel the mischievous grins from their faces, they made their way through the lobby and on to the restaurant. It was 9.50 a.m. – the tail end of the breakfast session. Most of the staff were busy clearing the decks. No-one was standing sentry, waiting to greet new guests – or deflect them. Lisa followed Ryan's lead to the buffet. The spread was extensive. Beyond the greasy stuff, there was fruit, yoghurt, cereal, pastries, something called Bircher muesli, and muffins – which seemed like an odd breakfast item to Lisa.

They filled their plates with all the necessary components of a full – to overflowing – English breakfast, along with glasses of juice, and took their wares to a vacant table.

The lady who approached them was large, but carried it in that bubbly, friendly way that made it endearing.

'Room number?' she asked politely.

'Two-O-seven,' Ryan responded with a smile.

She wrote it down on a pad. 'Can I get you tea or coffee?'

'Coffee, please.' He looked at Lisa, who requested the same.

'Lovely,' the lady said in a broad local accent, and trotted off.

And that was it. Free breakfast.

This appealed to Lisa's particular level of rebellion. Just

the right side of wrong. She glanced at Ryan with a smirk, and he smiled back.

'Who are we today?' he asked, out of the blue.

'Who are we?' Lisa repeated questioningly.

He looked up. 'We're in a hotel restaurant, eating breakfast, late on a Saturday morning. It definitely doesn't feel like we are a schoolgirl and a homeless guy.' He angled the hilt of his knife at Lisa then himself as he spoke.

'You want to be someone else?' Lisa enquired pointedly.

Ryan shrugged. 'Don't you?'

Lisa considered this for a moment. And she realised, somewhat to her surprise, that, no, she didn't want to be someone else. She wished things could be different, of course, but not that she was someone else. She wouldn't have wanted her mum not to have been her mum, even though she was no longer here. And she wouldn't want her dad not to be her dad even though he was … also no longer here, but in a different way. And although she had her own faults and idiosyncrasies, she knew that everyone did, and she wouldn't want anyone else's. So for the briefest of moments, in the reflection of Ryan's question, she felt a flicker of … what was it? … not happiness exactly, but *gratefulness* maybe. Because at least she was content with one aspect of her world, the one that could not be altered, not easily anyway. Her*self.* Her *mind*.

'Who do you want to be?' Lisa bounced the question back at Ryan.

He was quiet for a moment, looking around. Then eventually answered.

'That guy.' He pointed out of the window to a nondescript man walking along the pavement on the other side of the road. He was dressed casually, had a soft smile on his face, seemed to be enjoying the warmth of the sun. As the man approached the large doors to a building on the corner, a couple of people exited and the three exchanged a few words of conversation before continuing. Then the man disappeared into the building.

Lisa had assumed Ryan would fabricate a grandiose story about some successful artist or similar. She didn't see the significance of the guy that had now vanished out of sight.

'He seems normal,' Ryan said, knowing he owed an explanation. 'Seems at peace with himself. Maybe he's not, it's impossible to tell. But that's all I want.'

It seemed so alien to Lisa. She knew it was common for people to want to be in a different situation, to want more money or success, a different job or relationship. But to believe there is something so intrinsically flawed with yourself that you just want to be a different person, she couldn't imagine that.

After three and a half courses and two cups of coffee, Lisa decided she was full, and waited patiently for Ryan to finish his fourth. They were the only ones left in the restaurant now.

When Ryan finished his last mouthful he looked at Lisa with contented eyes.

'Let's go,' he said, and stood up purposefully.

As they passed through the lobby, they both smiled a *good-morning* at the receptionist who reciprocated. It was only as they hit the bottom step outside that Lisa collapsed into a fit of giggles.

'Welcome to the criminal underworld,' jested Ryan. 'There's no turning back now. By the end of the week you'll be running drugs and fencing diamonds.'

Lisa laughed. 'Cool. Where do I sign up?'

They ambled their way onto Queen Square, an oasis of green flanked by trees and Georgian architecture.

'So how's my tattoo design coming along?' Lisa probed.

'*Hypothetical* tattoo,' Ryan corrected.

'Of course,' Lisa responded with mock sincerity, followed by a wide smile.

Ryan raised an eyebrow in return before nodding toward a bench. They took a seat facing the grand equestrian statue standing on a plinth in the centre of the square. A mother and her toddler played peekaboo around its base, the kid giggling hysterically. It made Lisa smile. Innocence could be medicinal to the observer, she realised.

Ryan pulled out the sketchbook Lisa had bought for him and leafed through a few pages.

'Here,' he said, handing her the book.

She grasped the book in both hands and studied it wide-eyed like a child with a new toy. It was not what she expected. Not that she was sure what she expected. Maybe that's why she wasn't the artist. The pages before her, and those that followed, boasted a busy collage of symbols and shapes vying for position. All abstract. Nothing concrete could be determined, just forms that hinted at nature and chaos.

'I love them,' Lisa said genuinely. 'So you think these

represent me?'

'I don't know you,' Ryan stated flatly. 'But I knew you didn't deserve something trite like a butterfly or a dolphin or a flower.' He thought for a moment. 'An enigma. That's what you are, I think.'

'Look who's talking.'

Lisa's fingers reached out and gently caressed the texture of the paper, moving from one design to the next and eventually settling on one with a smooth spiralling motion.

'I like this one,' she announced.

The image had a sphere at its centre, but formed as if from a broad coiled structure – like the peeled skin of an orange. Around its edge were random curved points, which might have resembled flames.

'It's yours,' Ryan announced. Then added, 'As long as it doesn't end up on your skin.'

'Then what's the point?' She wasn't sure to what extent she was jesting, although she was a few years away from being old enough to get a tattoo anyway.

'Consider it your emblem,' Ryan said. 'Like a tag.' He snapped the sketch pad away from her playfully. 'You can draw it on your school books,' he teased, laughing and making his escape from the bench just in time to miss a punch in the arm from Lisa. She didn't feel like a schoolgirl, especially when she was with him.

Lisa and Ryan weaved their way through the hustle and bustle of the city centre and up towards College Green, chatting idly and ambling slowly. Neither had any place to be.

'Where are we heading?' Ryan asked.

'Brandon Hill, of course.'

'Of *course*.'

'If you've never been you're in for a treat.'

The two made their way up a very steep and narrow road, tall buildings either side. Then, suddenly, emerging from the urban streets, was grass, a park, a hill. The path zig-zagged its way toward the summit. Given the gradient and the heat they walked at a less than pedestrian pace. Halfway up there was a group of Lycra-clad ladies performing a variety of odd maneuverers as part of a boot camp.

Eventually, Lisa and Ryan made it to the top, and took a moment to enjoy the view. But the ascent wasn't over yet.

'Come on,' urged Lisa making her way to the base of Cabot Tower. Grey squirrels darted across in front of them, some so tame they sat happily beside the pavement as the two of them walked by. Stepping into the entrance to the tower they were welcomed by cool air, and started to make their way up the narrow spiral staircase.

'You never been up here before then?' Lisa asked.

'Nope.'

'One of the best views in the city.'

They emerged from the top to a spectacular sun-drenched panorama: rolling grass beneath them, Brunel's SS Great Britain sitting in the harbour, buildings stretching across the city, and green hills in the distance. They took a long time standing on each side of the tower, studying the outlook, Lisa pointing out the key landmarks each perspective had to offer.

When they were done, Lisa made an announcement.

'Time for an ice cream,' she said.

They returned to the cool interior of the tower and headed back for ground level. Back out in the daylight, Lisa bought them both a Mr Whippy from an ice cream van, without protest from Ryan who must have figured it was fair payment for breakfast. They were lucky enough to claim a bench overlooking the park and cityscape beyond, and sat in silence for a while.

'This is your canvas,' Lisa announced. 'Are you ready for it?' Lisa sensed Ryan nod slowly beside her. She turned to him. 'Do you have a plan?' she asked earnestly. 'A plan to get up?' Lisa had explained to Ryan the last time they met the rules of the game: how to become the king in this particular realm. There were three factors that could affect an artist's ascendency.

Proliferation: the more, the better.

Location: the more *audacious,* the better.

Execution: the more *time,* the better. Quality, of course, comes into it, and novelty too, but everyone accepts that this is subjective. The only universal rule when it comes to the artwork itself is: the grander the masterpiece, the longer the exposure to risk, the greater the kudos earned.

Ryan looked straight ahead, like he was staring into his destiny.

'I do have a plan,' Ryan said eventually. Then he turned to her with as serious an expression as she'd seen that day. 'But I'm going to need your help to pull it off.'

Twenty-five

Quaye placed a takeaway coffee on Wilcox's desk.

'Thanks,' she said, looking up with a smile.

'Good weekend?' Quaye said absently as he dumped himself at his desk.

'Yes, you?'

'Not bad, thanks.'

Wilcox was already beside him, coffee in one hand, tablet in the other. 'Here,' she said, offering him the screen.

'What's this?' he asked.

'Hot spots,' she exclaimed with a beam.

Quaye studied it more closely. An outline map of the region with an overlay graduated with colour: yellows, oranges and reds. He knew what it was.

'How did you generate this?' quizzed Quaye.

'You said it yourself. To generate a meaningful geographical profile of Gioco's work we'd have to walk down *virtually* every street in Bristol. So I did … virtually.'

Quaye wasn't sure what to say.

Wilcox continued. 'Okay, so I admit, I have some geeky friends. Used to share a house with a bunch of computer scientists at uni.' She dragged her finger across the display to pan the map. 'Every street of the city is available online, and together with all the geo-tagged tourist snaps, there is barely an inch of real estate which is not accessible programmatically. It was just a case of brute forcing it to find all the Gioco images.'

'Which your friends were happy to do?'

'They like a challenge at the weekends. Too much daylight makes them irritable.'

Quaye knew this was a phenomenal feat to pull off in a single weekend. Almost suspiciously so. But he let it lie, and studied the map instead. 'So what do we have here?'

Wilcox gave an overview. 'The pins show all the instances of graffiti writing resembling the name 'Gioco'. As you can see, pretty spread out across Bristol, but a definite higher density to the south. The spots with the highest probability are all south of the river. Southville, Ashton, Bedminster – that kind of area.' Wilcox looked at Quaye. 'So you think our artist lives in one of these places?'

Quaye pinched the screen to zoom in on one of the hot-spots. The brightest red covered an area of a few streets. Beyond that it faded to orange, then yellow.

'Could do.' Quaye shrugged. 'Or one of his comrades, where they regularly meet. These areas are mostly residential, but it's worth checking if there are any likely establishments where artists might congregate: youth clubs, skateparks, underpasses. I'll look into that.' He figured Alice might know the answer to that question. It was her area, both geographically and professionally. 'Not worth doing a door-to-door. We don't have a real name or a face to enquire about. And anyone who knows anything isn't going to talk.'

'I agree,' Wilcox added.

'We also need to have one note of caution regarding what this map is telling us.'

'What's that?'

'Our artist is more likely to be drawn toward the centre of town than away, so the distribution may be slightly offset if the model hasn't taken this into account. Otherwise, great work.'

'Really?' Wilcox seemed unsure.

'Absolutely.'

'But it sounds like it hasn't got us much further?'

'Maybe not with specifics. But rather like this map, eventually enough greys add up to black.'

Quaye stood up and grabbed a whiteboard marker from beneath the board on the wall. Not that he necessarily had any intention of writing anything.

'So let's go over what we know. Our dead man, Milner, was a novice, probably first-time, graffiti artist. Based on the testimony of his friend and the photo we found on his fridge, it would seem he was coerced, by the mystery lady, Cynthia, into going to a particular railway station bridge to write a particular name, Gioco. The name of an artist who seems to be based, we now know, in the *same* part of the city as the station.' Quaye looked at the board. Magnets held various artefacts to it: photos of Milner and the crime scene, a copy of the fridge note.

'Oh, I can add to that,' Wilcox said, grabbing a print out from her desk and affixing it to the board. 'Cynthia,' she announced.

'Ah, yes, good,' Quaye acknowledged. Wilcox had already informed him of a positive ID by Milner's friend, Rahman. The image had that blurred, distant quality expected of a security camera. He peered at it. It was hard to make out facial features, but if someone knew the woman they'd probably recognise her. More generally, she had long black hair. She was slender and showed it off: high boots, short skirt, white vest top. She carried a large handbag over her shoulder.

'I know what you're thinking,' Wilcox said. 'She really was out of Milner's league.'

'Couldn't possibly comment,' he shrugged with a slight smile.

'Do we release this?' Wilcox asked.

Quaye shook his head firmly. 'No. We don't know her name or have a clear picture of her face. If she's not a British national as we believe, she'll disappear into thin air. Right now she has no idea we've connected her to this, and with any luck she's still around.'

'But how else are we going to find her? I don't think canvassing the streets with a blurry photograph is going to work in a city of half a million people.'

Quaye paced away from the board thoughtfully. He knew she was right. 'I don't know,' he admitted eventually. 'But while we think on it, we have another task to keep us occupied.

'What's that?'

'Interview some scumbags.'

'The very reason I became a cop,' Wilcox responded. 'Which ones?'

'A couple that busted up the windows of a gallery in North Street, because the owner had talked to the police. Maybe they have something specific to hide.'

The lift was out of order, of course, so they had to climb the five storeys via piss-stinking stairwells. Quaye thudded on the door of Billy Cunliffe – Little Billy to his friends. There was movement inside but the door didn't open. Quaye thudded again, louder this time.

'Nocturnal, these kids,' he said to Wilcox as they waited.

Finally, the door opened a crack, and a pair of moley eyes peered out into the daylight. Quaye held up his badge.

'Your mum in, Billy?' he asked unnecessarily loud, enjoying the wince it garnered from the face at the door.

'No,' the boy said, cramming as much tetchiness into the single syllable as he could.

'Good.' Quaye pushed the door open roughly, causing the boy to stumble back, almost falling.

'Hey!' he exclaimed. 'Don't you need a warrant or summit?' He had a thick urban accent.

'Not to ask you a few questions, no,' Quaye confirmed as he pushed his way past Billy.

Billy grumbled expletives as he hitched up the sweatpants riding half-way down his backside. Quaye made his way uninvited through to the living room. It stank of pot. There was an ashtray full of dog-ends on the coffee table, surrounded by a dozen empty cans of cheap booze. The TV was blaring banal daytime trash. Quaye found the remote and shut it off.

'Looking forward to your trip to the magistrates?' Quaye enquired with a wry grin.

'Fuck off,' was the disdainful response.

'Charming.'

Quaye paced, studying the contents of the room, though

he wasn't really looking. It was just a tactic to make his host nervous. Everyone has something to hide from unexpected guests. Whether it be a pile of washing-up or a kilo of contraband.

'Why did you smash up the windows, Billy?'

'You know why.'

Quaye knew Little Billy had already confessed to the crime, under the advice of his counsel, and knew the kid was probably none too bothered either. It would cost him a slapped wrist or a few hours community service at the worst and yet earn him significant notoriety amongst his cop-hating associates.

'How about you spell it out?' Quaye continued.

'She's a pig-loving bitch,' he snarled.

'You mean she spoke to a policeman?'

'S'what I said.'

'Like *you're* doing now.'

The boy recoiled a little at the accusation, before collecting himself for a response. 'Don't have much choice do I?'

'Neither did she.'

'Yes, she did. She…' He stopped himself.

'She what?'

Billy remained silent. Just shrugged and hitched his pants up again. What Billy clearly didn't know was that the police officer who the gallery owner had talked to was the very man standing before him right now.

'Who's Gioco, Billy?'

The boy frowned quizzically at the sudden change of direction. 'What's that got to do with anything?'

'That's why you did this isn't it, to protect the identity of an artist?'

Billy was still frowning. Then shrugged. 'Hell yeah, why not. That sounds like a good reason.'

Either Billy was a great actor or the new line of questioning was unexpected. Quaye was confident in the latter, but played it out just to be sure.

'To protect the identity of someone involved in a murder,' he added.

'*Murder*? What the fuck? I ain't involved in no murder. All I did was smash up some windows.' A crack had opened up in his blasé posturing as he began to squirm.

'So who asked you to do it?'

'No-one. Got my own mind ain't I?' He prodded his temple with a forefinger.

Whilst Billy was rattled, Quaye continued to fire the questions fast.

'Was it your idea or your cohort's?'

'Mine.'

'How did you find out the gallery owner had talked to the police?'

'Just heard di'n't I.'

'From who?'

Billy just shrugged.

'Was it you who heard or your partner-in-crime, Daniel?'

Billy sniggered. '*Danno*,' he corrected.

'Okay, Danno. Who heard?'

Billy shrugged again.

'Hmm.' Quaye looked the boy up and down slowly, then

took a few more inquisitive paces around the room. He pushed aside the net curtains and peered out of a grimy window.

'People would pay a fortune for a view like this.' He turned back to Billy. 'If it weren't for the neighbours.' He flashed a grin then stepped forward until he was squarely in Billy's personal space.

'See you tomorrow, Billy.' He winked. 'I'll bring some uniforms.'

Quaye headed into the hallway. Wilcox followed.

'Wait, what?' Billy rushed after them.

Quaye's hand was on the latch of the door when he turned back. 'Sorry, I thought we had an agreement. You wanted to become a snitch?'

'What the fuck? I didn't…'

'You didn't?' Quaye cut him off. He made his way past Wilcox and into Billy's face, backing him up against the wall. For the first time, Quaye's voice grew aggressive.

'Billy, this is not a game. This is a murder investigation. I will enjoy making your life very uncomfortable with your groupies if you don't answer my questions. Who told you the gallery owner had spoken to the police?'

Billy looked away, then looked back with angry yet defeated eyes. 'I don't know,' he snarled. 'Danno found out, from some man.'

'Some man?'

'S'all I know.'

'He didn't say anything about who this man was?'

'No.'

'You just followed along blindly?'

Billy offered an exaggerated shrug. 'Some man. S'all I know.'

Quaye narrowed his eyes, studying the kid, watching the sweat bead on his forehead. Finally, he ended the exchange with a snarl: 'It'd better be.'

They left.

Making their way back down the grungy steps to the ground floor, Wilcox reflected on the discussion.

'So, do you think this incident is connected to the murder?'

Quaye shook his head. 'In all honesty, I don't know. But I'm programmed not to believe in coincidences, so I need to get to the root of it.' He held the door open as they ventured back out into the real world.

'Onto the next guy?'

'This Danno kid?'

'Yeah.'

'Absolutely.'

Before they got to the car, Quaye's phone rang in his pocket. His *other* phone. The one that rarely rang, but did so with an ominous air of foreboding. He took a few paces away from Wilcox before he pulled it out, and continued to walk away as he answered.

He was back seconds later.

'Fancy talking to Danno alone?'

'Umm…'

'You'll be fine. He'll be putty in your hands. Take along Geoff Deakin. He's a big lad. I'll introduce you to him back at the office.' He spoke whilst hurriedly getting into the car. When Wilcox was in, he wheel-spun out of the estate. 'Just find out who this man is who Danno supposedly got information from.'

'I'll try. Where are you off?'

'Work emergency.'

'Nothing serious I hope.'

He shook his head. 'I'll drop you at the station.'

The call had been a short one. The voice at the other end was the kind of voice you didn't argue with. It had told Quaye there was a job for him. There were few details. Just where and when. In fact, just where. The when was implicit.

Now.

Right now.

Twenty-six

Ryan reached into his bag and pulled out his sketchbook once again. This time, he skipped forward, passed the designs for Lisa's hypothetical tattoo. Then stopped, closing the book but keeping the page with his thumb.

'Just look at the design on the left,' he said, opening up the book, doing his best to obscure the right-hand page with his arm.

Lisa studied the image and smiled. The letters of Ryan's alternate moniker, NDA, could be made out, just, in what was otherwise a swirl of abstract shapes, conjuring thoughts of a future space-scape. It was nothing like she'd seen before. It was a mural-scale tag.

'I like it.' She looked up at Ryan with a glint in her eye.

'You haven't seen nothing yet,' he said, then slowly revealed the page opposite.

At first, Lisa wasn't sure what she was looking at. A graphic of dizzying complexity. She could see those three letters again repeated throughout it, in differing forms. But there was something else, she knew that. Some form attempting to coalesce in her mind.

Ryan noticed her hesitation and moved the book to a different angle, and slightly further away. Then the image snapped into place.

A face.

Her face.

In truth, it wasn't exactly her face. It was cartoon-like. But she could easily see the inspiration. She was confused. Not by the subject but by the scale. There was a hundred hours minimum in executing a piece like this. Probably a lot more. And it was large. Really large.

She made eye contact with Ryan. 'You're going to need the whole side of the M-Shed for a piece like this.'

'Yes,' he agreed. 'And no,' he added enigmatically. He slid down the bench a little, held the sketchbook up in front of his face, his fingers curling around the edge at each side.

Lisa stared at the pages. Then suddenly it was obvious what Ryan was planning to attempt. The first image, which had initially appeared as just letters and abstract lines, was a small part of the more detailed graphic.

It was a jigsaw.

Lisa reached out and lowered the book with one finger on top of it. When Ryan's face came into view, hers was showing wide eyes and an open mouth. It made Ryan laugh, as he snapped the book shut.

Lisa shook her head disbelievingly. 'That's a pretty ambitious challenge you're throwing yourself down there,' she pointed out.

'The hard bit's done.' He gestured to the drawings.

'No,' Lisa corrected. 'The *clever* bit's done. The hard part hasn't even begun.' She took the book from him. 'You've designed a skyscraper. Now you just have the small matter of building the thing.'

Ryan nodded acceptingly. 'With a little help?' he said, looking at Lisa.

'Hey,' she was quick to respond. 'I'm with you one-hundred percent on this project, but I'm no artist. I can't help with these.' She pointed to the plans before her. 'I can provide the paint. But that's about all I'm able to offer.'

'Not just the paint. You can provide the canvas too. Both real and virtual.'

Lisa furrowed her brow in his direction.

'You know every wall in this town. You know better than anyone where I can throw these up. I need forty-two locations. I don't know Bristol nearly well enough to scout these out.'

Lisa nodded, thoughtfully, already compiling a list of possible sites in her mind. 'Okay, I can help with that. But the virtual?'

'You may tell me different, but I'm willing to bet that even the gritty underworld culture of graffiti operates in more than just the physical space today. That even a lot of the illegitimate writers have their own websites, right?'

'That's true,' Lisa confirmed.

'So, I'm assuming that if an artist wants to *get up* in this century, it's more than just the art on the wall that counts. The art on*line* is just as important.'

'So you want a website?'

'Not exactly. I want a stalker.'

'A stalker?'

'Yeah, a fan. Someone who literally pieces these works together. I need someone telling the story. You said you put all your pictures on a blog already – that's all I'm asking.'

'I do. But I only have one follower. And that's me. It's a very … err … *personal* kind of blog.'

'Intentionally?'

She thought about this. 'No. But I haven't intentionally promoted it either.'

'Would you?'

Lisa pondered this. It was suddenly getting real. She'd only been a spectator before. Now she was going to be a promotor. More than that, she was going to be complicit in the act. That's what she'd wanted to begin with. When she met Ryan, she saw *him* as the blank canvas. She felt compelled to encourage his talent. And since hearing his story, even more so. It was the one thing that made him alive. Surely, the therapeutic benefit for him justified some paint on some walls?

It did, she decided.

'I'll help in whatever way I can.'

They spent the day idling through the streets of Bristol. Taking in the art. Ryan seemed happy, at ease. Lisa found she liked that. She had realised early on that he was a complex character. Complex wasn't the right word. Just different, maybe. And so harder to understand. Yet she found she could empathise with him, all the same.

'Do you want to come to my place?' Ryan asked out of the blue, verbally putting 'my place' in inverted commas.

Lisa looked at the time, then shook her head.

'I can't,' she said despondently. 'My dad will go ape if I don't get home.'

'Sure, another time.'

'I do want to, though,' Lisa added hastily, to reassure him it wasn't just an excuse.

He nodded. 'It's actually quite pleasant.' It was his turn

to reassure. 'Like camping. If it's a clear night, you can see the stars through the trees.'

They crossed the former rail bridge by the Create Centre. It was another of Lisa's favourite structures. It showed charm in its decrepitness, as many artefacts of the industrial era did. Paint flaked away, revealing rust beneath, yet it looked strong, with its chunky girders and proud rivets. Looked like it was willing to carry the weight of the world for another century at least.

They stopped on the other side. The point at which they would go their separate ways. And under normal circumstances, in this age of ultra-connectedness, that's exactly what they would have done. But with one of them off the grid, coyness was not an option. A plan of when and where had to be made right now, or not at all.

They stood in awkward silence for a moment, until Lisa said something she wasn't expecting.

'Tonight. I'll come back tonight.'

'What about your dad?'

'He won't know. I'll meet you here at midnight.'

'Okay.' Ryan smiled. 'I'll be here.'

Twenty-seven

When Lisa got home, her dad wasn't in. She figured he'd probably gone out for takeaway. It would give her time to plan her route out of the house later that night. She knew she couldn't go downstairs. Not least because the stairs creaked, but primarily because her dad had a habit of staying up late and falling asleep in front of the TV – another behaviour acquired since her mum had died. However much his actions frustrated her at times, this was one she couldn't judge him on. She couldn't imagine how empty his bed must feel with only himself in it now. It was probably the place he felt the loneliest.

The upshot was she wouldn't know whether her dad was awake and lying in wait downstairs, so she couldn't risk the front door.

She surveyed her potential route from the back garden. Her bedroom window opened wide. Outside it was the sloping tiled roof of the kitchen extension. Coming off the other side of the house was the garage. If she went this way she would have to make the jump from one to the other. This would be the tricky part. If she made it, it was simply a case of traversing the edge of the garage roof, dropping down onto the top of the garden wall, then along the wall to the back of the garden and down into the alleyway behind.

She knew she could make the jump. She had been a competitive gymnast up until … well up until the same event that everything seemed to be up until. Her only concern was the noise from walking on the roof above the kitchen. Would her dad hear it from the living room? Would he be in the kitchen? Was there any way she could dampen it?

Lisa rushed upstairs. She stole a glance out of the landing window to see if her dad was on his way. No sign yet. In her bedroom, she secured her door shut with a chair under its handle, then swung open the window. The roof was just a couple of feet below. She sat on the ledge and swung her legs outside, placing her stockinged feet on the tiles near the lead flashing. She realised she would have to carry her shoes in a bag for this part of her escape. She stood up carefully and took a step forward down the sloping tiles. She was light-footed and was confident she could make her way without any detectable thuds. At least, none so heavy as not to be dismissed as the local tabby. What she hadn't anticipated was the grinding of the tiles on top of one another, as she shifted her weight. She needed to do something about that.

Lisa climbed back into her room, then rushed downstairs and out the back door into the garage. She had always benefitted from being her dad's head helper in his maintenance activities, having no brother to fulfil the role by default. From this she had developed a decent engineering mindset and knew what she was looking for in the garage. A few years back she had helped in fitting some new units in the kitchen. She remembered that to compensate for the unevenness of the floor tiles in places, her dad had used plastic wedge-shaped spacers. These were what she was in search of. She rummaged around in the bottom of the big toolbox first, but couldn't find any in there. Then she systematically went through each of the little metal drawers on the workbench. Screws, nails, bolts, washers, Allen keys, randomly shaped bits of plastic and metal that belonged to long-since forgotten pieces of equipment. She couldn't find what she was looking for, but after about half a dozen drawers she struck upon something better. Lying next to a collection of dried up tubes of super glue and epoxy resin, there was a bunch of wooden clothes-pegs, grubby with oil and dirt but perfect for her purposes.

Just as she was about to reach in and grab a handful, she heard a car outside. She froze, trying to pinpoint the noise, trying to determine if it was pulling into their drive. It seemed to linger close-by for a while. Then it moved away and Lisa released the breath she had been holding.

She grabbed the pegs and made her way hastily back to her room. On the way she started to pull each peg apart, removing the metal spring, leaving her with two wooden wedges.

Back on the roof, with a fistful of wedges in hand, she mapped out her route, identifying which tiles she would stand on. At each one, she lowered herself carefully into a crouch and pushed two of her noise-dampening devices under its bottom edge.

Just as the last one was going in she heard the front door slam. Her dad was back. It made her start so much she almost lost her footing. She had been so intent on her task, she hadn't even heard a car this time. Lisa had no time to test her handiwork. She scrabbled back through the window into her room and collapsed onto her bed, her heart beating rapidly, but giggling to herself too.

She reflected for a moment and realised she was experiencing an emotion that she hadn't had for a while. Excitement. A swarm of butterflies in her stomach. Was it the plan of a clandestine escape? Partly, maybe. But she'd been doing the rebellion thing for a while now. That was nothing new. It was something else.

It came to her like a bolt.

It was a boy.

She found she wasn't entirely sure how she felt about this when she analysed it. She was not yet fifteen, albeit maturer than most her age. And the boy in question was … however old he was. Not to mention homeless. And bipolar. Her dad certainly wouldn't approve, which was usually reason enough to draw her to something. But that wasn't the attraction in this case. Her feelings were definitely deeper than such shallow motivations. Whatever, she harboured a warm glow, emanating from deep within her gut, and she welcomed it. It was comforting. And she lay with it, with a smile resting on her lips, until her thoughts were interrupted. Her dad was calling her down, in the impatient barks she had grown accustomed to.

Lisa made her way downstairs, conscious she would have to artificially depress her spirit so as not to arouse suspicions or even questions. It stated something about her home life that any flicker of contentedness would be such a noteworthy departure from the norm as to signal some mischievous act on her part.

Lisa shared a flavour-enhanced Chinese takeaway with

her dad, in the loosest possible sense that a meal could be shared. The most literal one. There was no exchange of conversation or emotion. They scooped helpings for themselves from foil containers and watched the news channel until it looped back to the start, her dad frustratedly jabbing at the remote in search of something more distracting.

When Lisa was done, she went up to her room. She had three hours to kill. She spent the first easily, showering followed by trying on every suitable combination of clothes in her wardrobe. All black of course. Then it was makeup. She didn't go in for the heavy look; just eyeliner, slightly thicker than average.

She began the remaining two hours lying on her bed, headphones on, listening to music impatiently, never getting more than half way through a track before skipping on to the next. When she was done with that, she managed to kill another half-hour serial-surfing inane videos on the web. By 11 p.m. she was just pacing.

Eventually, it was time to leave.

And that was exactly when something happened she hadn't anticipated. The security light at the back of the house came on, illuminating the garden. And it wasn't in response to urban wildlife. It was a much less welcome creature.

Her dad.

He was out the back of the house. Lisa watched him. He was jabbing something into his phone with one hand and holding a tumbler of whisky in the other. Lisa stepped back into the darkness of her room, out of sight, but still observing. She reflected on the plan she had made with Ryan. And panicked. In retrospect, she should have arranged to meet Ryan at a later time. Midnight sounded late and indeed poetic, but to get there on time she'd have to be exiting her bedroom window by eleven-thirty at the latest. Not late enough to guarantee her dad would be asleep, or safely settled in front of the TV. It was now quarter past and he most definitely wasn't doing either. She watched him intently from the shadows, trying to gauge his body language. Then he did something that made her heart sink to the pit of her stomach. He sat down. On one of the garden chairs which lived permanently on the patio. He put his phone away, leant back in the chair and took a long swig of whisky. It didn't look like he was going anywhere anytime soon.

Lisa paced in her room, out of sight of the window. She looked maddeningly at her phone, forever her lifeline yet completely impotent on this occasion. All it did now was relentlessly proclaim the passing of each minute as it ticked by, adding ever more weight to her anxiety.

It had now gone quarter to midnight. Lisa peeked out at her dad again. He had slipped down in the chair and put his feet up on the low wall around the raised bed at the side of the garden. It was another warm evening, and it looked like her dad was settling in for the night.

It was at this point that the realisation dawned on Lisa that this was not a problem. She didn't have to stick to her original plan. If her dad was happy in the garden. She could just sneak out the front door. It meant she wouldn't be able to secure her bedroom door from the inside, but that was a risk she would have to take. She cursed herself for not doing it sooner. Without another moment's thought, she hastily grabbed her bag and light-footedly skipped along the landing and down the stairs. Halfway down she realised her fundamental flaw and froze dead. She had planned to get back into her room in the small hours of the morning the same way as she left – through her window. But the window wasn't open. At least, it was only open about six inches to where it stopped on a security latch that could only be reached from the inside.

She had to go back to her room.

She looked out the window. Her dad was still there. The security light had gone out, so he was just a shadow now, save the little pool of light at his feet from a solar candle near the ground. His body position was suggestive of slumber, but she couldn't see his eyes. She reminded herself that there was nothing suspicious about opening a window wider on a sticky night like this. Nevertheless, she preferred not to attract his attention. She approached the window, very softly depressed the catch in the frame with one finger, and pushed out the pane just far enough to pass it. Her dad didn't seem to stir.

Lisa slipped back into the darkness of her room, down the stairs and out of the house, closing and locking the front door as quietly as possible before disappearing into the night in her bare feet. Only on the next street did she stop to put on her shoes, as hastily as she could. She looked at the time. It was gone midnight now. She started to run.

The park down the road was dark and eerie as she entered, but Lisa didn't let it trouble her. She ran through barely slowing her pace, despite the risk of tripping on the uneven surface or getting a tree branch in the face. Out the other side she crossed the road, went down the slope studded with solar lights, and arrived at the bridge where they were due to meet.

There was no-one there.

Her body deflated, both from disappointment and exhaustion from the run. She breathed heavily as she looked around in all directions. She couldn't see anyone.

Her shoulders slumped further as she resigned herself to her return journey.

Then there were footsteps. And a voice.

'Hello.'

Lisa spun around. It was Ryan.

'I thought you'd gone,' she said to him.

'I don't really have any other place to be.' He smiled. 'I was just keeping out of sight. Didn't want to scare any little old ladies and get moved on for loitering.' He took a step closer. 'Glad you made it.'

'Glad you're still here.' She gave a final deep sigh to catch her breath. 'Had a little trouble getting away.'

'Not to worry. You're here now. Let's go.'

Ryan led Lisa along the path beside the river. The view of Clifton and the bridge at night was as scenic as ever. Soon the path transitioned from asphalt to gravel, and then to a trail. By this point, they were shrouded in trees. Lisa had walked this path hundreds of times, but never in darkness, which was now almost total. There was no moon and the clear sky meant little of the city's orange glow was reflected back down.

Lisa felt Ryan's hand reach out and feel for hers. She took it gladly. It felt natural.

'I've done this route quite a few times now,' he said.

'No monsters then?' Lisa jested.

'Not so far.'

The trail they were walking used to be a towpath long ago for boats travelling to and from Avonmouth docks. The route was still used for shipping freight, but not along the river anymore. It came in along a rail line that ran along a high embankment to their left.

After about ten minutes they reached one of the many arches under the rail line that gave access to the steep woods on the other side. Lisa could just make out that this one was fenced off.

'This is where it gets a little tricky in the dark,' Ryan announced as he produced a torch from this pocket.

'Oh, so you do have a torch?'

'Of course. I live in the woods. It gets dark.' He shone the light under his chin to reveal a grin. 'But batteries are a precious commodity.'

Ryan peeled back a corner of the fence to make an opening just wide enough to squeeze through. Beyond was a flat clearing filled with boulders and discarded remnants of railway repairs. They made their way across by the light of Ryan's torch and then up into the woods via a steep narrow trail.

'Almost there,' Ryan assured Lisa, as they took a right into thick undergrowth. 'I wanted to be off the beaten track,' he explained. 'To afford myself some privacy.'

Eventually, they stopped.

'Wait here,' Ryan urged, as he took a few paces forward and reached into a tree. All of a sudden there was light, from a lantern hanging overhead. Then another.

'I don't usually allow myself two lights at once, but as we have a guest.' He spread his arms to welcome his visitor.

Lisa took a look around in the dim glow. There was a tent. Beside it, a tarpaulin was strung between trees, with a blanket on the ground beneath. There was an ash-filled fire pit made out of stones, with a small stove suspended above. And, as might be predicted, there was art: pages from Ryan's sketchbook pinned to tree trunks in places, spray-painted images dancing across the bark in others.

'Not quite what you were expecting, huh?' Ryan observed.

Lisa shook her head. 'It's slightly more … *established* … than I was expecting'.

'Well, not all homeless people are the same. They … we … all have our own unique story. Some may suffer from substance abuse. Some are between places. Some just have a spot of bad luck. In my case, I was completely aware of what I was doing when I stepped off the merry-go-round. Indeed, I was literally manic about the possibilities it offered. I used to camp a lot, so I had some equipment. I was determined to make my homeless experience as sustainable as possible.' He caught himself rambling. 'Sorry, take a seat.' He gestured to two sections of tree trunk acting as stools. 'I don't usually entertain. I got the second one in preparation for your visit.'

'Thanks,' said Lisa perching on one.

'There's a felled tree up the way. They chainsawed it up

to clear the path but left it in place as a habitat for the local wildlife.'

'Of which you consider yourself among?' Lisa jested.

'Exactly.' He smiled.

They stayed up until the small hours talking, until sleep beckoned and Lisa had to decide whether those hours of sleep would be in the woods or in her bed. She knew she didn't want to leave and decided that this was where she belonged tonight.

She slept soundly in the tent, her head resting on Ryan's chest, the sound of nature around her. The morning came all too soon. She'd set her alarm for dawn so she could get back to her room in time.

Everything looked different in the light as she emerged from the tent. She could see the extent of Ryan's decorations, sympathetic with the surrounding environment. She felt calm here. At rest. She didn't want to leave. Didn't want to return to the real world. But knew she would have to go now, if she ever wanted to come back.

Ryan guided Lisa out of the woods and then she made the rest of her way home alone, with a skip in her hurried stride and a warmth in her heart. It was early. Only the most hardcore joggers and dog-walkers were out when she passed through the park. She raised a smile to each one.

Not all was right with her world. But it was *more* right. And more right was good enough for now.

Back at her house, she executed her planned escape route in reverse: scaling the wall from the back alley, edging along to the garage roof, leaping across to the extension and climbing in through her bedroom window. And finally, she got into bed. Though, for ceremonial reasons only. She was way too wired to sleep, and it was only fifteen minutes until her alarm would go off.

She allowed excitement to consume her. Thoughts of Ryan, of sleeping in the woods, of hatching plans for his assault on the street art scene.

That was all to come.

And it couldn't come soon enough.

Twenty-eight

It was very early in the morning when Quaye picked up the young woman. The sun had yet to rise, and there were no lights in the remote location he'd been told to meet the other guys. It only took a moment. She was bundled unceremoniously from their vehicle to his, with nothing more than a few grunts to accompany the proceedings. Then he was driving. Just him and her, deeper into the wilderness.

Quaye didn't say anything when they set off, just glanced across to assess the woman's condition. Her hands were bound. She was gagged and blindfolded. In the dim glow of the dashboard he could see she looked grubby and had bruises up her arms. She was shivering with fear and cold.

It made him feel sick.

It always made him feel sick.

He turned up the climate control a couple of notches, then uttered his first words as softly as he could.

'You'll be warm in a minute.'

She flinched at his voice, but otherwise did not respond.

After five miles or so Quaye pulled the car off the road. He could only imagine what must run through the mind of a woman in her situation at such an event as pulling into a layby; an event normally so mundane.

He let the car come to rest for a moment, then spoke in as reassuring a voice as he could muster.

'I'm going to untie your hands, okay?'

There was no immediate response, then a slight downward nod, indicating her comprehension.

She had been bound with a couple of industrial cable ties. Quaye leant across and made two swift snips with a pair of wire cutters. The woman rubbed her raw wrists in relief.

'You can take off your blindfold and gag now,' Quaye said. He didn't want to encroach on her personal space any more than he had to. He felt compelled to build trust even though he didn't need to. He knew he could treat her like the other guys had, all the way to the end of this and it wouldn't make a difference to the outcome. In fact, it would make it easier to arrive at the right outcome. But something within him couldn't bear the thought of someone having the wrong opinion of who he was. Even though she would never know who he *really* was. It was not such an odd compulsion. In fact, it was an evolved trait. Like leaving a tip in a restaurant you'll never go to again, or waving another car out at a junction. It's not altruism, it's something much more powerful.

Manners.

Manners make the world a bearable place to exist, and Quaye was not about to abandon them now. That was the beginning of a slippery slope. And he didn't have the appropriate footwear.

Quaye stole a brief glance to study the girl. She was young. She had the defined bone structure reminiscent of her homeland. One that radiated beauty, even from behind tired reddened eyes and dirt marks on her cheeks. All the same, he knew she'd be horrified at her present state. In gaining her trust, he knew he could do no better than giving back control of her own appearance.

'If you want to freshen up,' Quaye said, nodding toward the glove compartment. In there were some cleansing wipes and a hairbrush. He stopped short of providing a selection of make-up. That would just be weird.

His passenger didn't say anything, but she pulled down the vanity mirror to study herself. As she set about fixing her face up, he reached over to grab something from the back seat. The woman flinched at the movement, and he apologised for not forewarning her.

'Here, if you're hungry,' he said handing over a selection of pastries and a flask of coffee.

She clearly hadn't been fed that well by the way she started devouring food. She was halfway through her second pain au chocolat by the time she finally found the confidence to speak.

'Who are you?' she asked.

'I'm the negotiator,' Quaye replied matter-of-factly. 'You're going home today.'

She studied the ever-diminishing and steepening track they had been following into the rural hillside. 'This isn't the way home,' she said nervously.

'No, I'm sorry. But … we have to go through the motions.'

'I don't understand,' she said with an obvious crack in her voice.

Quaye looked at her. 'I know.' He unfastened his seatbelt and got out of the car. 'Enjoy your breakfast.'

He sat on a grass bank, facing back toward the car. Besides his guest, he was alone. There was probably no-one for miles in any direction, such was the remoteness of this place. But the situation brought to mind many vivid memories of people.

The worst of people.

And the best.

And as he strained to concentrate on the latter, it only seemed to bring the former into sharper focus. Sharper, colder, darker.

He closed his eyes, tried to will the thoughts away, but he couldn't shake them. Instead, he felt the cold tip of a gun barrel firmly pressed to the back of his skull, as if it were really there.

The day the deal was struck.

'Tell me where she is,' the voice had said behind him, calm yet menacing. It was Myco. The worst of people. He was talking about Jessica. The best.

'You know I can't do that.'

Quaye was on his knees, facing the wall. He hadn't seen the face behind him, but then it wouldn't have made any difference. Myco was a man of many faces.

'Mr. Quaye, you don't seem to understand the seriousness of this situation. We have invested a lot of time and money in Jessica.'

That was true. They played the long game, these people. 'She is in our debt. She can't just walk away. That's not part of the deal.'

'I understand. But *you* must understand that I can never hand her over to you.'

'Then you are willing to exchange your life for hers?'

'That's exactly the deal I am offering.'

Myco had meant it by way of death, of course. Quaye had not.

There was silence for a moment as the crime lord considered this.

'What are you suggesting?'

'I'm a detective. She's a doctor. I must be worth at least as much to you.' It sounded like a game of chess. And that's pretty much what it was, on a grander scale. A knight for a rook. 'So, let me take her place,' Quaye continued. 'Take on her debt to you. In return, she is free of any further obligation.'

The gun barrel had been pressed against his skull all this time. Now the pressure was finally gone. Quaye took this as an acceptance of the offer, but he remained motionless – did not dare to turn around. He heard footsteps, a door open, and then, just before it shut again, the words:

'You will be hearing from us.'

He did.

When he came back to the present, Quaye found himself staring at the patch of grass in front of him, elbows on his knees, fingertips rubbing his temples. He flicked his head up to the car opposite and locked eyes with his hostage. The gaze lingered for a moment until Quaye snapped himself free, and pulled himself into an upright position, assuming the appropriate stature for today's role. Whatever that was. Hostage taker, negotiator, common thug, good citizen. He wasn't sure anymore, just played along to the beat. Waiting for the music to stop, so he could finally take a seat.

He checked his watch.

It was time.

He got back into the car. The girl studied him but didn't say anything. The engine burst into life at the turn of the ignition.

'Let's get this done,' he said out loud to himself, as the car skidded away.

Twenty-nine

Quaye dragged himself up the three flights of stairs to his apartment. His ribs were bruised, his face was battered and his mind was scrambled. Things hadn't quite gone exactly to plan, but the job was done. He could get back to pretending his life was normal.

Until the next time.

Back in his flat, he bypassed the scotch and went straight for the hard stuff. Tea. Strong. Two sugars.

He'd been off-grid for two days and knew he had to touch base with Wilcox. He pulled out his phone and called her up. She answered promptly.

'Hey, stranger. Thought you'd been kidnapped.'

Quaye let the irony wash over him silently. 'Sorry, I was called out of town. Forgot my phone.'

'Missing person?' she asked, assuming it was work related.

Quaye remembered the young woman who'd been in his care for the last couple of days. 'Yes, missing person.'

Wilcox updated Quaye on her progress in his absence. The interview with the second tearaway who had smashed in the gallery window hadn't borne any fruit. But, more positively, she was confident in tracking down some better images of Cynthia.

'Details can wait until you're back,' Wilcox insisted.

Quaye was more than happy with that arrangement. It

was as much shop talk as his muddy mind could take right now. He signed off the call, telling Wilcox he'd see her on Monday. Then he crashed onto the sofa and flicked on the TV.

Suddenly he was overcome by a sense of loneliness. Not unusual in itself, but this time it was different. It was more immediate, more acute. He wasn't sure why. Not to begin with. But then he realised.

It was something he'd have to do something about.

Although feared he couldn't.

Next day, he waited.

Near the top of Ashton Court Estate there was a wooden bench under an old oak tree. It was a simple bench, just a block of wood atop two sturdy legs. Quaye sat there, taking in the view of the city. It was another warm summer evening. People streamed by in both directions. Dog walkers, runners, cyclists, kids on scooters. *Lots* of kids on scooters. Occasionally, a whole entourage passed by, taking over the entire pathway: children, parents, friends of parents, grandparents, uncles, aunties, dogs. The sunshine had brought them out in droves, like an insect invasion.

Quaye registered each individual and watched them until they were gone. None of them lingered a suspiciously long period of time. None of them were looking at him in an overly familiar fashion. Not today. If they had been, he would have known about it. That was the point.

In possession of this fact, Quaye could strive for a state of mind in the vicinity of relaxed. As near as he was able to at least.

He didn't have to wait long. Until one individual in particular came into view. One who *was* looking for him. Her eyes met his at a distance. She made her way in his direction and sat down beside him.

'Lovely evening,' Alice offered as her opening cliché.

'Indeed.'

Quaye turned and smiled at Alice, providing her with her first close-up look at his recently battered features.

'Jeez!' she exclaimed. 'What happened to you?'

Quaye shrugged. 'Well, that's a very long story.'

'Does it relate to the clandestine nature of our meeting?'

'Yes,' he said flatly.

'What's her name?'

'Ha.' Quaye laughed. 'There *is* a girl involved.'

'There always is.' Alice delivered the line in a playful tone. She had a way of putting Quaye at ease. Somehow there was a level of understanding between them even though she could not possibly understand the first thing about him.

Quaye wasn't sure exactly what he was going to reveal to Alice. He only knew that he wanted to talk to someone, and for some reason he wanted it to be her. At the very least, Silvia had judged Alice as having a good soul – as she put it – and he was inclined to take heed of his neighbour's assessments. She was particularly shrewd on such matters. All matters, in fact.

He looked to the sky for inspiration.

'I'm not quite sure where to start,' he admitted.

'Then, at the beginning seems like a good idea.'

He nodded. 'In which case, it begins … oddly enough …

with an apartment. *My* apartment. You remember that it was the scene of a crime. The crime that first brought me to Bristol. Where the previous owner was…' He paused.

'*Diced*?' Alice suggested.

'Indeed. Into twenty-seven pieces to be precise. Some would say deservedly so.'

'Really?'

'Well, I'll let you judge for yourself,' Quaye said. 'The man owned a number of other apartments, over the other side of the green in front of mine. And he was very discerning about the *quality* of his tenants. Or should I say, *qualities*.'

'Let me guess: young, female, attractive?'

'Yes, that seemed to be his type.'

'I've got a feeling I'm not going to like why.'

'Probably not,' Quaye confirmed. 'He had a penchant for a spot of voyeurism in his spare time. Had a number of telescopes trained on their windows, which would be bad enough in itself. But the peeping Tom apparatus was not for his eyes only – not solely for his own pleasure. The scopes were all hooked up to video cameras, streaming live to the heart of the dark web. Anyone could take a peek if they were willing to pay for it.'

Alice winced. 'Eww.' She had an understandably guttural response to hearing this.

'And just to make sure he didn't miss a thing, he had one-way blinds fitted at each of the windows, only the opposite way than intended. So when the girls closed them, they couldn't see out, but he could still see in.' Quaye shuffled a little. The combination of the hard bench and the subject matter made him uncomfortable. 'The whole hidden-cam genre is big business … so I'm told. You'd be amazed at how many men out there will pay to watch this kind of thing. And not only watch. On *this* site, they could even control the scopes – panning and zooming to the best vantage point.'

'Sick.' Alice screwed up her face in disgust. 'Although, still not sure it warrants being chopped up into twenty-seven pieces.' She made a dismissive wave of the hand. 'Twelve at the most.'

Quaye smiled at her. He realised it was her sense of humour that put him at ease.

'Come on,' he said. 'Let's walk.'

They headed up the hill at an ambling pace, in silence for a while until Alice picked up the topic.

'So, we have a gruesome crime at the apartment you now live in. What bearing does that have on your life today?' Alice asked. 'Oh, is it haunted? Is that why I can't visit: the Ghost of the Chopped-Up Pervert? Dismembered body parts floating around the room in the dead of night?'

'I think a ghost would be a more tangible threat.'

Quaye deftly side-stepped an oncoming yappy-dog-chasing-scooter combo, and smiled at the apologetic and mildly embarrassed parent/owner in tow. Quaye was more than happy to tolerate errant canines and offspring so long as their handlers at least showed some signs of awareness. Indeed it pleased him to watch families making use of these outside spaces.

'It's hard to imagine in this idyllic setting,' he remarked, turning back to Alice, 'that Bristol is not always the wholesome and innocent ball of fluffiness that you might expect.'

'Really?' Alice feigned mock surprise.

Quaye knew she was well acquainted with the more subversive aspects of the city's culture, given the nature of her gallery. Not least its recent hammering by local thugs.

'But I'm not talking about your regular breed of criminal, stealing tools from lock-ups and dealing drugs in dark alleyways. There is an altogether more sinister kind of villain operating in this city. The *organised* kind.'

'Organised like *mafia* organised? In Bristol?'

'Like mafia yes. But not the mafia.'

'And Peeping Tom was involved?'

'Not directly. But he should have known better. Should have known who he was dealing with. The apartments he let weren't paid for by the tenants. Funnily enough, there wasn't a letting agent or tenancy agreement in sight. As far as we could gather from his bank records, they were all paid for by a single entity, in cash, in advance, on a rolling six-month basis. And at well above market rate. That sort of arrangement means only one thing: no questions asked.'

'So the girls were prostitutes? The flats paid for by the pimp?'

'Good deduction, but not quite right. Not exclusively anyway. It's more subtle than that. The women were…' – he faltered as he recalled the word – '…Assets.'

'*Assets*?'

Quaye nodded. 'With a capital A.' He realised some background was needed. 'Before I got involved in all of this I thought the term organised crime was such a pathetic and unthreatening way of describing something so brutal and merciless. I figured that a criminal's mastery of a nice Gantt chart or profit-and-loss sheet was not what made them so scary. Compared to, say, their mastery of a flick-knife or semi-automatic. But, in truth, it is precisely their organised nature that makes them so insidious. They are structured, distributed and faceless. They exploit and destroy innocent lives much more completely than by merely *ending* them. They burrow their way into your world like a tick into flesh, impossible to get out. And once they get hold … they *own* you. There's nothing you can do about it.' Quaye turned to Alice with a steely expression. 'These guys are smart. And they're patient. They play the long game. And it's real long.'

It was clear Alice didn't fully understand, but knew enough that there was no scope for flippancy now. Not at this point in the conversation.

'You're speaking from experience,' she observed.

He nodded, but didn't say anything more for a while. By this point, they had reached the initial summit of the stately grounds. Here, following the road around would lead them to the old gatehouse. Instead, they took a left, up a gravel track that led past a golf course and on to some woods. They walked in silence for a minute, allowing the new tone of the proceedings to bed in. A couple of mountain bikers flew past them in the other direction, kicking up dust from the dry ground. As the dust settled, the mood settled with it. Quaye drew in a deep breath. He knew he had to say her name, but it was never easy. He'd spent the recent years of his life trying to convince himself that she never existed. It would be easier that way.

But it wasn't the truth. He knew it. So he had to acknowledge it.

Out loud.

'Her name was Jessica,' he said, the last word sticking in his throat.

Alice waited patiently for more to come.

'She was a junior doctor when I met her, training to be a surgeon. Not from a privileged background. She was the first of her family to go to university. It was a tough career choice, but she was determined from a young age. Her grades at school allowed her to secure a bursary from a charitable trust, which helped pay her tuition fees. When she was struggling to make ends meet at university, she got a job as a croupier at a local casino. Then, at the casino, she befriended a wealthy businessman. A couple of years later, when she'd finished her degree and needed a place to stay, this businessman said he had an apartment she could use. Told her it was a capital investment, that he couldn't rent it out for tax reasons, and that she'd be doing him a favour by looking after the place for a few months.'

'Lucky break.'

'They were all lucky breaks, seemingly. But, in fact, none of them were. Like I say, they play the long game this particular criminal organisation. That supposed charitable trust was nothing of the sort, it was their own sham. The casino was real enough, but it was theirs too. And the fact that she learned of a job going there was no accident. And the businessman with the apartment, of course, was one of them. All planned. All staged.'

Alice shook her head. 'I don't understand. Why go to all that trouble?'

'Because, if they go to that much trouble, by the time you find out who is really behind all these seemingly unconnected acts of benevolence, you discover you've been on the payroll of an organised criminal gang for X number of years. Not only are you implicated, you *owe* them. And they'll make sure they cash in their debt. And then some.'

'But what are they after? What did they want from Jessica?'

'Skills. Although sometimes I wonder if it's just for the fun of it. These guys make so much cash from their various enterprises they couldn't spend it all in a lifetime. They literally have to either give it away or bury it. So, after a point, it's not about that anymore. It's about power and influence. Like some massive real-world role-playing game. And a critical aspect of the gameplay is strategically placed professionals to call upon at their behest. Prized pieces to lord over; to control. A lawyer, a cop, a council official, a surgeon.'

'Why a surgeon?'

'Because their business is a lot messier than normal business. And when one of their thugs gets a suspicious looking wound, from say a bullet or a blade, they can't just rock up at Southmead Hospital. Not without questions being asked, or the police being informed. So that's why they have doctors on their books, to patch up their heavies when needs be. In all, they have a vast multi-skilled army of professional consultants at their beck and call for any such emergency. And they call these individuals Assets.'

'And these *Assets* can't just go to the police?'

'Not unless they want to walk away from their lives. Full on witness protection. New name. New identity. No contact with their friends and relatives. It's not like one arrest and it'll all be over. Even if an arrest could be made at all, it would only ever be a bottom-rung foot-soldier. And for that you'd have a price on your head.' Quaye waved a hand to dispel that course of action. 'But they're smart. They don't push their Assets too far. They don't want to break them, to drive them over the edge. That would be a wasted investment. They just want them on their books for when they need them. So every once in a while an Asset will get called upon to do something they'd rather not do, but know it's better than the alternative. They live with it.'

Alice nodded slowly, before asking the obvious question. 'So, what's the story with Jessica?'

'She chose the alternative.'

Quaye paused. He knew he'd reached the point in the story where he had to tread carefully. Where it would be unwise to trust his companion – or anyone – with the whole truth. The truth that he'd done a deal with the devil, with Myco. Traded his service for Jessica's.

He was the Asset now.

Jessica had still decided to go. Hadn't trusted the word of an organised crime outfit, surprisingly enough. She may well have been right. Quaye didn't know them well enough. But he figured if he kept up his end of the bargain they wouldn't go looking for her. That was all he could do.

Besides, he had another motive. His only goal in life now was to bring this regime down – if that was possible. And the only way they were going to fall was from the inside. Not that he was on the inside. He didn't know how the machine operated, any better than cabin crew know how to fly a plane. But he was better placed than the passengers.

He continued with his story.

'Jessica joined Medecins Sans Frontieres. She set off for Africa, but that's as much as I know. I don't know where, or whether she is still there. I haven't heard from her in five years.'

This was all true.

They'd reached another fork in the path and Quaye gestured for them to follow the route that took them into the woods.

Alice asked the next question. 'So how much do you know about these guys?'

'Not a great deal, it's true. And a lot of what I think I know is merely personal conjecture. But I've done a fair bit of conjecting. They are far-eastern in origin and headed up by a man calling himself Myco. Although, it's not quite as straightforward as that. Unofficially, I've managed to gather half-dozen descriptions of this guy, and none of them match.' Quaye neglected to mention to Alice, or any of his colleagues for that matter, that two of these descriptions were from him. 'The only consistent element is his distinctive hat. From what I can determine, this is what identifies him as Myco.'

'But it's not him?'

'Well, we can't know. And that's the beauty of it. Most of my fellow detectives assume they are merely his representatives, doing his bidding. Or, at least, all but one are. But I'm not so sure now.'

'How do you mean?'

'Well, there is another alternative. They're *all* him. That is to say, they are all Myco. Myco is not an individual, it's a collective – a *concept*. They act as one, have a single goal. It makes them less tangible – less accountable for any crimes. Remind you of anything?'

Alice saw where he was going. 'Graffiti crews.'

'Exactly. Same model. That's what made me think of it.'

Alice contemplated this for a moment. Then her contemplation obviously strayed to another topic.

'So why are you telling me all of this?'

Why *was* he telling her this?

'Largely because…' – he looked at her – '…my elderly neighbour told me to.' He smiled.

Alice smiled back. 'I can quite believe it.'

The exchange invoked a timely lift in the mood, just when it was needed, like an extra kick when treading water.

'Jessica was unlike anyone I'd met before. I hadn't believed in the whole *The One* thing until her. And…'

Alice helped him out. 'And, what are you going to do about that?'

He shook his head in frustration. 'In the long run, I have to bring these guys down. That was the plan. *Is* the plan. I can't do anything else.' He threw his hands out wide in exasperation.

'Then go find her and bring her back?'

'That was always my thought, I admit. But now…'

'But now?'

'Now, I don't know anymore. Now, I question the

validity in that. I question myself in general. How real were my feelings? Have I raised her up onto a pedestal in her absence? Was she *The One* at the time or only after I lost her? Is the fantasy now far greater than the reality could have ever been? It's like a genius artist who loses their life tragically young. Were they really destined to change the world, or would they have faded into obscurity after their seminal work? Was it the *loss* that made them so loved?'

'You're wondering, if you'd been able to hear Jessica's second album, whether it would have been as good?'

'Right,' Quaye confirmed.

'Well, it probably wouldn't be as good as you've been building it up to be over five years.'

This was logic that Quaye could not deny.

Alice continued. 'So it may be time to stop obsessing and move on.'

Quaye smiled. 'Ha, now you're sounding like Silvia.'

'Then maybe we both have a point.'

'You do,' agreed Quaye. 'You do. But…'

'But?'

'But, that doesn't change one thing. Myco and his empire need to be brought down.'

'By you?'

'By me,' he confirmed.

Alice didn't know why it had to be by him. That it was just as selfishly motivated as benevolent. He had to get his life back.

Quaye stopped walking. He looked to the sky through heavy foliage and sucked in a deep breath. They were walking alongside a high fence surrounding a deer enclosure. He put both hands against it and bowed his head. He had one more thing to say. He knew now why he was really telling Alice all of this. It was so she would understand.

He turned back to face her. He couldn't find the words immediately, but Alice waited patiently. Eventually, they came.

'I can't see you anymore.' He paused a moment before qualifying his statement. 'I'm not a safe person to be around.'

Alice nodded almost imperceptibly, as if she'd been expecting this. She didn't speak, just did that thing where she twiddled her hair around her finger.

Quaye wasn't sure what the appropriate action was now. Shake hands and walk off? He'd never been adept at handling these situations.

Alice, evidently, was much better. She leaned forward and initiated a hug.

'Phew,' she said as they embraced. 'I thought you were going to say you were buying your art from someone else!'

Quaye laughed, and in an instant, the tension drained into the soil. And, to an even greater extent, he grew aware of how Alice could be a healthy element in his life.

But it was not to be.

'Take care,' Quaye said as they parted.

As he turned to leave, Alice took hold of Quaye's hand gently.

'Hey,' she said as Quaye turned back. 'Go get 'em, tiger.'

She winked; trying to bring light to the situation; trying

to say it was okay.

All Quaye could do was muster a weak smile, and walk away.

Thirty

Lisa poked the tin of boiling beans as they bubbled in a pan over the camp fire.

'Look, the truth is, in the eyes of the general public, any graffiti, however elaborate and skilful, if it's just letters they don't appreciate it. I used to feel the same until I read up on it. But your average Joe isn't going to know the history – they're just looking for pretty pictures. So you've got to decide who your audience is. If it's your peers or the public.'

'Can't it be both?'

Lisa sighed. 'Rarely. It would require becoming popular with the public without selling out. Because you can't retain respect from your peers if you sell out.'

'And what would *that* take?'

'It would take *everything.* It has to bring something new to graffiti. It has to stay real but be beautiful. You would have to hit the walls hard and fast and high. Walls that are chosen well. Walls that impress the peers but don't alienate the public.'

Ryan pulled out his sketchbook, flicked to the page of his grand piece. An assimilation of tiles. Each tile a work of art in itself, featuring the letters NDA. But bring the tiles together and a new grander artwork formed. A face emerged.

Lisa realised that this jigsaw graffiti was the unique

factor that might achieve his aim. But how was such an elaborate piece going to be executed at the frequency required to generate a buzz in this quicker-than-instant world? This had always been important to the writers. That's what tags were all about. Volume. Now the public demanded it too. Lisa was sure that if a pictorial story didn't develop at the speed of a flipbook, people's interest would wane.

'Ideally, you need spaces of regular size,' Lisa said. 'So each one could map to your design in a standard way. That would make the translation easier, right?'

'Right,' Ryan confirmed. 'The first job is to measure out a square. Size doesn't matter, just proportions. It's not like anyone is going to be cutting them out and sticking them together. Well, only virtually. Then I need to mark out where any parts of the design meet the edges, so they line up when put together.' Ryan ran a finger down a grid line of his sketch.

'But that's gonna take *ages*,' Lisa exclaimed. 'You need to be quick. You've got, what, seven-by-six … so … forty-two images. Ideally, you want to be hitting say two a night for twenty-one nights. Three weeks. *That* will get you up. That will get you noticed! But with all this prep, you're going to be doing less than one.'

Lisa thought for a moment as Ryan took charge of spooning beans and sausages into plastic bowls. They had been meeting in the day most of the time. It was easier to bunk school than climb out of the window every night. Sometimes she could stay out in the evening, but that would involve fabricating a story, and she wasn't so good at lying.

Deceit was easier when it wasn't face-to-face.

Conversation turned to other things as they ate, and time slid by without Lisa noticing. When she finally thought to look at the time, she grimaced.

'School's out,' Lisa announced, glumly. 'I guess I need to show my face at home.'

She felt trapped between two worlds. Between her elective one and her obligated one. However much she tried to assume the role of bad girl, she couldn't shake her feeling of obligation. She couldn't stop *caring*. That's what she wanted to do, if only for a while. Do whatever *she* needed to do, to affect *her* healing. To move on. But she couldn't move on. Her dad was still where he was, and as the duty-bound daughter, she had to stay with him.

She finished up her beans and grabbed her bag. 'Same time tomorrow?'

Ryan nodded and smiled.

Lisa couldn't reciprocate.

Lisa arrived home. She took off her shoes and carefully lined up the heels with the others in the hallway. Then she made her way into the kitchen.

Her dad was waiting for her.

Something about the look in his eyes made her stop dead. Anger tinged with something else. Fear maybe.

'Where have you been?' It was almost a shout.

'School!' Lisa replied firmly.

'Don't lie to me.' His hands were gripping the back of the dining chair in front of him, making his knuckles turn white. His eyes were tired. His stubble neglected. He looked like a man about to crack. It scared Lisa a little. Not that he might do something to *her*, but that she was the only one that could help *him*.

'I got a phone-call from your headteacher. You've been playing truant.'

The accusation stung, even though it was true. As if Lisa felt her absence was justified.

'So what do you care?' There was no point in denying it, she knew that.

'What do *I* care?' he emphasised the words as if they were incredulous. He shoved the chair hard against the table making Lisa jump. 'Do you know the pressure I'm under right now? With the business? With keeping this roof over your head? With finding a home for your nan. I haven't got the capacity to deal with a kid that should be old enough to know better.'

And that was it.

That was why he cared. All her cries for attention that had gone unheard over the months since her mum had gone. All the rebellious acts against the system. And when her dad finally deigned to notice, it was because it inconvenienced *him*.

In an instant, standing there with tears welling in her eyes, she knew that this was the final fracture in their relationship. The crack that made it irreparable. That one last failure in a cantankerous but once-loved vehicle that would consign it to the scrapheap.

A write-off. That's what they called it.

Lisa screamed. It was the only response that came naturally. Not a long blood-curdling primal scream. A brief deep scream of frustration and anger. It did enough to stem the overwhelming flood of sadness that came over her as she stormed toward the foot of the stairs and up to the sanctuary of her bedroom. She slammed the door behind her and stood breathing heavily for a moment. As her world descended around her, she followed it down, sliding to the floor with her back against the door, sobbing heavily.

After a while, she made an effort to lift her head out of her hands and rest it with a heavy bump against the door behind her. She took a long hard breath and the rush of blood behind her ears slowed. Only then did she hear her dad crying in the kitchen too.

Her emotions were conflicted, riven deep to the pit of her stomach. She felt her father's pain, but her anger toward him seemed impossible to overcome. She was not emotionally mature enough. She shouldn't *have* to be. Should she?

They were in the same place but a generation apart.

She knew deep down that her real anger was not at him but at the world. She considered the thirteen stairs between them. That was all it would take. All it would take to reconcile a broken bond.

For one fleeting, shameful moment, Lisa caught herself wishing her dad was no longer here either.

And suddenly it was clear.

She knew what she had to do.

She climbed out of the window and left the house. Left her dad behind.

When Lisa returned to Ryan's camp, he was standing

and alert. One thing about camping in a dense wood was that no-one could creep up on you. Ryan let out his breath at the sight of Lisa as she emerged through the final piece of foliage. They locked eyes for a moment, neither of them saying a word, almost as if they both recognised the significance of this moment. That it marked a turning point in both their lives. And that this moment needed to be introduced appropriately, with the grandeur it duly deserved. This was an honour that fell to Lisa.

'Let's go paint some walls!' she declared.

Ryan looked at her, confused. 'What are you doing back? What about your dad?'

'My dad doesn't matter,' Lisa said, stepping forward.

Ryan considered whether to address this further, but clearly sensed it was best left alone on this occasion. He reclaimed his log seat, beside which his sketchbook was laying on the ground.

Lisa remained standing.

'There is only one way to pull this off,' she announced. 'And you know it.'

'I do?'

'Teamwork. You already said you need me to scout locations, but you need more than that.'

'I do?'

'Scouting is more than just pointing at a wall. You need me to assess access to it, and prepare it.'

'I can't ask…'

Lisa raised a hand against Ryan's protestations. 'We need to draw on our strengths. Yours is art. Stick to that. Something I've not told you before is that up until a few years ago I used to be a county-level gymnast. Specialised in the beam. I can survey these sites without getting hurt or caught. I can take up paint and maybe crates or planks if I think it'll make access easier for you. Then I can give you details of how to get to each site.'

'But…'

Again, Lisa didn't stop. This was not a suggestion. This was a plan. *The* plan. It was going to happen. She paced back and forth.

'But that's just the start. I can mark out your template. I'll take a copy of your design, paint the frame and the markers for where the lines meet the edge. This is all stuff you won't have time to do. I won't be able to get out every night, so I'll have to lay the groundwork for three or four when I do. That'll give you enough to do one or two every night.'

Ryan had given up trying to halt Lisa's progress. His head was dropped looking at the ground.

Lisa continued. 'To speed up your work I can create you a harness for your cans. I'll load it up and leave it at the site, and you can work your magic with them.'

Lisa finally noticed Ryan's demeanour and stopped talking. She kneeled down in front of him and forced him to make eye contact with her. She knew him well enough by now to know what he was thinking.

'I want to do this,' she said firmly but in a softer voice. 'This is not about you *making* me. In the same way that it wasn't you who dyed my hair black or pierced my tongue. You're not the only one who wants to make a mark on the world. Who wants to be *noticed*.' She lightened her tone.

'In fact, you'll be letting me down if you don't let me do this.'

Lisa smiled.

And after a brief moment, Ryan lifted his head and smiled back.

And so it began.

Thirty-one

'What happened to you?' Wilcox asked, referring to the bruise over Quaye's right eye. A question he was getting used to.

'The rough and tumble life of a detective.' Quaye grinned. 'What's happening here?'

'Got something that will cheer you up,' Wilcox said, angling her screen to him. 'In more ways than one.'

The screen had a picture of a provocatively dressed woman on it, strategically scrolled to crop her at the waist. The image was not rendered with the graininess of a CCTV mugshot but the ultra-high-definition of a photoshoot. Pixel perfect. Not a blemish left to the imagination.

'I usually search for these sorts of images on my own,' Quaye quipped. 'You're telling me this is Cynthia aren't you?'

Wilcox nodded.

'And I'm assuming this didn't just land in your inbox?'

'No,' she confirmed with what appeared to Quaye to be an attempt at nonchalance. 'The web.' She turned away before adding: 'The dark one.'

Quaye processed this with a furrowed brow before closing the office door and pulling a seat up close to Wilcox.

'And I suppose you just happened to stumble across this browsing the entire dark web at home last night?'

'It's not as big as the other one,' she said sheepishly.

'Tell me, these so-called geeky friends of yours, from where do they hail?'

'Err, Cambridge.'

'Which one?'

'Massachusetts,' Wilcox admitted.

'Thought as much. I read your resume. One year sandwich course at Harvard right?'

She nodded. 'We did some collaboration with the geeks at MIT. I'm fairly tech savvy, but these guys have brains like planets. I'm still pretty close with my ex and his roommates.'

'And so you just emailed a picture of a subject from a private security camera to these guys?'

Wilcox sighed and pushed herself away from the desk. 'I know, it's slightly outside of protocol. But I didn't give them any context. And I couldn't get in contact with you for like two days so…'

Quaye put his hand up. 'It's okay,' he said. He turned away in frustration at himself. He knew he'd have done the same. Worse in fact. But he hadn't wanted Wilcox to deal with the consequences of such actions due to his absence. 'I'm sorry I went off grid. Long story.' He pointed to the screen. 'So, how did they find this?'

'Well, the face recognition bit is easy. All the big web giants can snap a photo of a person in the street and find every picture of them on the web in real-time. Probably their name, address and medical records too, if I were being cynical. The hard part is doing the same with the dark web. But the guys at MIT – and I dare say elsewhere too – are trying to index it.'

'And they found this picture?'

'They found hundreds, on both the open and dark web. The CCTV picture was not particularly clear, so we got a lot of hits. A lot of false positives. But I emailed a bunch of headshots to our witness, Rahman, and he identified this as her. I can't access the website it was found on from here, of course, but I took some screen grabs.'

Wilcox opened up an image of a website, featuring the picture of Cynthia embedded in a profile page.

Quaye studied it briefly. 'An escort?'

'Yup, a high-class escort for hire. Works in London and Bristol. That's why I'd added her to the shortlist.'

Quaye skimmed the text on the screen. 'Definitely operates at the high end of the market. Smart, talks several languages. Comfortable at glitzy social events. Able to hold a conversation with powerful well-to-dos. Her clientele will be middle-aged balding bankers needing a well turned out plus-one for an invitation-only fundraising gala. That sort of thing.'

'Right,' Wilcox agreed. 'She's sexy, intelligent, wealthy. Mixes with the elite. So the question is, what was she doing with Milner?'

'A slightly tubby, middle-management wannabe, who's usual type is bimbos.'

'Exactly,' Wilcox agreed. 'Maybe he hired her to make himself look good. But that doesn't fit with what we know already. That *she* encouraged *him* to attempt his fatal act of graffiti – to compete with her previous boyfriend.'

'So, the only explanation seems to remain: she targeted him specifically with this act in mind.'

'But what would be the motive? She didn't know him. Or at least, he didn't know *her*.' Wilcox closed her eyes to think through what they knew. 'Maybe she did know him, or of him, and had some retribution to deal out. Seems elaborate, but then, if she wanted to stage it as an accident, it would have to be elaborate.'

'That would make sense, if it wasn't for one detail.'

'What's that?'

'Gioco. Why that name? Why not anything? She was very specific in what he had to write.'

Wilcox let out a big sigh.

'This is not a time to be deflated,' Quaye reassured. 'This is good progress.'

'It is?'

'Always expect to uncover more questions before we find any answers. More questions mean more avenues to follow. And in this case, it's very clear what avenue we have to follow next.'

'And which one is that?'

'The one where we have to hire an escort.' Quaye grinned broadly.

Wilcox rolled her eyes at him. 'Well, I'd like to know how. The site through which Cynthia promotes herself prides itself on providing a discrete service,' she explained. 'As you might expect.'

'Of course.'

'But to ensure the safety of their agents and prevent time-wasters, they require full details of any potential clients for the purpose of personal vetting, or…' She let it hang.

'Or?'

'A hefty deposit in a cryptocurrency of your choosing.'

'Figures,' he said. 'I'm not sure I'm going to get an expense claim approved for meeting up with a hooker.'

'*Escort*,' Wilcox corrected.

'Not sure that's the word the tabloids will use.'

Wilcox mused. 'Maybe it's a *refundable* deposit?'

'Hmm, yeah, one thing shady outfits on the dark web are known for is their industry leading returns policy.'

'What's the other option? Using someone else's identity?' posed Wilcox. 'Given you're a cop and all. Might give the game away.'

Quaye shook his head. 'Then as soon as I turn up with the wrong face, my cover will be blown.'

'But at least we'd have drawn her out into the open. Can't we just pick her up for questioning then?'

'If we were playing it straight, maybe. But I was rather hoping to talk to her with her guard down. Besides, whose identity would we use? We don't know what potential trouble that would get them into.'

Wilcox nodded in agreement.

Eventually, Quaye concluded there was only one option.

'Okay, fuck it. I'll sort the money. Let's hire a hooker.'

Thirty-two

The place Quaye had arranged to meet Cynthia was public but sparsely populated. Quaye waited at the bar, already furnished with a light beer. Wilcox was there too, at a window table, ostensibly reading from a tablet.

The woman they had known as Cynthia was due in five minutes. That was not the name she went by on her profile. Nor was it the one she would use with Quaye. Cynthia was a character especially crafted for Milner – her last, and now late, client.

A fashionable few minutes after they were due to meet, a tall elegant woman approached Quaye at the bar. She glided with grace and confidence, on heels that clicked meaningfully with every step. She wore a dress, slightly more formal than the time of day would typically warrant, and more sophisticated than they'd seen on the security footage. Quaye assessed her in the brief seconds he had. On first impressions, could she fulfil the archetypal role of *femme fatale*? It didn't seem out of the question.

'Gretchen,' she announced confidently, reaching out a hand to greet him.

'Lleyton,' he responded as he took her hand. 'Can I get you a drink?'

'Thank you. White wine spritzer.' She smiled. Her voice was mellifluous and exotic with an eastern European accent.

The moments until the drinks arrived were filled with small talk. Then they took a table, a few down from where Wilcox sat.

'So, what is it I can do for you?' Gretchen asked.

Quaye smiled. 'You can tell me about yourself.' It wasn't an answer to the question she'd asked, but he couldn't provide one for that.

'About myself? Which self? It's you who decides who you want me to be.'

Usually, she had a role to perform for her clients.

Quaye shook his head. 'Your *real* self.'

She gave a quizzical smile. 'You can ask anyone to play themselves. For free.'

'But anyone would not be *you*.'

She toyed with her glass playfully, rolling it between her fingers.

'Okay, what would you like to know?'

She would play along for a while, but Quaye knew her patience would be limited, even with a potential customer. He pondered for a moment, before asking the kind of slightly perverted question she might expect from a typical consumer of her services.

'Tell me about your first kiss?'

'Boy or girl?'

Quaye laughed. 'Just the first.'

'I was fourteen. He was my best friend's older brother. It was … *unreciprocated*.'

Quaye raised his brow. 'By him?'

'By me.'

Quaye gave a considered nod. He understood what she

was implying.

The chit-chat continued for a while. Quaye was finding it hard to glean anything concrete from his companion. She was an accomplished performer. The best he could do was try to get a sense of her. The *real* her.

At a brief lull in the conversation, he noticed her glance up at the walls of the establishment, adorned with the works of local artists. Quaye pounced on this tiniest of opportunities.

'Are you a fan of the arts?' he asked. An ugly segue, but he knew he was running out of time.

'Of course. The ballet especially.' Her eyes lit up, and for an instant Quaye saw a little girl dreaming of a different life. *This* was the real Gretchen, he was sure. Someone whose creative soul longed for lace and sequined taffeta, not grungy walls and spray paint. It was true that street art transcends the class boundaries, but there was a difference between million-pound gallery pieces and tags in a subway tunnel. For the 'Cynthia' they knew about so far, her supposed intimacy with the art form was such as to suggest she was not merely acquainted with it, but deeply ingrained in the underground subculture. The name she chose, the stories she told, the method of execution. And the artist to mimic: the elusive Gioco. Yet the Gretchen before him now was every inch the high-class stereotype that went along with her profession – or, at least, the end of the market she served. Penthouses, swanky functions, ballet, caviar. All the clichés of high society.

It was increasingly clear that every part of Cynthia was an act. But an act for what audience? For what purpose?

'Well, it's been nice chatting,' Gretchen announced. 'But our time is almost up. We can either discuss your requirements now, or you know how to get in touch.' She smiled sweetly trying to close the deal.

The thirty-minute meeting had cost Quaye a pretty penny, and another meet would do the same. It was time to make a choice: let Wilcox follow Gretchen and see what more they could discover subversively, or blow his cover now.

Quaye made his decision.

'What do you think of graffiti?'

There was an almost imperceptible change in her expression. Her eyes returned to meet his rather quicker than might be expected.

There was a moment of pause before she responded. 'I don't know much about it, to be honest,' she said.

'Any favourite artists?'

She shrugged. 'There's only one anyone's heard of isn't there?'

'Not in this city,' Quaye pointed out. He wondered whether she was claiming ignorance of the scene because of recent events or because she was genuinely ignorant. It was becoming increasingly apparent to him what the answer was.

'It's been lovely,' Gretchen announced, theatrically looking at her watch. 'But, I'm afraid our time has come to an end.' She leant down to grab her bag from beside her feet.

As she did so, Quaye produced a photograph from his pocket and slid it across the table. 'How about this piece?'

he asked.

Gretchen's gaze landed on the picture. The bridge over the train line. The name Gioco in arcane lettering. This time, her reaction was obvious, albeit brief. She recomposed herself almost immediately, but it was clear the image meant something to her, and that she wasn't expecting to be presented with it here.

Briefly, Gretchen's eyes met his and paused, as if studying his intent, working out her next play.

She figured out what it was.

She ran.

Quaye rolled his eyes. He wasn't sure exactly how swiftly Gretchen expected to affect her getaway in four-inch heels over the harbourside cobbles, slaloming her way through ambling tourists. Wilcox came hurtling past him in pursuit of the escapee. Quaye followed.

He rounded a corner to find Wilcox restraining Gretchen up against a wall, who only struggled for a moment before resigning to her fate. Wilcox backed off, and Gretchen straightened herself up.

Quaye spoke calmly but firmly. 'Either way, you're coming to the station to talk to us. It's up to you whether you do so in cuffs or not.'

Thirty-three

Raymond was in his usual spot at the amphitheatre near the docks. This was finance district.

It was a school day so skateboarders were few on this occasion. Limited to those playing truant, and not worried about getting caught. They hung around in groups, in odd juxtaposition to the suited professionals who owned this place on a weekday lunchtime.

Despite his age, Raymond looked more in place with the boarders than the bankers. Though that hadn't always been the case. The memory of shirt sleeves and shiny shoes was not so far-off.

He watched them. The workers. Scurrying back and forth. Some of them daring to catch ten minutes of sunshine with their lunch, sitting on a step with a Tupperware box and a takeaway coffee. Some stood in pairs, vaping over the docks.

He despised them.

Not for the same reason everyone did. For a specific reason. The one that had brought him here. To this city, in these clothes.

But *indirectly* it was the same reason. What they represented. What drove them. The pursuit of a hollow buck. Adding no worth to society. Just moving resources from A to B and creaming off a bit in the middle. Spinning the machinery of finance, not worrying about who gets sucked in and chewed up in the process.

That was the reason.

He had spent a lot of his life *not* contemplating this. About worth. About what someone adds to the world. Only now did he realise that a graffiti artist was more productive than a day trader, on almost any scale.

He'd be the first to admit, he'd realised this too late.

Suddenly, amidst this horde of individuals, he understood how his only two objectives left in his world could be brought together. How the one could enable the other.

But neither could be cast in motion until he'd found Gioco.

And that was when he spotted the kid. Sat there, watching his mates do their tricks. His left arm was in plaster. His board was by his side, balanced up on its edge such that Raymond could see its underside. That was what had first drawn his eye. It was a work of art – and a kind he recognised. The stylised block lettering of a graffiti writer. Raymond peered closer at the kid's plaster cast. It was covered in the penned signatures of his friends. But not the spidery scrawls of your average kid, these were the tags of the graffiti world too.

He realised that the youths he'd been watching all this time, were the very people who might be able to help him find who he was looking for. This was what the graffiti crews did when the sun was up.

Raymond walked over and sat down next to the broken-armed skater kid, at enough of a distance so as not to freak him out. He was aware enough to know that most people weren't comfortable in the presence of folk like him. But this was a cool kid. Raymond was pretty sure he wouldn't be overly flustered.

'You out of action?' Raymond said nodding to the other kids practising tricks on their boards.

The kid nodded in return.

'Me too.' Raymond held a deadpan expression for just long enough before cracking a smile. They both laughed.

'I'm official cameraman now,' the kid said, holding up an action cam in his good hand.

'Sucks. This your board?'

'Yeah. Still my mode of transport, even if I can't do tricks.'

'It's nice.' He knew the culture well enough that he might have said *rad* or *sick*, or even *rad-to-the-power-of-sick*, but he also knew it would have sounded ridiculous coming from a man in his fifties – homeless or otherwise.

'Thanks.'

Raymond decided not to mention the artwork. Not yet. It was too soon. He opened up his bag and fished out two cans – beer not paint.

'Here.' He handed one to the kid.

The kid looked suspicious.

'Go on. It's cheap, but it's still beer.'

The kid took it. 'Thanks.'

They both popped them open and took a swig.

'You know, we watch you kids all the time. My friend Eric especially loves to. You'd probably recognise him. He's a nice guy, but, you know, a little bit…' Raymond whistled and spun his index finger at his temple, to the amusement of the kid.

They talked about skateboarding after that. About the names of the moves.

Eric turned up after a while, and he and Raymond watched the skater-boys attempt to capture a range of tricks on camera, failing more often than not, but in a good-natured way.

There was a time when Raymond would have despised these boys, this sub-culture. A time when his own son was the age they were now. But he was willing to accept now that they were not quite the axis of evil he had painted them to be. He could actually imagine liking some of them, and that wasn't just because he needed something from them.

In the days that followed, Raymond chatted to the skaters regularly. They were all under age, so would give him cash to buy them booze. It was a couple of weeks before Raymond raised the topic of graffiti. They were not cagey about it in the slightest. On the contrary, it was a badge of honour. And after all, he was just a homeless guy. On one occasion he met them at the skatepark. This was a place where writers got to practice their skills legitimately, in daylight. But the crew he'd befriended were of the old-school mentality, of the thinking that a legit site was a waste of good paint.

When Raymond was sure he was well inside the trust boundary, he'd ask more probing questions about their clandestine exploits. In truth, they would probably have opened up much sooner, but he wanted to be sure not to spook them. He needed to get to *that* question – naturally, without it sounding incongruous. And eventually the opportunity arose:

'Who is Gioco?'

He asked just one of the guys, but it soon grew into a debate that encompassed the whole crew.

This time, Raymond was sure, he would get his answer.

Thirty-four

The only items of furniture in the small windowless interview room were four plastic chairs and a Formica-topped table. The only *colour* was the red light that blinked on the camera in the top corner of the room. Other than that, grey prevailed.

Gretchen sat with poise opposite her apprehenders.

Quaye produced a tablet, and summoned an image of a man to its screen.

'Do you know this man?' he asked, showing it to Gretchen.

'No,' she replied petulantly, barely glancing to look at it.

'For the tape, I am showing a picture of Tobias Milner to the interviewee,' Quaye stated, before prompting Gretchen again. 'Do you know him?'

'No,' she repeated.

Quaye acknowledged the answer. Moving methodically, he slid the tablet to one side and positioned two glossy photographs in its place.

'For the tape, I am showing two photographs of the bridge formed by Bedminster Down Road as seen from Parson Street railway station. One of them is a photograph taken prior to the incident in question. The other was taken at the scene of Milner's death, showing graffiti believed to have been applied by the victim on the night of the incident.' Quaye looked up from the photographs to

Gretchen. 'I think you can tell me something about the events that occurred between these two pictures being taken.'

The interviewee remained stoic.

Quaye fetched a pen from his pocket. 'Tobias Milner died creating this artwork,' he stated strongly, tapping the picture to Gretchen's right. He let that statement hang for a minute before flipping over the other picture. On the back was the message that had been left for the victim:

GIOCO. SHOW ME WHAT YOU CAN DO. CX

'Is this your handwriting?' Quaye asked.

Gretchen looked at the words and furrowed her brow.

'No,' she responded firmly. 'I've never seen this before.'

There was a hesitance to her denial this time. Was this the first question she was not expecting to be asked? Quaye remained silent for a moment, trying to needle any meaning from this observation.

'Gretchen, I'll be straight with you,' Quaye announced, knowing he wasn't intending on being *entirely* straight with her. 'We have security footage. We know you were with Tobias Milner at a restaurant in town. We have a witness that informs us of the nature of your relationship with him, and with the world of graffiti. We have a note, goading the victim into the act that would be his last.' Quaye tapped the end of his pen on the table a couple of times. 'You see, to us you are intrinsically linked to this crime. You are our number one suspect. If you have anything to say relating to this incident, I suggest you do so now. I remind you that it may harm your defence otherwise.'

Gretchen's expression looked intense and sorrowful, but her eyes were still firm. She lifted them to meet his.

'Gretchen,' he said in a softer voice, 'ultimately the truth will come out.'

She didn't respond. Quaye studied the steely expression of his adversary. She was a professional. He needed to know what she knew, but she wasn't going to crack easily. If at all. More leverage was required if he was going to convince her to talk. He didn't have it. Not yet.

Eventually, she spoke. 'I want to exercise my right to legal advice'.

Quaye nodded. 'Fine,' he said, hiding his frustration. 'Interview suspended.' He clicked the recording device off and left the room.

Wilcox followed.

They found themselves in the kitchen. Quaye absently poured two mugs of coffee from the jug on the hot plate.

'What are you thinking?' Wilcox enquired.

Quaye found it was something he hadn't been expecting.

'She didn't do it,' he stated matter-of-factly.

'Really? We know we got the right Cynthia because she recognised the bridge.'

'Did she?'

'She ran.'

'People run for different reasons. At that point, she'd just realised I was a cop. Or, at least, a weirdo. Sure, she certainly has things to hide, but doesn't everyone? And anyway, we know exactly what she wants to hide – her client list.'

They headed down the corridor toward the back of the station. The door at the end opened out onto a sunny courtyard, shrouded in a haze of smoke and vapour from the nicotine enthusiasts standing at the threshold. They crossed to the other side.

'Think about what we have,' Quaye said. 'What we actually know for sure. We have an acquaintance of the victim who told us a story, who supposedly identified a character from that story, from a set of women pre-selected by you from security footage in the vicinity of the story's setting.'

Wilcox considered this for a moment. 'But what about the note you found at Milner's place? That validates the story.'

'Exactly, it validates the *story*. But is the story true? Was there ever a Cynthia?'

Wilcox paced over to the tall fence around the back yard, stared through to the street beyond. Quaye gave her time. Eventually, she turned back.

'For what it's worth, I think there was a Cynthia. And I think that's her in there,' she said.

Quaye took a dramatic swig of his coffee. 'For what it's worth, I agree.'

'You do?'

'I do. I think Gretchen is our Cynthia. I think she played some part in setting Milner up for his fall. But that doesn't necessarily mean she is guilty of anything.'

Wilcox turned to Quaye with a puzzled look. 'How come?'

Quaye claimed the recently-vacated bench facing the

sun, and Wilcox joined him.

'Consider her occupation,' he continued. 'What does she *do* for a living?'

'I'd rather not think about it,' Wilcox quipped.

'Aside from that,' Quaye said. 'If I were being generous, I would say she was an actress. If I were being *accurate,* I'd say she was a stooge. Hired to play a role – to pretend to be someone else. Normally, this would be at the side of the client, but…'

Quaye turned to Wilcox, whose expression gave way to realisation.

'Someone hired her to be an escort for someone *else,*' she said. 'For Milner. Without him knowing.'

'Right.' Quaye cocked his head. 'Maybe?'

They sat in silence for a moment before Wilcox spoke again.

'But if this is the case, why is she playing so dumb? She was duped as much as Milner was. Why would she not open up to clear her name?'

'Ah, and that right there is why. Her *name*. Protecting her name, her *business*. The currency she trades in above all else is discretion. Her clients are all wealthy. And with wealth comes power. Amongst her portfolio will be high profile individuals: business execs, judges, politicians…'

'Detectives,' Wilcox added wryly.

'Indeed. If word got out she ratted on a client, that would be it for her. Goodbye high-life.'

'Even if the client she ratted on was a murderer?'

'She works on an ask-no-questions basis. I'm not saying she'd be thrilled to have been a pawn in this game, if that turns out to be the case. I dare say that *accomplice to murder* is not on her list of offered services. But it's happened now, and if there's any chance of getting through this by keeping schtum, then she will do everything in her power to do so.' He looked at his watch. 'For about thirty-two hours.'

'So where do we go now?'

'Go hunting for any evidence we can find in the next thirty-two hours. Anything that will give us grounds to charge her with something or get her to talk. Firstly, now that we know her real name and address we should dig up as much about our suspect as we can. See if we can't generate any leads from that.'

Quaye's phone buzzed in his pocket. He answered it and spoke for a moment with words of acknowledgement, before thanking the caller and hanging up.

'That was the lab,' he said to Wilcox. 'No match.'

Quaye had gotten them to run Gretchen's fingerprints against those on the spray-can found at the scene.

'So, we know there's at least one other person involved,' Wilcox commented.

'Right.'

'Which confirms your theory and potentially Gretchen's story. The final push – the spiked can and probably the note – didn't come from her?'

Quaye nodded, but not enthusiastically.

'That's good, in a way, isn't it?' Wilcox suggested. 'Find the matching fingers, find the killer?'

'Maybe. I was kind of expecting them to be Gretchen's actually.'

'Really?'

'Yeah. Well, the note was clean. Which didn't surprise me. The killer is smart enough to not leave his, or her, prints all over the evidence. So why on the can? I'd assumed this had been passed on by Gretchen, knowingly or otherwise. And that this would give us the ammo to get her to talk, or charge her. There were no prints other than Milner's on the other cans, and only two sets of prints on the can with the fatal additive. Assuming the killer was smart enough to wipe down his own prints and those of anyone else involved in spiking it, then they could just mean nothing.'

'So what other angle do we have?'

'We have motive. Well, somebody does. Who in Milner's life wanted him dead and why? Was it money, vengeance, jealousy? We need to talk to his friends, family, colleagues.' He looked at his watch. 'And we don't have much time.'

Thirty-five

Lisa took one last look at the sheet of paper ensuring she'd faithfully committed it to memory. After Ryan had completed his final design, she had scanned it and printed out an enlarged version of each cell, each piece that would form part of the citywide puzzle. She'd figured a corner piece would make a good starter square, being that the design only crossed two of the edges. She had measured the positions of each crossing point at the scale of two metres square, marked-up the design and memorised them. She had done the same for three squares, as many as she could hope to complete in one night.

That one night was here.

She chose an easy location. Access was straightforward: hop up onto a dumpster, along a wall for about ten paces, around a corner and then up onto a ledge. No security camera nearby. Out of view from people walking directly underneath. Mostly the darkened windows of offices across the street. Given all that, she thought it would be easy. But suddenly it didn't seem so. Despite the darkness and relative seclusion, she was underprepared for just how exposed she felt. She may as well have been on stage at the Hippodrome.

For a while she did nothing. Just sat on the ledge with her legs hanging down, surveying the surroundings. Was there someone lurking in the shadows? Was there someone peering out from the window opposite? Or was the darkness just playing tricks on her eyes? Just because it was three in the morning didn't mean people weren't up. *She* was. Everyone had their own motivations for not conforming.

She felt herself shiver with nerves and grew frustrated with herself. She had to do this. She couldn't let Ryan down. Or herself. Else what kind of rebel would she make?

She took a deep breath and shuffled around onto her knees, facing the wall. The first thing she needed to do was draw a square. She produced a can of black paint to mark a dot at the bottom left corner and immediately realised her first mistake – not pre-mixing the paint. Rationally, or otherwise, she was hyper-sensitive about making any noise. She had to resist the urge to shake the can, instead just turning it slowly end-over-end, hoping that would be good enough.

She squeezed the nozzle, not hard enough at first, but then slightly firmer until the tiniest jet of black paint made itself to the wall. With the tape-measure she'd brought along, she measured its height from the floor to assist in making the line level, then made a similar dot two metres to the right. It was more awkward than she had anticipated.

She realised how challenging it was going to be to paint a straight line between the two marker dots with a spray-can, shuffling along the floor and trying to keep her arm steady. She would need some more guide marks in between, the same height from the floor. She measured one at half-way, but stopped herself just in time. A mark here might be confused with the marks she needed to make on this edge of the frame to guide Ryan's artwork.

She recalled the position of the first of these marks –

fifty-two centimetres. She measured across by this amount, then up from the floor to align it with the others. It was a fiddly process. She made a mental note to bring a marker pen next time. After double-checking her measurements, she made a finger-length vertical mark, and then set about repeating the process for the other four points on this edge. When done she did her best to paint a straight line through the marks she'd made, moving slowly, holding her body rigid. At the end she let her body fall back as the tension left her muscles.

Looking at the line, she wasn't satisfied. It felt like she'd been up here for almost an hour and only had one badly-drawn line to show for it. She'd underestimated how hard this would be. The vertical edge would be harder too; harder to keep it straight because there was no edge near enough to use as a guide. Only then was she struck by what should have been obvious so much sooner, what vital tool was missing from her armoury: a length of string. That was all she needed to make straight lines. But she wasn't going to give up on this one now. Even if she had to abandon it as a canvas, it would still serve as a good learning experience – as already proven.

Eventually, when all four lines and their markers were complete, she jumped back down to the street and disappeared into the shadows. She'd left home over two hours before. There was no more time to do another frame. She had restricted her window of painting to be between 2:30 and 4:30 a.m. – being as close to dead as a city could get. She knew herself well enough to know she had to get *some* sleep to function, and there was no option of not going to school in the morning, being under such great scrutiny from her dad.

On her way home, she left a note for Ryan at an agreed location, a nook in the old iron bridge near where they'd first met. It was the point where the routes between their respective homes and the city converged. This is how they would communicate at times they could not meet in person. The notes from Lisa would document her progress, with instructions of how to reach the locations she'd identified and which cells of the design they related to.

On this first night, it was just one.

The next day Lisa was tired at school, but she made it to every class. Since meeting Ryan and descending further down an alternate path, she had become even more isolated from her classmates. School felt like nothing but a penance now. But a penance for what, she did not know. Fortunately, the last period of the day was for study and so she could head home.

She passed the iron bridge earlier than she might usually and so Ryan wasn't there. But the note she had left for him had been taken. He would know what to do.

Tonight it was *his* turn.

But it would be hers again too, due to her poor performance on the previous night. She had two sites in mind. Close together and nearer home than last night, to give her more time than before. She knew she was still on the learning curve, and she *had* to get at least two done tonight to allow herself one night off.

With this in mind, she decided not to wait for Ryan. She

had to get home, study, sleep, be borderline civil with her dad. But most importantly, she had to prepare for another night on the town.

Preparation was key.

Thirty-six

'I like it,' Lisa said to Ryan when they met. The previous night Lisa had made her second and third templates, whilst Ryan had completed the first, in all its glory.

'Thanks. Your ground-work really helped.'

They walked along beside the river. Like they had done shortly after they'd first met.

'I don't have long,' Lisa announced with a glum expression.

'That's okay,' Ryan said, taking her hand.

They strolled in comfortable silence for a while before Lisa brought the conversation back to the other necessary part of the plan.

'I've been thinking about getting the word out.'

'I thought you were going to use your blog.'

She shook her head. 'I can't now. I'm too involved. I can't be the one to miraculously discover each piece of work you do. It would be too obvious.'

'I guess. Although, if it *were* someone else putting up these pieces, it would still likely be you who discovered them.'

'Maybe, but it's a tall story to believe. Bit like driving around in a stolen car and saying you bought it off a bloke in the pub.'

'Okay, I agree,' Ryan conceded. 'Too risky.'

'Your peers will catch on pretty quick, but if you want

to reach a wider audience, we'll have to get into the local media. They won't be interested. Not to start with. But I figure if they receive an anonymous email with a different piece of work every day, after a week or so they may pick it up. As soon as one does, then I can feature it on my blog without suspicion.'

'Sounds like a plan,' Ryan confirmed.

And that's how it went.

Lisa left it a few days into their project before contacting any media. Then she fired off an email from a fake account to a number of local papers. She attached photos of all the graffiti she and Ryan had created so far, with text aimed at engendering mystery. Who was this new artist, NDA? What did the graffiti mean? Of course, she knew it would be less than interesting to an everyday observer at this stage, but it was all part of the build-up.

Each day or so Lisa sent another email with the new NDA pieces that had appeared on the walls of the city. Then, after one week, it was time for the hook. There were ten artworks in total now, and this was the point that the anonymous informer supposedly figured out they were all part of a greater whole. Lisa arranged the graffiti created to-date into a single image, fitting together those pieces that neighboured each other. Now the mystery was a puzzle, literally. And everyone likes a good puzzle.

More days passed with no success, and Lisa was growing concerned that the media would never pick it up. Then, two weeks into the project, her web filter scored a hit on the Bristol Post website. She clicked through, and there it was. A couple of paragraphs and a few pictures. It wasn't much, but Lisa was confident it would be more. It was the start of something.

Sure enough, after a few more days of hard graff, the ultimate accolade was attained. The story made it to the print edition. This crystallised their achievements to a much greater extent than a mere note on the internet. *Anything* could be on the internet. *Everything* was on the internet. But not everything was worthy of two short columns and a tiny picture on page sixteen of the Bristol Post. Curated by an editorial eye, rendered in physical media. This was lofty success indeed.

Lisa rushed a copy to Ryan. His reaction was more than she had expected. He beamed at seeing his artwork in print. Even though it was only a local rag, it was clear what this meant to him. As if this was the first time in his life he had been appreciated; that he'd finally created something of his own wont – and been recognised for it.

Lisa collapsed onto the blanket outside Ryan's tent. Lying on her back, she looked up through the flickering leaves above her. She was tired. If there were such a candle with three ends, she'd be burning it at all of them. She was attending class to ensure no suspicion was raised with her dad. She was doing her time at home. And every second or third night she was out on the town. After two weeks she was almost broken – and they were only half way there. She had considered taking a break; convincing Ryan that a few days off wouldn't hurt. But seeing him now, she couldn't bring herself to do it. There was an energy to him, a spark that had never been there before, not until this moment. And who was she to extinguish it?

Ryan joined Lisa on the blanket, locking smiling eyes with hers, lingering for a moment as if savouring the closeness, before collapsing down beside her.

'Thank you,' he said.

They remained in silence for a while, resting peacefully side-by-side, staring up at the same sky, sharing the same destiny.

Lisa made up her mind. They *had* to finish this.

But not right now. Right now, she was beat.

She rested her eyes.

She really should be moving.

Should be going home.

But it felt so good to stop.

To be still.

She slept.

More than an hour passed before she woke up. Ryan was sitting watching her.

'I couldn't face waking you,' he said softly.

Lisa rose to a sitting position. She looked at the time with blurry eyes. It was late.

Ryan echoed her thought. 'It's late.'

She looked at him with unemotional eyes and shrugged.

'You should get home,' he said.

She shook her head slowly. 'I can't do it all. And we have to finish this.'

'But your dad…'

'My dad will go ape shit. If I miss school and don't go home every night, yeah. He'll probably disown me. But it's only two weeks. And what do I need him for?'

Ryan was uneasy. 'I can't let this come between you and your father. It's not worth it.'

Lisa leaned forward and rested a hand on his arm. 'Ryan, the last thing I need right now is someone else in my life telling me what's worthy and what isn't.'

Ryan nodded. 'Point taken.'

'Come on. I need to show you something.'

Thirty minutes later Lisa and Ryan were in town, looking up at the wall of a tall building.

'What's this?' Ryan asks.

'This is the grand finale.'

Ryan looked at Lisa disbelievingly. 'You want me to get up there?' he asked. 'And paint?'

Lisa grinned. 'I've been working on it. The access. Since the start. I've figured out a way. From the back. It's just … umm … there's a…'

'A what?'

'A move.'

'A *move*?'

'Yeah, it's not hard. Not really. Just a technique.'

'You don't sound too sure.'

'It'll be fine. I'll teach you.'

Lisa had given up gymnastics when her mum died. Continuing without her was not even an option. In a strange way, she didn't miss it. It was put in that box along with everything else that came before. Her body, though, did long for the movements. And to fill the void she had visited Circomedia for a while – a circus training school. It was less formal and competitive, which suited her mindset.

Something she could get lost in – pure physicality driven by sub-conscious thought. Muscle memory was the only memory she wanted to exercise.

In the end, though, it was still a performance. And it was this aspect that became too much – the expectation to 'put on a show'. Lisa was tired of acting, of being someone else. So she quit that too, to become herself. Whatever that may be.

Her interests shifted to free-running, parkour; what some may consider a kind of urban dance. Although, it wasn't *dance*. It wasn't about *performance*. It was about *freedom*. About pushing your physical abilities. It appealed to Lisa. The loner she was becoming. But as a fourteen-year-old girl it was a scene she felt very much on the outside of, as with graffiti. Ultimately, it was Ryan who became a conduit to both these worlds. At night when she snuck out into the darkness, she was free-running the town; its obstacles – the physical barriers it threw up between her and the canvases she sought. The challenge was liberating. She finally felt alive, felt she had a purpose beyond being a daughter and a schoolkid.

That was why this was the priority now, regardless of the consequences.

After a couple of sessions with Ryan at Circomedia – jumping, tumbling, falling – it was time to hit the streets, where there were no crash mats. Lisa had identified an obstacle at ground level that simulated the one Ryan would have to overcome on the roof of their final site.

'It's a wall,' Ryan pointed out sarcastically.

'Right, get on top of it.'

Ryan sized it up. It was about the same height as him, six foot. He approached it, jumped, scrabbled with his legs for a moment, then dropped back down. For his second attempt, he took a few paces back. With the short run up he managed to get his body higher up the wall in the first move, such that his right shoulder was far enough above the top of the wall that he could lock his arm and then extend it with some effort, pushing down and pulling himself up. In a final move, he swung one leg onto the top, then over, and pulled himself into a sitting position. He grinned at Lisa.

'That it?' he asked. 'That all I have to do?'

Lisa cocked her head. 'Kinda. In essence.'

Ryan jumped down off the wall. 'In essence?'

'It's bigger,' Lisa admitted coyly.

'How much bigger?'

'Hmm, about fifty percent.'

'Fifty percent? That's like nine foot. I can't climb up a nine-foot wall!'

'Yes, you can. It's just technique. I've seen kids scale brick walls over twice their height. Don't worry, I'll show you.' She paused for a moment before giving him another coy look. 'There's also a gap.'

'A gap?'

'Between the roof you'll be jumping from and the wall of the next building. It's very small.' She indicated how small with her hands and smirked at Ryan.

'So, it's like nine feet up or *twenty*-nine feet down?'

Lisa shrugged by way of confirmation. Ryan shook his head and rolled his eyes playfully. They had reached the point in their relationship where communication didn't always need words; where their humour aligned to the extent that the punchline could often be left unspoken.

Lisa took a moment to explain the technique of scaling a wall. There were two aspects to it. First was the skill of converting *forward* momentum into *vertical* – by literally running up the wall. The second aspect was the pull-up. Those who were well-practised could haul themselves to the top so long as just their fingertips made it there first.

'Okay, get your ass up it again,' Lisa instructed.

Ryan did as he was told. It was a smoother performance this time.

'Better,' Lisa credited.

Over the following days, Lisa helped Ryan work on his parkour skills. It was not just the last piece of their project he would need them for. As they worked their way through the pieces, one-by-one, the locations got harder to find. The access became tougher. Lisa knew what her priority was and what it would take to achieve it. If she needed to spend daylight hours scouting locations or training Ryan – or sleeping – then that was what she would do.

And that was what she did.

She spent less time at school, got home later, if at all – went further down *that* road. Her relationship with her father reached breaking point, but that was not her concern for these next two weeks. Only the project was. And so she solved that problem quite easily – by going home even less, avoiding the confrontation. She knew the fallout would be bad. But, equally, she knew it would be worth it.

Her other task as the days progressed was her blog. Given that her bedroom was in hostile territory, she had to resort to writing most of it at the library on one of the public computers. She didn't want to take her laptop out of the house as invariably she ended up scaling urban obstacles.

The story was starting to create a buzz – within the street art community at least. The average person in the city wasn't aware of the story as it unfolded – but the reach was global. By day twenty her blog subscribers reached four digits. It may be nothing compared to the teeny-bop sensations, but to Lisa it was unbelievable; that at the push of a button a thousand people would be notified, would read what she had to say. With that came a sense of responsibility she hadn't expected – and a sense of self-doubt. She found herself anxious about what she was saying, about whether her opinions were valid. She had to remind herself that opinions could never be invalid – that was the beauty of them. She just had to remain true to herself.

Her blog was not just about their project – she didn't want to give it disproportionate coverage. And a happy by-product of scouting for locations was the discovery of many other works of street art. She dutifully photographed and catalogued every one she encountered, no matter the artist – or the quality. And with her newfound focus and freedom she had the time to add her own commentary to them all as well. It was this comprehensiveness that fuelled the site's popularity, once it had been discovered.

Knowing that her project with Ryan was only going to be temporary, this grander undertaking gave her a sense of purpose like nothing else in her life. It was an assignment not entirely of her own choosing, driven as she was by the same obsessive compulsions that lay behind her other less productive behavioural ticks. The ones that had manifested shortly after her mum passed away.

When she allowed herself to assess things objectively, she knew she wasn't responsible for her mum's death. Yet some deeper process within her thought differently – *told* her differently. It was not so much a voice, more an *instinct* – a *pernicious* instinct. It told her what certain tasks must be carried out in order to avert other bad things from happening. So she dutifully carried them out. She made sure the shoes were always aligned in the hall; that she always reached the top step with her left foot; and that each piece of street art she encountered in the city was assiduously catalogued. In this respect, her blog was more than a hobby, it was a medicine. Without it her mind felt like Swiss cheese, full of holes that only got bigger. Now that she could focus on it more fully, she felt better. And better still with her new found audience, because that came with an added bonus. Her fellow city dwellers would post to her site their own pictures of art they had discovered. It was like she had outsourced her necessities – her healing.

It felt good.

Thirty-seven

'Let's release her,' Quaye announced as Wilcox returned to the office.

No avenues of enquiry had proven fruitful since their interview with Gretchen the previous afternoon. Quaye had knowingly plucked the short straw in opting to visit Milner's parents for an overview of the family situation. They were willing to help and pleasant. They offered him tea but didn't volunteer any skeletons from the cupboard. He didn't sense any insincerity. They didn't hide the fact that their son hadn't gotten on well with his half-brother. Nothing other than a clash of personalities. Nothing that would seem to justify murder. Either way, the brother lived in Manchester, and when calling upon bereaved family members to accuse them of murder, it was good etiquette not to do so over the phone. So that avenue was not a candidate for a quick win.

Calling up bereaved *acquaintances* by phone, though, was just about acceptable where necessary, and Wilcox had phoned around some numbers she'd obtained from Milner's friend, Rahman. She had also called into Milner's place of work to learn what she could.

'Nothing unusual,' Wilcox had reported. 'The HR director was quite frank about him not winning any boss-of-the-year awards. He managed a team of five or six, and it tended to have quite a high turnover of employees. But she was expectedly incredulous about him inciting anyone to murder.'

Quaye let Wilcox get settled at her desk.

'So why release her early?' she asked.

'Because we'll learn more from what she does outside of here than inside. And there's no way we're going to be able to charge her with anything in the next few hours.'

'You planning on tailing her?'

'It's a long shot, but I'd be interested to know the second thing she does after leaving here.'

'Second?'

Quaye nodded in confirmation. 'She's dressed for a date and hasn't had a change of clothes for a day. The first thing she'll do is head home for a shower.' He stood. 'Before that, we need to find a suitable spot to keep an eye on her front door.'

Quaye and Wilcox sat on high stools at the window of a coffee shop. Across the street was the apartment block where Gretchen lived. One thing to be said for the rampant proliferation of coffee vendors over recent years was that it made surveillance activities a lot easier these days.

They sipped long coffees from takeaway cups.

They waited.

Out of the blue, Wilcox asked an incongruous question. 'Where's Beanie MacAskill?'

'Hmm?' Quaye turned to her.

'You're the expert on missing children. The one with the special insight. In your opinion, where is she? Alive, dead? What happened?'

The name Beanie was synonymous with missing. Hers was the name that popped into the mind whenever a new kid disappeared. She was the sorry poster child for the vanished. She went missing two decades ago, but rather than the story fading from the headlines after a few weeks as many did, it stayed there. Something would bubble it to the surface every few months. A new lead, a new piece of evidence, a bungled investigation, an accusation levelled at the parents, the case being closed and re-opened multiple times by multiple forces. This went on for a decade. Some may call it distasteful but Beanie's parents knew how to wield the media to maximum effect, to keep it fresh in the public's mind. From magazine features to billboards to celebrity pleas. And the photo of Beanie was always the same. A frozen moment from a happier time. Everyone knew that sweet little face, with the mole under her left eye. A face that never aged.

Wilcox spoke again before Quaye could answer. 'I just can't imagine it. Waking up and your kid is gone.' Her eyes grew vacant for a moment, and Quaye didn't interrupt her thoughts. She continued. 'We took in a stray cat when I was a kid. It got lost for a whole day until we found the poor thing stuck behind the wardrobe. That was harrowing enough. Knowing that a living thing is in distress someplace, and you are helpless to do anything about it. But a child?' She shook her head as if trying to cast off the horror. 'The violation of it. Someone coming into your house and…' She couldn't end the sentence. She turned to Quaye with desperate eyes. 'I don't know how parents can even *live* after that.' She paused for a moment before asking the question again. 'So where do *you* think she is?'

Quaye knew the details as well as anyone else. It took place on a Greek island, at a luxury resort with a private beach. The villa was owned by the parents who were both lawyers. Their daughter, Beanie, just vanished in the middle of the night. No sign of forced entry. No useful security footage.

Quaye shrugged. 'I don't think it's such a mystery – just well executed.'

'Go on.'

'She was taken to order. A pretty little face like that. Picked out on the beach or at the pool. Clearly, there was someone on the inside to help source a key for the apartment, but that could've been any one of hundreds of people. Being so close to the ocean, a boat could've been moored up just a few hundred metres from the villa. Within a few hours, the girl would've been on mainland Africa, and that's that – gone.' He took a long swig of his coffee. 'The only thing that makes it seem so unbelievable is the audacity of it.'

Wilcox seemed to shiver at the thought. 'And then what?'

'Hmm?'

'In Africa? If that's where she ended up.'

Quaye shrugged. 'Impossible to say.'

'There's a window, isn't there?' Wilcox continued. 'With a kid so young. And it's only measured in months. After which there is no happy ending, even if she's found alive. If she's been treated badly then obviously that's horrific for the parents. But if she's been treated well –

adopted by a nice family, say – then after a year or so, she's somebody else's daughter, at that age. She won't remember anything of her life before. You can't swoop in and take an eight-year-old from her family and say "hey, we're your real parents." You can't expect her to be happy to see them.'

These were scenarios Quaye knew all too well from his previous role. 'And now you understand why I prefer dealing with dead people,' he said. 'At least you know where you stand with them.'

Quaye's phone beeped in front of him. He looked at it and rolled his eyes.

'I have a meeting back at the office,' he announced. 'Sorry to leave you. Keep me posted.'

Wilcox nodded.

Thirty-eight

When Raymond arrived at the skater hangout behind Victoria Park he was greeted warmly. Not a greeting normally reserved for homeless people, and indeed not one usually expected *of* the skater-boy types who were offering it.

'Hey Raymond man!' from one.

'How's it going?' from another.

'Not seen you over here before,' yet another.

This last observation was correct. It was the first time Raymond had come to this skatepark. He'd bided his time, not wanting it to seem too forced. But he'd needed to come here at some point. There were some new faces over here, some that didn't often venture to the centre, to the amphitheatre where he usually hung out. One face in particular.

Raymond dumped down his duffle bag on the concrete shelf of a half-pipe and pulled out a few six-packs of cheap beer. The response to this was even more positive. A group of boys crowded round and pulled out a pound each for a can. There was a chorus of pssts as ring-pulls were popped, and the boys began swigging eagerly from their contraband; the surge of satisfaction from the rebellion just as potent as that from the alcohol.

They kicked back for a while, talking about nothing in particular, until one boy remembered a specific interest of their homeless friend.

'Oh, see the guy sat over there, on his phone,' he said to Raymond. 'That's Spiky, the one I was telling you about. Had a run-in with Gioco, so he says.'

Raymond glanced over with feigned nonchalance. 'Thanks, I'll go speak to him maybe.'

He chatted for a few more minutes, until he'd emptied one can, then picked up a couple more and headed over to the kid they called Spiky.

'Hey,' said Raymond, offering a beer. 'On the house.'

The kid looked up at him suspiciously, but took the beer anyway. 'Who are you?'

'Just a friend of some of your acquaintances over there. Would like to speak to you about something.' He sat down next to the apprehensive kid.

'I'm looking for an artist named Gioco. I hear you might know something.'

Spiky opened his beer and took a swig. 'I had a run-in with Gioco yeah. What do you want to know?'

'Anything you can tell me.'

He shrugged. 'S'not much. I tagged over one of … err … his pieces. He took exception. One night, I was out tagging again, and this big guy came warned me off, then beat the crap outta me. So I stopped doing it.'

Raymond didn't say anything, just shook his head and smiled, as if with pity, although it was meant with condescendence. He slowly opened up his duffle bag and withdrew the black sketchbook. He opened it and began methodically leafing through the pages until he got to the ones adorned with *that* name. The boy watched, pondering on the significance of this act. Raymond rested on one of the pages, tracing the edges of the designs with the tips of his fingers.

'The thing is,' Raymond said eventually, '*you* know that's not true. And *I* know that's not true. But, as of now, *they* don't know that's not true.' He nodded to the lads larking about on the other side of the skatepark. 'Now, I'm more than happy for this to remain our little secret; for you to continue to tell your tall stories about the big bad thugs that beat you up; so long as you don't spin *me* any further lies.' He looked at Spiky, and with a much more direct tone of voice said, 'Tell me what you know about Gioco.'

The boy did.

And that was the final piece of knowledge Raymond required.

Thirty-nine

Quaye was in his office when he received the call from Wilcox on reconnaissance.

'She's leaving. And it doesn't look like she's planning on being back anytime soon.' She spoke with the breathless urgency of someone moving quickly on her feet. There were sounds of cars and people in the background. 'She's just got into a taxi with a suitcase.'

Quaye started moving. 'Which company?'

There was a delay, just the effort noises of Wilcox as she rushed to get closer before the car sped off. 'Abby Cabs.'

'I know them. Their office is on Church Road down from where you are. Get there, flash your badge and see where it's taking her. You're closest to the bus depot and train station if you need to head her off there.'

'Okay. What about you?'

'I'm going to make my way to the one place I hope she's not going, but fear she is.'

'The airport.'

'Right.' Quaye was in his car by now, speeding off single-handedly.

'What do I do if I catch up with her?' Wilcox asked as she ran.

'Don't know yet,' he admitted. 'Just keep me posted.' He hung up.

After ten minutes he got a text from Wilcox. A single

word: *Airport*. He was going in the right direction. Or, at least, he was *facing* the right direction. The traffic out of the city was bad and currently he wasn't moving. He knew Gretchen would be afflicted by the same slow progress, but he opted to flick on his blues-and-twos all the same and dramatically improved his momentum.

At the airport he abandoned his car at the taxi drop off and headed into the terminal. He spun around in a throng of aimless travellers all heading in different directions. The greatest concentration of people was at the two-hundred deep check-in queue for EasyJet. He headed for it, trying as well as he could to weave through the crowd without barging anyone out of the way, not always succeeding. At the queue, he began scanning faces in the zigzagging line. Fortunately, if there was one thing Gretchen was bad at, it was blending into a crowd. He could almost triangulate her position from the errant gazes of men in her vicinity.

There she was. Midway down the queue. Embedded in a dense mass of bodies and luggage.

Although he didn't have much of a plan, he knew it didn't begin with causing a commotion, with performing some attention-grabbing skit at the heart of an airport terminal.

Low-key was the watchword.

So he waited. Waited for Gretchen to make her excruciating way to the desk, go through the motions, insist there were no sharp objects, firearms or endangered animals in her hand-luggage, and ultimately check-in.

Then she headed in his direction.

When her eyes first met his, she stopped in her tracks.

But it was only for the briefest moment of calculation, before motioning to pass him by. Quaye took half a sideways step into her path.

'Neither of us wants a scene,' he said in a low calm voice.

'You can't stop me,' she said in a hiss, not breaking her stride.

She was right, to the letter of the law.

Quaye kept pace beside her. 'Really? One mention of the B-word from a guy with a badge and you won't be getting on a plane for a month.' He mellowed his voice. 'I just want a word, off-the-record.'

She stopped and turned to him with an anguished expression. 'I have a plane to catch.'

'I know. You have plenty of time.' His voice was softer. 'I know it's hard to believe, but I'm trying to be on your side. Currently, I think you're innocent. And I think you can help me. But if you run I'll have to assume the worst.'

Gretchen looked at pains with her dilemma.

Quaye understood. 'Come on, let me buy you a…' He looked around. 'A Subway.'

Gretchen pulled a face.

'Fair enough,' Quaye acknowledged. He glanced the other way. 'Okay, a cinnamon bun?'

Eventually, she accepted begrudgingly.

They chose a seat in the corner, away from inquisitive ears.

Quaye began.

'I understand your predicament,' he tried to assure her. 'All I need is a name. Just point me in the right direction and I can find other evidence. It won't have to come from you. I just need to know where to start. Help me with that and I'll do my best to keep you out of it.' Then he looked her in the eye. 'I can't expect you to trust me, but I can offer you something else. All you need to do is refuse it.'

Gretchen looked confused. That was the look Quaye was hoping for. Out of view, he discretely thumbed a bunch of twenties from his wallet, then slid them across the table.

'I don't understand,' she said, almost recoiling from the gesture.

'Don't you?' he probed.

She shook her head. 'No.'

'Perfect.' He withdrew the money quickly and returned it to his wallet. 'Now you have leverage. This airport is packed with security cameras. There's footage of me offering you money. Trying to bribe you, or hire you, or pay you off. Whatever story you want to spin, should you need to.' His tone softened. 'Who is he?'

Gretchen looked up to the heavens as if for guidance. When she eventually started to talk, she seemed to do so with cathartic release.

'I don't know his real name. Only the one he used to contact me with via my profile, which was Philistine. I followed the same protocol as I always do with new clients. One you are aware of. If they insist on using a fake name, then *I* insist on a crypto-currency payment in advance before our first meeting. The same if I take on a job. It pre-filters out some of the time-wasters and weirdos.'

'And you deemed him to be neither?'

'Indeed. It's a judgement call on the latter. My

profession does not come without its risks, but the rewards are significant.'

'Where did you meet?'

'Somewhere without a security camera, I'm afraid. You're not the only one hyper-aware of those things.'

'So what did he look like? Old, young?'

'Middle-aged. Say, in his fifties. He was … kind of smooth. Wavy, silver hair. Rimless glasses. Tall, slim.'

'Clothes?'

'Smart. Trousers, open-collar shirt.'

'Long-sleeve or short?'

'Long.'

'Cufflinks or buttons?'

Her eyes flicked up as she recalled. 'Buttons, I think.'

'Any distinguishing features?'

She mused for a moment as she slowly shook her head. 'Not that I can remember.'

'Okay, so continue with your story. What happened? What did he ask you to do?' Quaye had to fire the questions. Knew he was on the clock.

'He was polite but formal. I sensed he didn't really have time for small talk. Got down to business straight away. What he asked was unusual, but not so much that I was concerned.'

'Unusual?'

'Wanting to hire my services for someone else. Other than that it was nothing I hadn't handled before. Revise a backstory, play a role. And, you know, the other stuff.'

Quaye nodded. 'And what was the role?'

'Play the hard-to-get conquest.'

'And the backstory?'

'That my ex was this world-famous graffiti artist. That I was clearly still obsessed with that world and with him.'

'Gioco.'

'Yes.'

'In reality, was this Philistine man Gioco?'

'Not as far as I know.'

'Do you know who is?'

'No.'

'What do you know about him?'

'Gioco? Only what the guy told me.'

'And what was that?'

'Mainly about how we met.'

Quaye knew this tale. 'You know that's based on a true story?' he said. 'About an artist and his Cynthia. Only the artist was one of the founding fathers of graffiti in America, and it happened forty years ago.'

Gretchen shrugged.

'And Gioco isn't world-famous,' Quaye added. 'Just a local artist.'

'Under *that* name maybe.'

'Okay, point taken.'

'So my role was to play the enigmatic, hard-to-get girlfriend. To talk about my previous life. To make his own seem dull and conformist by comparison. To suggest that being rebellious was sexy. That graffiti artists are these cool, underground anti-heroes. Like Batman or something.'

Gretchen was clearly a pro. The archetypal femme-fatal. Albeit an unwitting one. Quaye could well understand the power she could wield in such a situation. An almost unattainably desirable woman revealing the truth about what *really* makes a man attractive, to her at least. And, in particular, what made her previous man attractive. It would have impact. Like an emotional cattle-prod. He'd seen men crushed like this before. Not just men. It worked both ways, he knew that.

'So your influence was … significant … it would seem?' Quaye suggested.

'He was somewhat…' – she searched for the word – '…malleable. He had a brash, cocky exterior which belied a rather insecure core.'

'Would you describe him as a *nice* person?'

'Nice? That's not necessarily a word I'd use.'

'You could imagine someone wanting to kill him?'

'I can *imagine* it. Seems extreme. But then, funnily enough, murder always seems a bit extreme to me.' She smiled.

Quaye appreciated her candour. And that's how he read it. He knew he had to maintain an open mind, but he also had to make judgement calls. And his judgement here sided with the plaintiff. In fact, he found himself actually liking her. But was he just being sucked in by her professional charm?

'So ultimately your role was to convince Milner to create an artwork?' Quaye put to Gretchen.

'*Ultimately* maybe, but not explicitly. It was not part of *my* script.'

'Really?' Quaye was surprised.

'No. That must have come from somewhere else.'

Quaye considered this. The photograph with the

handwritten note on the back, the toxic spray-paint: they must have been delivered by this Philistine character himself. Maybe he thought getting Gretchen/Cynthia involved in the specifics was too risky.

'When was the last time you saw Milner?' Quaye asked.

'It was about a week before he died. Philistine told me that the job was done and that I was not to contact him again.'

'Milner?'

'Yes.'

'How had you been communicating?'

'By an email address Philistine had set up. He said I must not use a mobile phone or any other method. Only this email.'

'And you didn't check it after that last meeting?'

'No.'

Quaye retrieved a pad and pen from his pocket and pushed it toward Gretchen. 'Can you jot down the address and password?' He knew the password would likely have been changed the day Gretchen's role came to an end. Philistine would have used it over that final week to ratchet things up to the next level, pile on the pressure, spur him to his final act.

After scribbling, Gretchen looked at her watch.

'I have to go,' she said.

Quaye nodded. He had more questions to ask, but he didn't want to lose the little trust he had of his only witness by making her miss her flight.

'Thanks for your time. I appreciate it.'

Gretchen grabbed her hand luggage. Quaye walked with

her towards the escalator that headed to departures.

'Just one question for you,' Gretchen said. 'What's the B-word?'

Quaye smiled in amusement on learning she hadn't fully understood his threat from earlier. Lost in translation. He responded by way of mime, placing the fingertips of his hands together and exploding them apart.

Gretchen laughed a little at herself as she realised.

'Have a good flight,' Quaye signed off, as they went their separate ways. Then he immediately pulled out his phone. There were a couple of missed calls from Wilcox. He called her.

'Hey, what happened?' she asked.

'Nothing,' responded Quaye, sounding as breathless as he could. 'She wouldn't talk.'

Forty

By the time the last day of their project arrived, Lisa knew Ryan was ready to pull off the move needed to access the final canvas. And she knew *she* was ready for it to be over. It had been a fulfilling but full-on experience, and now it was time for her to re-group and re-coup. But not until one last artwork was in place. And this time – for the first time – they would be there together. Her work was already done, with respect to preparation. No more groundwork was required. And she needed to be with Ryan on this occasion to guide him to the final location. Access was a little more involved than on previous nights – via two neighbouring buildings. Making it to the top of the first was straightforward enough. But now they were looking down to the roof of the second, and Lisa realised her mistake in focussing so much on the final ascent, in overlooking the descent that stood before them. Studying it now, in the context of Ryan's apprehension, she could be willing to concede it wasn't an insignificant drop. But they were here now, and it wasn't going to get any smaller by looking at it.

'Just jump,' she urged, like it was nothing.

'Just jump?' Ryan questioned.

'Yes,' she confirmed. Unfortunately, she knew there was no alternative route down. It wasn't even possible for Ryan to lower himself down and drop because there was also a small gap to negotiate. 'I'll go first,' she announced confidently.

In an effortless fluid motion, she leapt, landed, rolled forward and returned to her feet, raising her arms and giving a winning smile for the judges. Ryan shook his head at her showmanship before hurling their supply rucksack at her to wipe the grin from her face.

It didn't work.

Ryan had to accept his fate. He rocked back and forth on his heels, trying to summon the nerve to take the leap, opposing biological mechanisms within him competing for supremacy. Eventually, a surge of adrenalin tipped the balance of power in favour of action, and his muscles exploded into movement, launching his body into the air, then crashing him heavily to the ground below with a yelp.

Lisa was about to laugh at the unceremonious landing, until she saw Ryan grab his ankle and wince.

'Shit, you okay?' she asked, crouching down beside him.

'Not sure,' he responded flatly.

'Try to stand,' Lisa encouraged, helping him to his feet.

Ryan put weight on the injured side and then tried a step. He tipped his head to one side and pouted.

'It's not so bad,' he admitted. 'But it's not tip-top either.' He slumped back to the floor. 'I'm not sure it's in suitable shape for running up that.' He pointed at the wall of the next building – the big one.

'Seriously?' Lisa sat down beside him with a heavy sigh. 'We have to do this tonight. We can't fall at the last hurdle. No pun intended.'

'I know,' Ryan said glumly.

They sat in silence for a while. If Lisa were being honest

with herself, she would have admitted that Ryan had only ever been borderline ready for the maneuverer he had to pull off next anyway, even fully fit. Now, with a potential injury and, more importantly, a dent to his confidence, she knew it would be irresponsible to push him to do it. But wasn't that the whole point of her little rebellion at the world? To be irresponsible? To not give a damn about the consequences of her actions? Wasn't the idea to just do what she wanted regardless of how it might affect other people? To skip school, to clamber over rooftops with a near stranger, committing acts of vandalism?

But she wasn't *that* kind of rebel. And it wasn't *that* black-and-white. For instance, her respect for architecture didn't allow her to graffiti on a building she admired. Nor indeed would she dabble on road signs or street furniture. That was just crass.

So it would appear she was not that much of rebel after all. Just a girl with an agenda – guided by a relatively healthy moral compass. As such she could not push Ryan to continue, however frustrating it would be to quit now.

But they didn't *have* to quit now.

'We just need another location,' she blurted out. 'One with easier access.'

Ryan looked at her with a furrowed brow. 'Unfortunately, genius that you are, there is *nowhere* in the city with easy access, if you happen to be already sat on the roof of a Superdrug with a busted ankle.' Lisa couldn't help snorting with laughter at the ridiculousness of the situation, and Ryan joined her. 'Besides, *this* is the grand finale.' He gestured to the building before them. 'We can't do it anywhere else.'

'But we can't do it on any other *night* either. The finale is right here, right now.'

'Then we have only one option. The show must go on.'

Lisa looked at him questioningly.

'The understudy has to step up,' he added.

It took a moment for Lisa to grasp exactly what he was suggesting. Then her eyes widened.

'Me? I can't do it. *You're* the only artist around here. I'm the assistant, not the understudy. I can't paint.' The words came fast as she recoiled at the suggestion.

'Then you'll have to learn pretty quick.' He looked at his watch. 'We have three hours 'til sun-up. And there's plenty of walls to practice on.'

It was true. They were surrounded by surfaces out of view from the street below.

'But … it won't be as good as yours. And it won't be yours, period.'

'So? It'll add a twist to the tale if the last picture is completed by a different artist. A little intrigue. The forums will go mad for it.'

As crazy as it sounded, they were semi-famous now. Well, NDA was. The average Joe on the street wouldn't know the name, but artists and the graffiti geeks sure did. They were following the story. And they were expecting it to end. Tonight. Someplace.

Ryan tried to re-assure her. 'Look, we'll simplify it. You'll be okay. Let's give it a go.' He pulled the design out of the rucksack and handed it to Lisa, who took it apprehensively, like it was a court summons. She studied it.

She held it up with a hand on either side and tried to project it mentally onto the wall in front of her.

It was not like she'd never wielded a can before. She'd been out on the roof every night preparing the frames for Ryan's artwork. She could paint a mean straight line – if she did say so herself. Moreover, she'd dabbled with more creative works on cardboard in the garage at home when her dad had been out. She wouldn't class herself as an artist, but she had a feel for it.

She threw a sideways glance at Ryan. 'There's only enough paint for one practice,' she said.

'Best make the most of it, then.' He smiled broadly. 'No pressure.'

Lisa threw him a petulant look, then turned to the wall. This would be her first formal lesson. It was a clear night, with an almost full moon, which meant the light was as good as it could be – a mixture of white moonlight and the sodium orange reflected off surrounding buildings. Ryan sat and guided her approach as she attempted to recreate the design in her hand. Fortunately, spray paint is a forgiving medium. Opaque when layered on, any misdemeanour could be covered up.

'Just focus on the shapes,' Ryan encouraged. 'The fancy effects can come later, if you have time.'

After forty-five minutes Lisa stepped back to admire her handiwork. It wasn't finished, but she didn't feel that continuing was going to make her any better.

Ryan obviously agreed with her assessment. 'I think you're ready,' he said.

Lisa turned to see him smiling at her like a proud father,

then turned to face the wall she had to scale. Suddenly it looked much more daunting. But she had come this far – *they* had come this far – and she wasn't going to hesitate now. She scooped up the cans into the rucksack and put it on her back, pulling the straps tight.

'See you on the other side,' she said. 'You be alright getting down?'

He shrugged. 'Down's easy. Gravity will see to that.' He smiled. 'You concentrate on keeping it at bay.'

'Gotcha.'

With a hand from Lisa, Ryan got to his feet and gave her a hug.

'Good luck,'

'Thanks.'

She turned. Took the briefest of moments to size up the wall one last time then started running. Her first few steps of acceleration skidded in the gravel on the rooftop, but she was soon at top speed. The timing of the take-off was crucial for this move. At the edge of the flat roof was a low wall, the width of one brick. She had to plant her launch foot squarely on that without losing momentum. The brain has a long-evolved mechanism for subtly adjusting stride length to plant a foot in a specific place some ten paces out. Traditionally, it was for the avoidance of tree roots when chasing a wild boar, or such like. Lisa's scenario was somewhat different, but her survival depended on it to an equal, and far more immediate, degree. So it was a rather inconvenient time for two primal parts of her brain to conflict. Her hunting instinct was guiding her strides to hit the wall with her more powerful right leg, but her OCD suddenly classified her launch point as a Top Step, which meant she had to land with her left. She faltered momentarily but something drove her forward, told her she was too committed to stop now. Her legs would work themselves out. And, sure enough, her right foot landed squarely where it needed to, launching her into the air. In a cat-like motion, she made two strides up the wall, her fingers scrabbling for the lines of mortar between the bricks, before one hand found its way to the top, followed shortly by the fingertips of the other. Her legs kept running, making her bum stick out from the wall until, finally, one leg could be thrown over the top, leaving her straddling her conquest like a horse. It wasn't pretty, but it was effective.

Lisa looked back at Ryan and saluted, before disappearing into the shadows.

The next move was to lower herself down the side of the building and drop onto a narrow ledge. This was a one-way trip, no turning back. She executed it cleanly. Finally, she edged along the ledge and around a corner to her destination, where her groundwork from a couple of nights ago was already waiting for her. She didn't hesitate on setting to work. This was second-nature now. She only wished that when she'd practised this piece, moments before, she'd done so with her nose to the wall, because that's where she was going to have to execute it now. Regardless, it didn't faze her. This was it, do or die. Rather more literally than she cared to imagine. But on this night she seemed to be driven by a force that made her feel invincible. Not in a dangerous way that made her careless, but one that seemed to place her feet and hands surely, wherever she needed them to be.

She was *in the zone*. That's what it was. This must be what it felt like. She figured she'd best get the job done before she left it.

Occasionally, as she worked, a drunken couple or rowdy group of revellers would stumble past beneath her. All she had to do to avoid being spotted by such astute individuals was to shrink into the shadows and stop moving.

When she was satisfied that the final jet of paint had been sprayed, she had no way of stepping back and surveying her work. She had to trust her instinct and her close-up view. She assumed Ryan would be down there somewhere, watching her, but she couldn't see him.

She had to make the call alone.

She was done.

It was done.

There was just one move left. But before she attempted it, she had to lose the rucksack. She didn't want it on her back. She was going to have to drop it. She knew it was going to make a noise, but she wasn't planning on hanging around much longer. She let it go, making sure it was off to one side and wasn't going to impede her landing.

Then, carefully, she sat down on the ledge. She twisted her torso to allow her to put both hands on the ledge to one side of her, fingers pointing towards the wall. Then she took her weight on her hands, slid her bum off the ledge and lowered herself down, twisting to face the wall, until she was hanging by her fingertips. The ground was still too far to drop to directly, but there was a windowsill a couple of metres below her feet. It was too narrow to land on, just enough to break her fall. Without hesitating she let herself go. Her toes came in contact with the windowsill, at which point she was supposed to bend her knees then jump in a twisting motion to take her towards the ground facing forward in a reasonably controlled fashion. That was how it had worked before. This time was different. She was rushing, and as she tried to perform the manoeuvre, her foot slipped. She couldn't turn and was heading towards the ground backwards. She put a leg out behind her instinctively, but by the time it made contact with the pavement, her body was already at a steep angle, and she came crashing to the ground. Her wrists and elbows took the worst of it before her back and then head hit the deck. She lay there motionless for a moment, until a shadowy figure appeared above her. It was saying something. She couldn't make it out to begin with, but then it came again.

'Are you okay?' it asked.

She recognised the voice. It was Ryan.

She came back to reality.

'I'm okay,' she said, and Ryan helped her into a sitting position. The backs of her arms were grazed and bloody. Ryan winced at the sight of them.

'They look worse than they are,' Lisa reassured. 'Nothing broken.'

Usually, at this point, they'd be high-tailing out of there, especially with the clatter Lisa had just made. On this occasion, Lisa doubted she could even medium-tail it anywhere. But, at the same time, it didn't seem necessary. The job was done.

Both battered and bruised, they limped across the street

to a bench where they could sit and admire the final piece of their story. After a moment of silence, they looked at each other, smiled and then laughed. Still laughing, Lisa looked up at her artwork, shaking her head in disbelief.

'Maybe this site was a little bit trickier than I thought.'

'Maybe,' Ryan agreed. 'But … you did it.' He put his arm around her.

'*We* did it.' She turned to him with beaming eyes, holding still for a moment, part of her wanting to mark the occasion with a more meaningful gesture. Then a recollection snapped her thoughts away. 'Oh there's a couple of *special* cans in the bag,' she said, nodding toward the rucksack.

Ryan frowned as he opened up the rucksack beside him and rummaged around. His eyes widened as he found two cans of beer.

'These weren't here earlier!' he exclaimed.

'I know,' Lisa responded with a cheeky grin. 'I left them on the roof the other day.'

'You are a genius,' he said, as he cracked open one of the cans and covered himself in beer, shaken up from the fall.

'And *you* are clearly not.' Lisa laughed uncontrollably.

When she came to open her own, she did so at arm's length, then sipped off the foam before raising the can for a toast.

'To…' Ryan began.

'…Getting up,' Lisa concluded in graffiti parlance.

'To getting bloody-well up,' Ryan repeated triumphantly, and their cans came together with a dull metallic thud.

As they sipped their drinks, they regaled each other with tales of their conquest. The scrapes, the near misses and, of course, the brilliance of their execution. They felt they'd earned some mutual back-slapping. It'd been a hell of a ride.

It was after four in the morning now, and the sky was beginning to get light. The two renegades started to walk back in the direction of home hand-in-hand, both sore and aching, both glowing with a sense of accomplishment, in their own individual ways.

'I was planning to come back to yours, but I feel so battered and in need of cleaning up.' Lisa gestured to her bloodstained arms. 'I think I'll head home.'

'That's fine,' Ryan said. 'I think you should.'

After crossing the bridge where their paths diverged, they embraced in a hug, which Lisa held for longer than she might have on any previous occasion. Finally, she knew it was the right time. She stood up on tiptoes and kissed Ryan on the cheek.

'See you tomorrow,' she said.

They went their separate ways, both looking back several times with a smile and a wave – like two lovers not wanting to hang up the phone first.

Eventually, the curvature of the path they were following in opposite directions took them out of each other's line of sight.

As she turned away, Lisa could not have known she would never see Ryan again.

Forty-one

Lisa felt nothing but contentment on returning from the finale night of her project with Ryan. Proud of what they'd achieved together. Two souls rallying against the world and the paths it had preordained for them.

As Lisa reached her house, she decided to risk the front door, the threat of being grounded no longer such a concern. Yet, still keen to avoid confrontation, she entered the house as stealthily as her weary limbs would permit. She doffed her shoes and aligned their heels with the rest in the hallway, as her instincts mandated, then tip-toed through to the foot of the stairs.

Foremost in her mind, as always at this moment, was the desire not to wake her father. But on this occasion, only seconds later she would be desperately wishing she *could*.

In her sleepy stupor and the half-light she might almost have missed him. But something in her periphery was out of place as far as her inner compulsions discerned; something needed righting. As she placed one foot on the bottom of the stairs, she turned her head and saw him. Her father, lying on the sofa, his face and arm hanging off the side, a trail of drool leading to a pool of vomit on the floor. The shock of the sight was so visceral it made her scream even before she rushed to his side. Shaking him she could get no response, but his body was warm. She picked up his wrist searching for a pulse. At first, she felt nothing, but after a few attempts, she thought she could detect the faintest of flutters. Or was she just imagining it in her panic? He was on his front so she couldn't see if his chest was rising and falling. She leaned down close to his face and was sure she could sense a breath.

She didn't know what to do. She knew she should, but she didn't. If she'd had time, she might have felt ashamed of this fact. But in the midst of her frantic fear, all she could feel was useless. She grabbed for her phone, pulling it out of her jeans pocket clumsily, sending it spilling onto the floor. She chased after it on her knees and punched 999 into it as soon as it was in her hands.

The man she got put through to on the phone kept her talking whilst she waited for the emergency services to arrive. He asked Lisa if she knew what her dad had taken. Lisa listed the items on the coffee table. Four empty beer cans, an empty vodka bottle, a half-empty whisky bottle and a blister pack of over-the-counter sleeping pills with four tablets missing.

The events of the following hours were a blur. People arrived at her house dressed in green jumpsuits. They acted rapidly but fluidly. They checked things, administered things. They moved her dad to an ambulance.

She rode along with him, floating between worlds like it was a dream.

Reality only began to return to sharp focus a couple of hours later, when Lisa found herself sitting on a plastic chair in a hospital corridor. Found herself wondering who she was.

Merely hours before, the only important thing in her

world was graffiti. Nothing warranted her time unless it furthered her goal of creation, of making her mark on the world – literally and figuratively. She was sure that the one noble thing to be in life was individual. Free. That just doing what other people wanted her to – her dad, her teachers, whoever – was to disrespect the very notion of freedom. That surrendering to authority was to squander the life she had been given.

Now everything was different. Now, nothing could seem more insignificant, more trivial, than squirting paint at a wall – however well-aimed the squirt or high the wall. Lisa had literally come within minutes of becoming an orphan. And this time it *was* her fault. Her actions had very nearly caused the death of another human being. What could possibly be *more* important than that?

Just as Lisa's mind was about to implode with self-destructive thoughts, a woman approached her. She wasn't dressed like a nurse, but Lisa could tell she worked at the hospital because she had a badge on her lapel.

'Lisa?' the woman enquired.

Lisa nodded.

'I'm Andrea, a social worker at the hospital.'

Andrea was a kind-looking Asian lady. She sat down, leaving one chair empty between herself and Lisa.

'I've spoken to the doctor,' she said in a flat but warm tone. Lisa's stomach flipped over at the words. 'Your father is still unconscious, but stable.'

'What does that mean?' Lisa asked frantically, her mind racing. 'He's going to be okay, isn't he?'

'The first twenty-four hours are critical.' That didn't

answer Lisa's question and the woman knew it. 'Until he wakes we can't be sure.'

'Sure of what?'

'Every case of coma is different.' Andrea took on the tone of a primary school teacher. Not in a condescending way. In a caring, authoritative way. 'There is always a chance of neurological damage, but the extent is very difficult to predict.'

Lisa flipped out at this phrase. She stood up abruptly and began to pace. Suddenly she had visions of her father as a vegetable, of pushing him around in a wheelchair for the rest of her life.

'What kind of neurological damage?' she asked with urgency, but then wasn't so sure she wanted to know.

'I'm sorry, we just can't say at this time.'

Lisa continued to pace backwards and forwards. Part of her wanted to know more; more about what the future may hold. But at the same time, she wasn't sure she was prepared to hear the worst-case scenario. In the end, she chose to wimp out and not probe any further; just kept pacing silently.

'How are you holding up?' Andrea asked softly.

Lisa stopped moving and looked at her. The best she could do to answer the question was shrug.

'One of the paramedics said you might be injured too?' Andrea questioned.

Lisa wasn't expecting this line of enquiry. Her arms were now covered by long sleeves, but she touched them instinctively, without thinking.

'I'm fine,' she said.

'Do you mind me asking how you hurt yourself?'

Lisa had to think quickly. She knew how bad it looked. Not for her, for her dad. And not just the injury, the whole thing. A fourteen-year-old schoolgirl rolling home at four-thirty in the morning covered in blood to find her dad comatose on the sofa from alcohol.

Frantic thoughts of a different nature were now running through her mind. She was going to get taken into care. Her dad was going to get prosecuted. It was all her fault.

It was all her fault.

Lisa sat down beside the social worker; tried to compose herself as best she could; tried to fabricate a believable story that would not get her taken into care.

'I'd snuck out in the middle of the night,' she admitted guiltily. 'My dad didn't know anything about it.'

'A boy?' Andrea guessed.

Lisa nodded with a hint of shame in her face. 'A *skater-boy*, in fact. Hence the…' She pointed at her forearms. 'Trying to impress him, you know. Stupid, I guess.'

'I see,' Andrea made an expression of acceptance and placed a hand gently on Lisa's knee. 'Not so stupid, love.'

'He's a good dad,' Lisa insisted after a moment of silence. 'I've just been a bit…' – she paused, searching for the words – '… messed up … since mum died.'

'That's understandable.' Andrea was obviously aware of that part of Lisa's history. 'Your dad too, I expect. Does he drink a lot?'

Lisa didn't like the way this was heading. 'No, not really,' she lied.

Andrea didn't say anything for a while.

'This was an accident, don't you think?' Lisa asked.

'Yes, I think so,' Andrea agreed. 'From what you told us, he'd taken at most four sleeping tablets, possibly less, which tends to suggest he was just trying to sleep. Trying to forget his troubles maybe. Is there anything else going on at home that might be troubling him?'

Lisa said nothing. She managed to shake her head calmly, as if she couldn't think of anything, but inside was a different matter. Inside she was screaming at herself. She knew exactly what was troubling him. It was *her*. It was the fact that he couldn't control his wayward daughter. That not only had he *lost* his wife, but he had *failed* her too, in not being able to bring up their only child.

Lisa was struggling to deal with the mix of emotions. The guilt, the sadness, the fear. Her hands were trembling and clammy. She clasped them together to try to hide it. But then she erupted into tears. She couldn't help it, and she couldn't stop. It felt like she would never be able to stop.

Andrea slid across to the seat next to Lisa and put an arm around her. They sat there like that for a long time. Until Lisa felt she could stem the flow of tears, for a while at least. She sucked in a few deep breaths and pulled herself upright in her chair.

'When will I be able to see him?'

'You'll be able to see him soon. But bear in mind that it is likely to be a while before he is aware enough to communicate. And if he does begin to regain consciousness, it might only be for short periods at a time. And we can call you when that happens. In the meantime, it would be best for you to get some rest. Do you have anyone you can call to be with you?'

'Umm, yes, my grandparents can come pick me up.' Lisa knew this was what the lady would want to hear. In truth, all her grandparents were too senile or too dead to be of any comfort right now. But she was okay with that. Okay with being on her own.

'Good,' Andrea said. 'Would you like me to get in touch with them?'

'No, that's fine.' Lisa produced her phone as if that were proof she was going to use it.

'Okay, I'll let you get on and call them then. Remember, if there is anything you need to discuss I'm always here.' Andrea stood to leave. 'And I'd like to talk more next time you're in.'

Lisa smiled weakly. She did not relish the prospect. When Andrea had turned the corner, Lisa put her phone away and left the hospital. It was a long way home, but she walked anyway. She knew straight away that things had to change, and by the time she got home she knew exactly how.

Forty-two

Lisa stood in front of the bathroom mirror, studying herself solemnly; knowing for the first time in a long while who was being reflected back at her. And that it was not who it needed to be.

Only hours before, she had returned home to find her father hanging on to the last vestiges of life.

Everything changed for her in that single moment.

Everything.

Just like they had a little more than a year before.

When her mum had died, she had taken it as a personal slight on her existence by the universe. Took it as justification to choose a different path, to reject authority, to rebel. She figured that if being good didn't bring goodness, then she may as well be bad. Or, at least, as bad as she liked.

Looking at herself now, at the wise old age of almost-fifteen, she realised how immature those reasonings had been. Recent events had rendered into sharp focus the reality of her world – of *the* world. The reality that no individual was *truly* individual. That no-one lived in total isolation. That every action had a consequence, and those consequences could be felt far and wide. Like ripples in a pond. She was just a single pebble, but she was sending out shockwaves in all directions.

A transformation needed to occur. Back to who she once

was. Who she *should* be now. The compulsion to change was overwhelming and urgent. She couldn't have put into words the nature of the urge if she'd had to, but it was much like her other idiosyncrasies. She knew she was lucky compared to others who experience such obsessive compulsions. Hers were not debilitating. In fact, she found them kind of comforting. And although they were irrational by definition, she had always believed they had their roots in rationality. Like her need to line up the heels of the shoes in the hallway – she knew exactly where that had come from. When she was five she had rushed out of the front door when her father had arrived home one day, tripping over some shoes left untidily in the hallway, sending her crashing down the steps outside and planting her face into the pavement. She lost her front teeth which went right through her bottom lip. She still had a small scar.

So, however obscure at times, she trusted her inner compulsions. They were like her shepherds. And right now they were telling her how to change, *what* to change. And it had to be right now. The changes may be merely cosmetic, but they were symbolic. And in life, as in graffiti, symbolism was important.

Sometimes, it was *everything*.

Lisa took one last lingering look at herself in the mirror. And then the transformation began.

First, the dark eyeliner would go. When she had applied it the previous night, she was full of excitement, about to set off to paint the city, to complete her project with Ryan. That was now done. Over. And so was that Lisa. With a couple of cleansing wipes the dark circles around her eyes were gone for the last time.

Next, superfluous metalwork would be banished from display. Lisa removed the piercing through her tongue, the ring through her lip, and the studs from the top of her left ear. All she left behind was a pair of understated silver earrings.

When it came to her clothes, it wasn't just a case of stripping them off into a heap on the floor as she usually might. Instead, she peeled off each of the black garments one-by-one, ceremonially folding them into a neat pile, topped off by the leather bangles that almost perpetually adorned each of her forearms. She stood in nothing but her underwear. Naked of her former identity.

Almost.

Now it was time for the final statement.

Now it was time to say goodbye to Lisa Noir once and for all.

She snapped on a pair of blue latex gloves and read the instructions on the bottle of bleach one last time. She couldn't wait for her dyed hair to grow out. It had to be blonde right now, so she was going to Marilyn Monroe the shit out of it.

One hour later, Lisa Le Blanc was back. Not quite her natural colour, it had a greyish quality to it, but good enough.

The next day Lisa left a note for Ryan at their bridge, telling him what had happened and saying she could no longer be who she had been with him. She promised she would come see him soon to explain. Then she headed back to the hospital to begin her vigil, even though she hadn't yet heard word of improvement in her father's condition.

Lisa recoiled when she first arrived at her dad's bedside. An oxygen tube trailed under his nose and a drip into his arm. His skin was almost as pale as the bedsheets. He looked so vulnerable, and Lisa had never been able to consider her dad in this way before. This, she realised, was the naivety of a girl – a daughter.

The lifecycle of the parent-child relationship was bookended by periods of one-way dependence. The child in need at the beginning; the parent at the end. And in between, a long meandering journey through co-dependence, a generation-long transition of roles, so gradual as not to be noticeable. But recognising the inevitably of this process was an important step to adulthood. One that Lisa had just taken, sooner than most.

The hospital staff had warned her not to expect too much. To be prepared for the worst. Apparently, it wasn't like in the movies: lucidity returning in the opening on an eyelid. Instead, she was told, signs of consciousness would be fleeting to begin with, and any awareness of surroundings was likely a long way off.

It was true. It was a slow process. But Lisa was sure there was a flicker of recognition in her dad's eyes when they made contact with hers from time to time. And eventually, Lisa's patience was rewarded with two raspy, laboured words.

'Your … hair.' The sounds were barely audible, but she could just about make out her father's voice. And that was all it took for Lisa to know he was going to be okay. The sense of relief was so overwhelming she couldn't stop herself bursting into tears, and collapsing to his chest.

'I'm sorry,' she said through sobs. 'I'm so sorry.'

Her dad was not strong enough to put his arm around her or even say anything in return, but Lisa knew he would have done so if he could.

The weeks that followed were tough for Lisa, but at the same time, they were the best she'd had in the last two years, her escapades with Ryan aside. By the time her dad was released from hospital, it was almost summer holiday at her school. After long and tiresome consultations with social workers, it was concluded that Lisa would be able to care for her dad until he was back to fitness. The weather was still good and in the beginning they spent most of their time just sitting in the garden talking, or making the short walk to the park and getting a coffee from the man with his little three-wheeler van. In the evenings Lisa would cook, and she came to really enjoy it. She'd let her dad choose a recipe from one of her mum's old cookbooks, and Lisa would try to recreate it – not always successfully. She'd buy all the ingredients from the local independents and sometimes the market.

They talked a lot. They talked about her mum. If not for the first time then definitely for the first time *comfortably*.

And, most importantly, they laughed.

By the end of the summer, Lisa had a dad again. And, more importantly, her dad had a daughter.

One frank exchange would always stay with Lisa. After a long silence, he had just come out with it; obviously feeling an explanation was overdue, of why he had remained so distant from her.

'You remind me of her,' he had said, softly. 'That's why ... why I couldn't look at you.' He swallowed hard, dew welling in his eyes.

Lisa could see how hard it had been to admit. Admit that he'd not been able to bear the presence of his own daughter. She understood.

'I know,' she responded, pulling her chair closer to his and resting a hand on his arm. 'I know I remind you of her. But that's because half of me *is* her. And you still have that. It's still here if you want it. But if you let it go, she really will be gone for you. Completely. All we'll have left is our individual memories of her, with no-one to share them with, no-one to reinforce them. And over time they will drift, diverge, fade even. Until they are no more than our own personal fiction.'

Her dad nodded, slowly, almost imperceptibly, then turned and give the weakest of smiles. 'How did you get to be so wise?' he teased.

'Must get it from my mum,' she replied, with a smile of her own.

They laughed.

And that was the moment Lisa knew they would be alright.

She couldn't possibly have known about Ryan.

Forty-three

There was no natural light. Just the hazy glow of a city after dark.

But that was enough.

Enough to carry out his work. To create his final masterpiece.

The can of spray-paint resonated comfortingly in his hand as he shook it – an action more of reflex than necessity. He knew the sound would not betray him. Cities like this never fell silent. There was always a hum, a backing track to his clandestine endeavours, sufficient to shroud his every move.

With his free hand, he clung to a support on the outside of the bridge; his feet edging slowly along a narrow ledge. This was his office. The underworld office of an urban artist.

Precarious.

Solitary.

And exhilarating beyond compare.

The artist began to paint. Deftly. With natural sweeping movements. Like the master of an ancient martial art. And like those timeless disciplines, there was honour at stake in his works too. Not just from the mastery of the craft, but from the audacity of the canvas. Illicit, unreachable, perilous.

This would be his finest creation. It had to be. There

would be no more after this one.

No more art. No more days. Not even the coming sunrise.

Not for him.

He worked intensely, with the flair of a dancer but the precision of a machine. Until the last mark was made, and the work was complete.

When the end came, it was swift. To the observer, had there been any, it would have been over in a moment. But to the artist, as he fell, he was no longer bound by the rules of time. He felt a great relief – a release from all worldly pain. He sensed the Earth coming up to reclaim him, and he welcomed it. And then there was nothing. He was one with nature again.

For him, the event was the most significant of moments on his journey. The final moment. The end.

For most, it barely registered, on the day that followed. The merest flicker of firing neurons. A morsel of news that obscured the consciousness only long enough for it to be rapidly swiped from view to make way for the next.

For one unknowing individual, it was the beginning of a new chapter of her life.

Forty-four

As Quaye entered his office, Wilcox turned to face him; a motion that seemed more an automatic response than a conscious gesture of greeting. Her eyes stared through him; her mind clearly elsewhere.

'Earth to Wilcox,' Quaye quipped, and her eyes finally came up to meet his, wide and piercing, set into an ashen face. 'What's up?' he asked.

'Well, either I'm experiencing a serious case of déjà vu, or…'

'Or?'

'It's happened before.'

'What's happened before?'

Wilcox paused as if running a mental calculation, then concluded: 'All of it.'

Quaye came to join Wilcox. She turned back to face her screen and began delivering facts in staccato fashion from the news article displayed upon it.

'Graffiti artist. Ryan Penrose. Fell to his death whilst working on his masterpiece. Onto a *train line*.' She emphasised the significance of these two words. 'This time from Clifton Suspension Bridge.' Wilcox paused momentarily as Quaye skimmed the article over her shoulder. 'Granted,' she continued, 'it could just be a coincidence. But look what he was painting.'

Wilcox scrolled down until a picture of the artwork came

into view. Abstract lettering. Almost illegible unless you knew what letters to make of it. And they both did. It was ingrained on their minds. In a game of word-association, they would both respond the same to the word 'graffiti'.

GIOCO.

And there it was again.

What did this mean?

'When was this?' Quaye asked firmly.

'Three years ago. It was recorded as a suicide. No suspicious circumstances.'

'Suicide? Not misadventure?'

'Apparently not.'

Quaye nodded, silently berating himself for not finding this sooner. The case would never have come to his attention at the time. Incidents on the train network were usually the sole preserve of the Transport Police. And, as a suicide, it would have warranted no further investigation. But was that excuse enough? Had his professionalism been compromised? Was the increasing preoccupation of his mind impeding his due-diligence at work? He shook the thought from his head.

Wilcox turned back to Quaye. 'It has to be related right?'

'I can't see how it couldn't be.'

'So what are we thinking? Two murders? The first one being misidentified, just like the second one would have been if you hadn't got interested?'

Quaye shrugged, pensively.

'Oh, there's one very curious detail about this first incident, though,' Wilcox added.

'Go on.'

'Well, the paint used by the artist was not the usual kind.'

'In what way?'

'It was water-soluble.'

'Meaning?'

'Meaning that a few heavy rain-showers later and the piece of artwork the guy died for was all but washed away.'

Quaye frowned. 'You're right, that is curious. Temporary graffiti. Hardly the MO of your average vandal.'

'Indeed, that's what I thought.'

'Okay, excellent work Wilcox. Let's dig out that old case and see where it takes us.'

While Wilcox was doing that, Quaye disappeared in a bid to fetch coffees, getting waylaid in the process by various other office matters that demanded his attention. On his return, he could tell Wilcox was fit to burst with further revelations. Cases could be like that; picking away at the threads until one of them caused the whole thing to unravel.

'What's up?' he asked, depositing a coffee on her desk.

'So, Ryan Penrose was bipolar. He went AWOL from his job a few months before his death. Coroner's report suggested he was going through a depressive stage prior to going missing and wasn't happy in his workplace. So far, so normal. But, here comes the bombshell. Guess where he worked?'

'Where?'

'Trinoviant. The very same finance company as Tobias Milner.'

'Shit.' Quaye allowed this new fact to settle in as he took a seat at his desk. After a while, he decided he needed to study the coroner's report in more detail, before he could draw any new conclusions. In particular, he was interested in further evidence for the suicide verdict. There was little. No suicide note was found. Although, shortly before his death, he'd sent his sketchbook to his parents. An admittedly symbolic act for an artist, but hardly conclusive. The window of foul play was still open in Quaye's mind.

Now he was ready to assimilate all the new pieces with the old. He leant back in his chair, cupping his hands around his coffee mug and slipping into deep thought. When he came back to reality, it must have been noticeable, as Wilcox was poised to ask a question.

'So, two murders?'

'Maybe,' Quaye said hesitantly. 'But there is one obvious difference about the Ryan Penrose incident that makes this seem less likely.'

'Go on.'

'The artwork.' He pointed at Wilcox's screen. 'It's finished.' He went over and pulled up a chair next to her desk. 'Milner barely got half way through his attempt before intoxication led to his fall. With Penrose, it looks like he was done. He might have been moments from climbing down. So either the culprit got incredibly lucky, or…'

'Or Penrose chose when he jumped,' Wilcox concluded.

'Exactly.' Quaye stood, abruptly, and with purpose. 'Right, we have jobs. We need to get back to Trinoviant and find out the relationship between Ryan Penrose and Tobias Milner. We need to track down Penrose's parents and find out their perspective on their son's death. But first…' – he grabbed a set of keys off his desk – '…let's visit the bridge.'

Quaye parked up on the Clifton side of the suspension bridge – the opposite side to where Penrose had fallen from.

'Your neck of the woods,' Wilcox remarked on the proximity to his apartment.

'Indeed. I feel personally invested in any suggestion of wrong-doing on my bridge.'

They made their way onto the iconic structure. At either end were two large towers, supporting the industrial-scale cables that suspended the deck. The two passed under the east tower, walking along the left-hand side of the bridge. The drop beneath them was breath-taking. On the east side, there was a road beneath, cars like matchboxes speeding in either direction. Then the wide expanse of the River Avon, murky brown from silt kicked up by the strong tidal currents. They walked slowly to the centre. The bridge hadn't been built with cars in mind. Or tourists. The pedestrian pavements were narrow and progress was slow, dodging between sightseers, dog-walkers and joggers. But Quaye was in no hurry. He was taking in the scene in a way he hadn't before; gauging the physics of the grand structure and its setting.

He knew the problem with the murder theory, before he'd gotten here, but he wanted to see to be sure.

Ten metres from reaching the west tower, he stopped and looked down from the bridge. Wilcox stopped beside him.

Now she recognised the problem too.

'The train track,' she observed.

'Right. A good way from the tower where the graffiti-ing was carried out.'

Quaye already knew Penrose couldn't have fallen from

the tower. At its base was a wide paved area. If Penrose had fallen onto it, he might still have died, but he would never have made it over the side of the bridge into the valley below. Even if he'd made a concerted effort to clear the plinth, he wouldn't have made it. He certainly wouldn't if he'd fallen passively. The fact that the train line wasn't directly below just compounded the fact.

They walked further to reach the base of the tower and looked up. Quaye was well acquainted with the mechanics of it. Inside the top of the tower was a saddle over which the giant chains hung, allowing them to move as load passed over the bridge. To the right, the chains descend in a shallow curve to the centre of the span, down to about eight feet at its lowest point. To the left, the chain came down at a similar angle to meet the ground.

Wilcox walked around to the left of the tower. 'I have no idea how he managed to paint the thing,' she exclaimed, 'but he must have climbed up the chain from one side or the other. There's no other way up. Either way, after the job, he decided to climb down toward the middle. That's how he ended up in the valley.'

They navigated the base of the tower and took a few strides back to the point on the bridge that was directly over the train track, where Ryan Penrose had ended his journey.

Quaye's eyes wandered up, following the long steel rods that hung from the industrial chain above. It was enough to give someone vertigo just looking at it. Someone. Not him, of course.

'Pretty extreme,' Quaye muttered, mostly to himself. He turned back to Wilcox. 'That's another difference between this victim and Milner. *This* guy was a hardened graffiti artist, not a newbie.'

'But that makes some sense,' Wilcox suggested. 'If the first victim was an artist, then the whole intoxicated spray-can idea for masking a murder as a suicide was kind of logical, and to be fair, kind of successful. So much so, the killer orchestrated a plan to get his second, *non*-artist, victim into the same position. But upped the dose this time, to make sure it kicked in before the job was finished. Otherwise, it's a bizarrely elaborate plan.'

'Bizarrely elaborate,' Quaye repeated, deep in thought. He took one more moment to study his surroundings before arriving firmly at what was now blindingly obvious. He walked off shaking his head to himself.

'Not murder,' he concluded. 'Definitely not murder.'

Wilcox scurried after him. 'Why not?'

'Well, you're suggesting that the plan almost failed because Penrose was almost down before the intoxication kicked in. But it was precisely this timing that meant he ended up in the valley. If the incident had gone to plan, he'd have fallen onto the buttress at the bottom of the tower.'

'Which, as you said, would probably still have killed him.'

'Right. But the point was not just to kill him but to make it look like suicide. This is an infamous suicide spot. But suicidal people don't come here to climb all the way up that tower only to fall back to the bridge again. They come to a bridge to jump off the bridge, yeah? To climb over the fence and jump into the valley. There's a symbolism to it. Not to mention height.'

Wilcox was silent for a moment. 'Well, maybe he wasn't trying to dress it up as a suicide. We're only being swayed that way because of the iconic location and the coroner's verdict. Maybe it was supposed to look like an accident.'

Quaye considered this option. 'Okay,' he conceded. 'I'll give you a maybe on that one.'

'Gee thanks.' Wilcox smiled.

Quaye smiled back.

When they got back to his car, Quaye threw his keys to Wilcox, who caught them deftly.

'Drop me off at Trinoviant,' he said. 'I'm going to find out the connection between Penrose and Milner. I'll see you back at the office. See if you can track down Penrose's parents and get their take on his death.'

'Sure,' Wilcox confirmed.

Forty-five

Lisa admired the view from the bench beneath Cabot Tower once again. Her fair hair played about her face in the gentle breeze. She liked to come here at least once a week, since Ryan. Always on her own. Anything else would seem like a betrayal.

Yet, today, she was here with someone else. Luke. It wasn't pre-meditated. It was just the way the wandering had taken. The muscle memory of her legs guiding her steps, like a dog on its daily walking route. It was just that this time another pair of legs had been in step. Right to the bench where they sat now.

It didn't feel quite right. Not yet. But it didn't feel wrong either. Did that mean she could feel comfortable with Luke?

Trust him?

Trust him with the truths that were only hers and Ryan's?

Or even trust him with the truths that were only *hers*?

Maybe she would have to. Maybe the choice would be taken from her.

But not yet.

Now it was just a place. With a view.

And an ice cream.

She let her mind float back to those times. Those times of Lisa Noir. But then after a while, the thoughts became more than thoughts. They became words.

And the story was told.

Lisa had never talked about Ryan before. About their project. Not to anyone. It felt good when she finally had. Like a wound had been lanced; the pressure released. She didn't know Luke very well, but she felt she could trust him with her secret. Not that it was a particularly damaging secret. It wasn't like her life was at stake. It was just that the Lisa back then was a different person. One who bore little resemblance to who she was now.

Her companion had listened patiently to the tale as it had unfolded, allowing Lisa to continue at her own pace. Now she was finished, an obvious question was left hanging in the silence.

Luke posed it. 'So what happened to Ryan?' he asked. 'To NDA? On your website you speculated that he'd left the city. But you didn't need to speculate – you *knew*?'

Lisa nodded solemnly, then sat quietly for a moment before pulling out her phone. She made a few deft jabs and swipes and then held the screen up to Luke.

Luke studied the image before him and frowned, trying to understand what it meant. He recognised the location, of course. It was one of the towers of Clifton Suspension Bridge. And covering almost the entire width was an ostentatious work of graffiti.

'This was his last piece,' Lisa said. 'His last *anything*.' She steeled herself for a moment before continuing. 'After completing this, he climbed down along the cable.' A tear welled in her eye. 'And jumped.'

Luke recoiled a little at the revelation. Clearly he hadn't been expecting it. The story of the artist who had fallen from the bridge was at around the time Luke had started to get interested in the scene. He didn't know enough for the conundrum to be obvious to him back then. Now it was as clear as day.

'But … I don't understand,' he began. And Lisa knew exactly what he was referring to. It was the name Ryan had emblazoned across the bridge tower. It wasn't his own. It wasn't NDA.

It was Gioco.

'I know you don't understand. But you will.' Lisa stood up. 'Come on. I have to show you something.'

Forty-six

Quaye didn't waste any time. They had momentum now, and he didn't want to lose it.

'I need to speak to your HR director, Elaine Hodges,' he said to the receptionist at Trinoviant, flashing his badge.

The receptionist didn't seem fazed by the request, asking him to take a seat while she made the necessary calls. Five minutes later a lady appeared to greet him. She was short and round and sported a tight bob of hair that was almost white in colour.

'Thanks for your time.' He put out a hand which she took.

'Not at all.' She gestured him toward the elevator she had appeared from.

'You spoke to my colleague before,' Quaye pointed out.

'I did. I assume this is regarding poor Tobias?'

'Indirectly,' Quaye responded. Something about the way she said that, the way she used his first name only, seemed insincere to Quaye. Employees were just a number to these people, weren't they? He knew that experiences from his early career had tainted his view of HR directors. He forced himself to open his mind. Maybe he was prejudging unfairly. Maybe she really did know Milner personally, not just as a result of his recent untimely exit from the company and the stack of paperwork it had generated.

In her office, Elaine Hodges poured them both a cup of

filter coffee.

'Do you remember an employee of yours called Ryan Penrose?' Quaye asked, getting straight to the point.

She knitted her brow in thought for a moment before shaking her head slowly. 'I don't think I do.'

'He worked here until three years ago, and left under unusual circumstances.' Quaye was referring to the fact that Ryan had gone AWOL.

'I'll take your word for it. We have over two thousand employees here, and an annual staff turnover of eleven percent. So, as much as I'd like to, unfortunately, I can't know everyone on the payroll by name.' She applied a smile to her face about as naturally as she had applied her makeup that morning. 'I can look up his records if you'd like?'

'Please. I'd like to know if Ryan and Tobias worked together, or would have known each other.'

She clicked and tapped at her computer for a few moments.

'Ah, here we go. Hmm, yes. Well, I can confirm they did work together. Tobias was Ryan's team lead at the point he disappeared.'

Learning of a deepening connection between the two was perhaps inevitable, but it didn't get Quaye any further on its own.

'Okay, I need to speak to someone who knew them both,' he stated firmly. 'Preferably someone who was in the same team, then and now. And I need to speak to Arrash Rahman, one of your IT guys who was friends with Tobias Milner.'

Ms Hodges remained stoic in the face of Quaye's orders.

Sometimes in his role he had to be assertive and impersonal, bordering on rude. Sometimes he had to force himself to do it. On this occasion, he didn't find it so hard.

Quaye's host found him a meeting room down the corridor from hers; big enough for a table and a few chairs, with a window looking out onto the square below. Over the course of the next two hours, a procession of individuals were brought in to speak to him. The meeting with Rahman was brief. He hadn't known Milner at the point Penrose was around, so he couldn't help with any details regarding their relationship. Quaye made a note to ensure this story checked out fully.

Quaye also spoke to Milner's line manager, who knew both the deceased, but didn't seem emotionally capable of revealing anything beyond the corporate line. In fact, he seemed equally unaware of what was happening in the team as what happened in anyone's life outside of the office. He did, though, offer a team member to talk to, who he suggested might be more helpful.

Mel was a mousey young woman. Small in stature, mid-brown hair, glasses, neatly dressed. She'd worked at the company since university. Probably wasn't going to leave anytime soon. Wasn't the go-getter type, it seemed. She came across as timid in her mannerisms, but certainly wasn't shy in speaking out. Most importantly, she wasn't averse to talking ill of the recently deceased. If anything, she seemed to relish the opportunity to do so.

'Toby was a bully,' she said in no uncertain terms.

'Did he bully you?'

She nodded glumly. 'He used to. Although he backed off

a little when he got concerned about the gender aspect. When Ryan turned up, he had a new outlet for his macho bollocks.' She apologised quickly for her language.

'What kind of bullying was it?'

'Verbal. General put downs. Schoolboy stuff a lot of it. But Ryan was sensitive, and lacked confidence, so I could see it was affecting him badly.'

'Did he make a complaint?'

She shook her head. 'No. He wasn't the type to snitch. To blame someone else. That was his problem. He'd take these things to heart – like it was genuinely his fault.'

'So HR never knew about this?'

'Oh no, they knew alright. Even Hodges knew.'

'How?'

Mel looked a little sheepish. '*I* told them.'

'*You*? Why?'

'I was concerned.' She answered like it was a dumb question.

'And did they take any action?'

She shrugged. 'Not as far as I know. They were quite dismissive. Almost like they were suggesting that it *was* Ryan's fault.'

'Why?'

'I guess because of his condition. I didn't know about it at the time. Not 'til … after. But I guess the HR folk in their ivory tower thought he was awkward to deal with or something. But he wasn't. He was late in occasionally, but he more than made up for it. And he was quiet sometimes. But that was it. Toby just saw him as weak. Like a lamb to the slaughter.'

'How did you feel when Ryan left? Or rather, stopped coming in.'

'I guess in retrospect I should have been worried. But I wasn't. I was pleased for him. I thought, good on him. Just assumed he'd had enough and fucked them over. Sorry. Didn't really know how troubled he was. We weren't close enough that I had his number, that I would have called him up. It's times like this you wonder whether you could have done something different; been a better person.' She looked down at her hands, fiddling with a ring on her finger.

'You did what you could in speaking to HR. You can't be expected to know what's going on in everyone's head.'

'I suppose,' Mel accepted half-heartedly.

Quaye scribbled furiously, and when he was done went over his notes with his interviewee, filling in gaps where needed. He saw the benefit of putting the time in with this one.

When they were finally done, Quaye thanked Mel for her time and for her honesty. Though he knew honesty was such a fluid concept. People's statements could never be considered as facts, however authentic they appeared. If not lies they could always be tainted with prejudice and misconception. The challenge was in working out to what extent. The key to this – the key to being a detective – was not in having a good judge of character, but in assuming that you *haven't*. First impressions of a person may be right ninety-five percent of the time, but it was the other five percent where the cases were cracked open. Quaye knew that.

He sat back in his chair and stared out of the window.

And he played his game.

What if everything he had just heard had been a lie? What would the liar have to gain? In the case of mousey Mel, maybe she had an axe to grind against HR Hodges. Maybe Ryan was a slack worker, and Tobias was a saint. And the conversation with HR never happened. That *could* be true.

Or, maybe Hodges was lying. Maybe she knew she was culpable in not following up the bullying accusation. And if there was no formal record of the conversation with Mel, she could deny it ever happened. Or, at least, claim she'd forgotten, which could never be disproven.

He knew who he was inclined to believe, but that wasn't enough. Fortunately, he also knew it should be easy to corroborate one story or the other. There were a thousand potential character witnesses in the building, and from previous experience, it would only take a handful to determine the truth with a sufficiently high degree of certainty.

Either way, it would have to wait until tomorrow. It was near knocking-off time, and the building was beginning to empty. Plus he wanted to catch Wilcox before she left.

On his way out he made the decision not to challenge Hodges. He knew what the response would be. The same as before: *My empire is so vast I couldn't possibly remember every trivial interaction with the minions*. He just smiled, bid her good evening, and promised he would be back.

When he'd left the building he called up Wilcox and arranged to meet her at a bar on the docks.

'Any luck with the parents?' was Quaye's first question as they sat outside with a light beer each.

'I got hold of the mum, but not the dad. She lives up near London, so it had to be a phone thing.'

'And did she have anything interesting to say?'

Wilcox pouted. 'Nothing you wouldn't expect. She always knew suicide was a possibility with Ryan's condition. She didn't expect it, but wasn't surprised either. If that makes sense. She blames herself, of course.'

'Why?'

'Ryan had a bad relationship with his dad. His parents ended up divorcing over it. After leaving home to return to Bristol, he was never in contact with his dad, and not much with his mum either.'

'Return to Bristol?'

'The family used to live here when Ryan was young. He came back when he got a job here.'

'Why didn't Ryan and his dad get on, do you know?'

'His mum said her husband was very authoritarian, controlling. In particular over Ryan's career path. She said he was always trying to squash his artistic pursuits.'

'Oh really?' Quaye raised his eyebrows in realisation. 'That's quite telling. Ditching his job, becoming a graffiti artist. Sending his dad his sketchbook before he died. That all stacks up with the suicide angle.'

'I agree. By then, his mum was getting a little upset. Thought that was as far as I should go over the phone.' Wilcox took a swig of her beer as Quaye took stock of the situation.

'Okay, let's recap where we are. Two very similar

deaths. Both look like suicide or accident. One, the second, is definitely a murder, by virtue of the spiked spray-can. The two deaths are connected, by more than just similarity. The second victim, Tobias Milner, was the team leader of the first, Ryan Penrose. And they were both painting the same name, Gioco. We know that neither of the victims is/was Gioco, because this artist was active *after* Penrose's death, and long before Milner had even picked up a can of paint, or was even aware of the graffiti scene, as best we know. So, whoever Gioco is, he is at least a key witness, if not the prime suspect. Let's go over what we know about the Milner case.'

Wilcox picked up whilst Quaye took a sip of his beer. 'Milner was targeted by femme fatal Gretchen, aka Cynthia, a high-class escort. She encouraged him into the scenario that saw his demise, we assume under the instruction of a client.'

'I have a confession to make there,' Quaye interjected sheepishly. 'She did speak at the airport.'

'What? Why didn't you tell me?'

'She was about to skip the country. I kind of offered her immunity if she gave me a lead. So it's way off the record.'

'And?'

'And it confirmed our thinking.' Quaye filled her in on the meeting, then focussed on the most salient point. 'The client called himself Philistine on his profile on the escort site. I gave the details to digital forensics, but there wasn't enough to go on.'

'But you got a physical description?'

'Yes. Late fifties, male, athletic, wavy silver hair.'

'Not much to go on there either,' Wilcox pointed out.

'Nope, standard human-shaped suspect as per usual. Never seem to get anyone with three legs or anything.'

Wilcox rolled her eyes in acknowledgement, then continued with her round up. 'As for forensics, we have one unidentified set of prints on the incriminating spray-can, besides Milner's.'

'But only his on the other cans found in his possession,' Quaye interjected.

'Right. And none on the crucial photo you half-inched from his apartment.' She flashed Quaye a mock disapproving look, which he returned with a grin.

'Today we learn, depending on who we believe, that Milner was a bully. And bullied Ryan.'

'So, what does that mean?' Wilcox questioned. 'We fancy Milner for Ryan's death?'

'Not directly. From what we know, Milner knew nothing of the graffiti scene, so it would have been a truly leftfield method of execution. Of course, whether he *contributed* to his death, given Ryan's condition, is a different matter.'

'Agreed,' Wilcox said. 'And that's about it for Milner,' she added in summary.

Quaye picked it up. 'Regarding Gioco, we don't have much to go on, other than your geographical profiling which puts the location of the artist in South Bristol, in the vicinity of the Milner incident.'

'Yes.'

'So, Ryan?' He prompted Wilcox. 'What do we know?'

'We don't know much about Ryan. Bipolar. Fell out with his dad over his art. Got bullied at work. Went AWOL. We

don't know what he did in the months between that and his
death, but I did a lot of reading today on the graffiti forums
and a few people seem to think he was an artist called
NDA.'

'NDA?'

'Yeah, an artist who was active during this period in
Bristol and not since. He gained notoriety in that short
period for doing forty-two large-scale pieces over thirty
consecutive nights, that all fitted together to form a single
image. Created quite a buzz in the community at the time.'

Wilcox pulled out her phone and after a few taps pointed
it in Quaye's direction. On it was a digital collage someone
had made of all the artworks pieced together. The result was
the image of a face. A girl's face. Quaye studied it for a
moment, but it didn't help.

'Did any of these wash away?' Quaye asked referring to
the paint used by Ryan for his last artwork.

'No. These were all traditionally permanent. Though
many don't exist anymore, of course.'

Quaye found himself wishing for a graffiti expert again.
Of which there were three options: PC Widdecombe, who
had not only left the force but changed his name; gallery
owner Alice, with whom he had imposed a communications
embargo for her own safety; and Lisa, who was a seventeen-
year-old schoolgirl. So, three options was somewhat of an
over an overstatement.

'Okay, let's wrap this up,' Quaye announced. 'I've taken
up enough of your time. Let's see what tomorrow brings.'
He finished the dregs of his beer.

'Need a lift?'

'Nah, I'm good. Do my best detective work when I'm walking.'

'I expect this thing solved by tomorrow then.'

'Count on it,' he said, and headed off towards home.

He couldn't have guessed he'd be right.

Forty-seven

It had been one of those heavy days, when, on arriving home, there was nothing left. Nothing left to give and nowhere left to go. When he felt like that, Quaye could almost imagine the frame of mind someone like Ryan must be in to do what he did, assuming it was of his own volition. He could *almost* imagine it. But not quite. His own inner darkness was different. Somehow he always believed he could be rid of it. Not that he was an optimist. He'd never describe himself as that. But he at least felt there was always something else he could try, even if it wasn't clear what it was yet.

Quaye stood on the terrace of his apartment, looking out over the city. At the edge, there was a low wall with slabs on top that followed the perimeter of the roof.

He stepped on top and looked down.

And felt nothing.

He edged sideways until it was no longer the terrace that was behind him but the sloping tiled roof of his apartment.

He stopped.

He let his weight sway forward a little. He was trying to feel what a jumper must feel, but he couldn't. Fear was an alien concept to him. He locked the heels of his shoes over the back edge of the slab, preventing his feet from shuffling forward should he need to re-address his balance. In any normal person this would initiate a surge of adrenaline through their veins; prompt their heart to race. But nothing came. Maybe then, he should just let himself fall. Teach his damned body a lesson.

He looked down and contemplated it. It's not that he had any compulsion to jump, but then, he didn't have a compulsion not to either.

He closed his eyes. Drifted inside himself. Into a kind of meditative state. Allowed some force beyond his control to decide which way his balance would tip. Just out of curiosity.

Then a noise startled him.

And he fell.

Backwards.

He ended up leaning on the tiled slope of the roof behind him, about thirty degrees from the vertical, the rays of the setting sun on his face, the warmth of the slate on his back.

It felt … nice.

It proved that although he may feel hollow, he wasn't a vacuum. He could still be warmed.

He smiled, almost chuckled at himself, and stayed there for a moment before he allowed himself to return entirely to reality, focussing his attention on the noise.

It was voices.

And laughter.

He returned to the safety of his terrace then up the small adjoining roof to his neighbour's.

When his eyes met Alice's, she answered his question before he had time to ask it.

'I'm here to advise on Silvia's art installation.'

Quaye nodded and realised he wasn't even going to ask.

He didn't care why she was here. He was just glad that she was. Alice began pouring wine into a third glass that was already sitting on the table. Quaye took that as an invitation and dropped down onto the neighbouring terrace.

He rested a hand on his neighbour's shoulder. 'Hi, Silvia. Hope you're well.'

'Perfectly fine son,' she replied with a smile.

Quaye turned to Alice. 'It's fortuitous I should bump into you,' he said with a hint of sarcasm. 'I have a question.'

'Oh really?'

'Yes. Do any of the artists you know use washable paint? For their illegitimate works, I mean.'

'I didn't know there was such a thing.'

'Neither did I. It's used for temporary markings, like on roads for sporting events and such. Why would an artist use this for graffiti, do you think?'

'Well, that's obvious isn't it?'

'Is it?'

Alice shook her head disappointedly. 'You're still thinking of graffiti artists as nothing more than vandals. The real artists among them – and there are many – actually appreciate art, in all its forms. So they might feel comfortable painting over the drab plastered end of a shop in Bedminster Parade, but they wouldn't paint over the gothic façade of a twelfth-century church. Where was this piece you're referring to?'

'Clifton Suspension Bridge.'

Alice flicked her eyebrows up as if to say, *I rest my case*. 'So your real question is, why was it so important for it to be there?'

'Oh, I can answer that one,' confirmed Quaye. 'That was where he was going to jump from.'

'Ah.' Alice paused for thought. 'Oh, that guy a few years ago?'

'Yes, do you know anything about it?'

'Nothing more than I read in the news at the time. And not even that now to be honest.'

At this point Silvia interjected. 'Is there a link between his suicide and the recent death?'

'Very much so. The two who died used to work at the same place. And they were painting the same name.'

'Gioco,' Silvia stated.

'Yes,' Quaye confirmed. 'There are theories on the forums that the first was actually an artist called NDA.' He turned back to Alice. 'Do you know anything about him?'

Alice shook her head. 'I'm not really down with the underground goings-on.'

Quaye whipped out the assembled picture of NDA's masterpiece and showed her.

'Ah yes,' she said with a vague nod. 'I recognise it. That's as much as I can offer, I'm afraid. I don't think I can shed any further light on it.'

Quaye pocketed his phone. He'd already resigned himself to this being the case.

'Oh, I have something to tell you,' Alice announced.

'Really?'

'Yes, it might not be important, but…'

'Go on,' encouraged Quaye.

'Well, you remember the very first question you ever asked me? Trying to identify the artist behind the graffiti on the bridge?'

Quaye nodded.

'Well,' Alice added. 'You weren't the first.'

Quaye sat up straight in his seat, suddenly alert. 'What?'

'I happened to be talking to Laurence – he looks after the shop on my days off – about the case. He said that a few months back a man came into the shop and asked if he knew who Gioco was.'

Quaye's mind ticked over rapidly for a few seconds. His eyes were wide when they locked onto Alice's. 'Fifties, smartly-dressed, silver hair?'

Alice nodded. 'You know who he is?'

'I wish I did. He's the key to all this.' It was the man who called himself Philistine, Quaye was sure. The man who hired Gretchen to play the role of Cynthia. 'I don't suppose your assistant knows the exact date he visited?'

Alice shook her head. 'We might be able to narrow it down based on the days Laurence was working, but he couldn't be sure how long ago it was. Sorry.'

'That's fine. It's a great help.' Quaye was well acquainted with the limitations of human memory – details deemed as irrelevances soon begin to fade. From the recent incident at Alice's gallery, he knew there was little CCTV in the area. And with a vague date, so long ago, trawling through footage from a wider area was unlikely to hit paydirt anytime soon. But it was worth a shot, and Wilcox seemed particularly adept at the process. Potentially more fruitful would be a tour of other galleries.

He sunk back into his chair, took in a deep breath and smiled softly at Alice.

'Did I do good?' she asked.

'You did,' he confirmed, and their eyes lingered in a non-verbal exchange for a moment.

He took a sip of his wine. More than a sip. It felt good. He was buoyed by a new lead. But that could all wait until tomorrow. Right now, he was experiencing a rare moment of calm, and nothing was going to interrupt it.

Then he made eye contact with Silvia, and something about the mischievous expression on her face made him think he could be wrong.

Silvia's mind was as sharp as a blade. More than that. It might be considered *special*. A fact intentionally few people were aware of besides Quaye. He wasn't one to believe in fate, but in the case of meeting her, he had to make an exception, else be plagued by paranoia – even more so than usual.

Quaye narrowed his eyes suspiciously at his neighbour.

'What is it?' he said, self-consciously. Silvia didn't respond immediately, and he turned to Alice. 'This is when you'll learn that it's Mrs Granby here who actually solves my cases.'

Finally, the old lady spoke. 'Well, I can't say much, other than there is most certainly a connection between Gioco and NDA.'

'Go on.'

'Literally a connection. Between the names. You should've put them together.'

Quaye looked confused.

'Literally,' Silvia reiterated.

He tried to do so, at first in his mind, then out loud. He

spoke them in turn. 'Gioco NDA.' He couldn't visualise them in any other way.

It was Alice who got there first. 'Gioc...onda? *Gioconda.*'

Quaye shrugged. 'And should that mean something to me?'

'It should if you were *educated*,' Silvia teased. 'Google it!'

He did. He whipped out his phone and typed it in. He scanned the snippet of the very first hit. And suddenly everything was clear.

Or at least *something* was.

Gioconda. The painting of the woman.

The woman with the enigmatic smile.

The Mona Lisa.

Now it was obvious who Gioco was.

The artist was a she, not a he. A girl. A *school*girl.

Lisa.

Gioconda was a team. A team of two. The painter and the subject. NDA the painter. Gioco the subject.

Then the subject became the painter.

The student became the master.

NDA's last painting, *Ryan's* last painting, was a message to Lisa. To pass on the baton.

'I have to...' Quaye couldn't finish his sentence. His mind was flooding with thoughts. He stood up with urgency, his chair scraping backwards across the tiles. 'I have to go.' He turned to Alice. 'I won't be long. Will you be here when I get back?'

'Maybe.' She smiled playfully.

'Good.'

Forty-eight

When the door opened, it was Lisa's dad.

'Is Lisa in?' Quaye asked.

'I'm afraid not.'

'Sorry to trouble you in the evening. I have a few questions your daughter may be able to help with.' His face remained emotionless.

'That's no problem. Come in, I'll give her a call. See how long she'll be.'

'Thanks.'

When Lisa's dad went through to the living room to find his phone, Quaye stayed in the kitchen. He assessed the room quickly. Nothing instantly jumped out as being obviously Lisa's. But by the sink there were two mugs: one empty, one with the dregs of milky tea. He knew from his last visit that Lisa's dad took his tea black. Quickly, he emptied the contents of the milky mug and concealed it: sucking in his stomach and slipping it down his waistband, under his shirt. It was a trick he'd devised at university for stealing pint glasses.

When Lisa's dad returned Quaye was casually gazing out of the kitchen window.

'She's in town with friends at the moment. Will be about an hour.'

'Oh, that's fine, don't make her rush. It can wait until tomorrow.'

'Are you sure?'

'Of course.' He gave another winning smile to cover a grimace. There was only so long he could hold his stomach in for. He bid Lisa's dad good evening and showed himself out.

Back at his car, Quaye carefully extracted the stolen item and placed it in an evidence bag. He dropped it off at the station on his way back, with a note asking for it to be fast-tracked for prints in the morning.

Then he went home.

It was less than an hour from the time he'd left his neighbour's terrace to the time he dropped back onto it. By now Alice and his neighbour were more than merry. They'd reached that giggling stage. And his presence only seemed to exacerbate the situation. Silvia had been playing Alice at Go, judging by the black and white stones scattered on the board between them.

Alice stopped. 'Saved the day?' she enquired.

Quaye looked at her. '*Finished* the day,' he responded, with a swiping hand-gesture to indicate as such. 'That's good enough for me.' He picked up the glass of wine that was still waiting for him and held it up to the other two. 'Cheers,' he saluted, and his companions reciprocated.

'I've learned all about you,' Alice declared.

'Oh, I seriously doubt that,' Quaye responded.

He didn't feel like sitting. He walked over to the edge of the terrace and looked out over the town, dusk falling over the rooftops. His mind was contemplative and detached, yet at the same time it was right here in the present. He half listened to the voices behind him. Silvia telling stories of her late husband. Of whirlwind romances and adventures in faraway places. Occasionally the stories would cease as a move was made on the board.

Eventually, Quaye returned to the table and just watched. Happy to be there without really being there. He got this sense at the back of his mind that things were coming to a conclusion. That answers were just around the corner. Maybe more than just answers. Resolutions.

But that was for tomorrow.

Tonight was for … nothing. Nothing, except maybe wine. And watching.

After a while, he stood.

'Sorry, I've not been much company this evening,' he announced. 'I shall leave you to your game.' And with that, he returned to his own rooftop, furnished himself with a stronger drink, and stood in the centre of his terrace looking up at the stars.

It was ten minutes before two feet landed softly behind him. He turned. The two looked at each other for a moment across a distance that was not far, yet far enough to be symbolic.

'So, you're *not* a vampire,' Quaye commented.

'Ha.' Alice smiled softly. 'I knew you wouldn't invite me. Knew you needed it to be my decision.' She took a step forward. 'It *is* my decision,' she confirmed.

Quaye nodded almost imperceptibly.

'I have Silvia's key. She said I could go back via hers.'

'She's a great lady.'

'She is,' Alice agreed, before allowing another moment

of silence to pass. 'And you trust her,' she continued. 'You don't trust people easily. But you trust *her*. Why?'

Quaye shrugged. 'Because she trusted me.' He paused. 'With a secret.'

Alice was far too well brought up to ask what the secret was, but added: 'And because you came knocking on her door, not the other way around?'

Quaye nodded.

'Because that's your rule,' she continued. 'Only trust people who have come into your life through your own action. If someone spontaneously appears in your world, you have to be suspicious. Right?'

'Right,' Quaye agreed, almost ashamedly. He knew she was eluding to him turning up in her shop one day, out of the blue, asking questions.

'But therein lies a paradox.' Alice took another step forward. 'By your rules, trust can only be a one-way thing.'

Quaye was well aware of this paradox.

By his rules.

In his world.

'I'm not asking anyone to trust me,' he said, eventually.

'But you have to let *somebody* in, right? Otherwise, you have no-one. So, at some point, someone has to take the plunge. Take a calculated risk.'

'It's not calculated if you don't know all the facts.'

'Like the fact that you're an Asset for Myco?'

Quaye recoiled a little.

'Just an educated guess,' Alice added. 'You traded places with Jessica, yeah?'

At this statement, Quaye exhaled a breath of

exasperation. He turned away, paced over to the edge of the terrace and looked out over the twinkling lights of the city.

Alice came and stood beside him.

'I've done bad things,' Quaye admitted.

'For the right reasons?' Alice asked genuinely.

Quaye paused on this question for a moment. 'I hope so,' he answered eventually. 'I really hope so.'

Alice allowed the silence to hold for a while as the gravity of the situation settled.

'Sometimes, hope has to be enough,' she said eventually, and she let the back of her hand brush against his.

She was right.

He knew she was right.

Forty-nine

Luke was aware of the building of course. Derelict, but somehow majestic. Such buildings held an eerie fascination. They had stories to tell – this one more than many. Luke didn't know exactly how long it had stood abandoned for, but it was at least as long as he'd been alive. As a canvas for intrepid artists over the years, it was nothing but ironic that the writing was very much on the wall for this old husk of a building. The bulldozers were assembling over the horizon, readying themselves to make way for a car park or an arena, or something. That was progress. But Luke, for one, would be sad to see it fall. Likewise, Lisa, it would appear.

The most recently added measures of security had been sufficient to keep out even the most daring of graffiti writers. Yet, somehow, Lisa had found a way in. Now he knew more about her, about her past, he wasn't surprised in the slightest.

Once inside the perimeter, they picked their way through overgrown terrain, mottled with the discarded detritus of an ageing industry. Then, at the base of the structure itself, they squeezed through corrugated metal sheets to gain access to the building. Lisa led him up crumbling concrete staircases until they were on the top floor.

As they emerged, Luke was taken aback. Every surface was covered in the marks of a spray paint can. From lines to letters to full-scale pieces. Luke studied it, walking slowly across the open space, turning, examining. One word – name – was more common than any other.

With its presence here, and with *their* presence, a fact that maybe should have been evident before was now undeniably vivid.

The ramifications of it, however, were anything but.

Lisa threw her arms out wide. 'Welcome to my lair,' she announced theatrically.

Lisa's form was silhouetted against the setting sun beaming through one of the glassless windows, framed by the vibrant letters of her nom de plume. Luke was left with no option but to state the obvious.

'You're Gioco.'

Lisa nodded. She walked over to a cabinet in the corner of the room, a relic of the building's former life. The rusted hinges of the doors creaked as she opened them.

Luke stepped forward to see the shelves lined with the tools and materials of an urban artist: paint, brushes, rags, straight-edges. It took him a moment to take it all in.

'You said you didn't know who Gioco was.'

Lisa turned to Luke.

'No, I said I didn't know anything about that incident. And I don't.' She looked at him with an apologetic expression. 'Besides, the whole point of a secret identity is, you know, not to tell anyone about it. Least of all an almost stranger you've just met in person for the first time.'

This made sense to Luke, but lots of things didn't.

'So why now? Why me?'

Lisa just offered a shrug.

Luke turned away frustrated and paced to the other side of the room before turning back pointedly.

'That's not good enough.'

Lisa was taken aback by his tone. 'What's wrong? Why are you angry?'

'I'm not angry, I'm–' He cut himself short. 'Look, two people wound up dead painting your name on a bridge. At its very best, this doesn't look good for you.'

'Shit, you don't think–' She couldn't even bear to say it. 'Whatever you're thinking. That's not what it's like.' She took two steps toward him, palms upturned as if symbolising her having nothing to hide.

'Then tell me, Lisa, what is it like? Every detail. If I know this,' – he pointed to the walls – 'then I have to know everything.'

She nodded solemnly. Then sat down crossed-legged on the dusty floor and patted the ground in front of her, beckoning Luke to sit. 'Okay, everything.'

It was hard for Lisa. For as long as she could recall, hiding something had been a way of life. More than that, a necessity of life. Maybe this time, the opposite was the case.

It was also hard for her because she'd had to be the strong one for so long now, she'd forgotten how to be vulnerable. Forgotten how to ask for help.

But she remembered.

'It only occurred to me later on,' she said, 'that on the last night of our project, Ryan hadn't really hurt his ankle on that jump. He'd planned it; faked it.'

'Why?'

'It was my rite of passage. He saw a latent desire in me to start writing, even before I knew myself. Properly, that is, not just boxes for his creations. So, he gave me the now-or-never moment. Baptism of fire.'

'And it worked?'

'Hell yeah, the rush was … indescribable. I think he saw what was coming. He couldn't have predicted what would happen with my dad, but that just brought it to a head. He knew our partnership wouldn't last forever; knew he felt more for me than I did for him. In *that* way. You know what I mean?'

Luke indicated that he did.

'So he wanted to set me on my path. His last piece, at the suspension bridge, was his parting gift. It was the name we had chosen for me, half in jest, way back when. It was in place of me getting the tattoo he'd designed for me. He said he'd rather I ink up the walls than my skin. So, he sketched loads and loads of examples of Gioco in his black book for me to study. I wasn't as gifted as he was, but I could copy, with practice.'

Luke looked confused. 'But that last night with Ryan, when you did your first proper graffiti, was the night your dad almost died right?'

'Right.'

'But I thought that was when you gave it all up, left the scene behind.'

Lisa shook her head. 'Ostensibly, yes. That was when I became a good girl again. Lisa Le Blanc. I dropped the anarchist image, hid all the non-legit stuff on my website, smartened up my act at school, and rebuilt a relationship with my dad. But I saved something for myself. I liked having that secret little side of me. If anything, it was more thrilling when it was so at odds with my everyday persona. So once a week or so, I'd sneak out my window at night, like I used to in the early days with Ryan, and bomb a couple of sites. It … I don't know … grounded me in an odd kind of way.' Lisa took a deep breath as her mind drifted back. Tears welled in her eyes. She looked through them at Luke. 'He's still with me, you know. When I'm up there in the dark of night. He's right beside me, looking out for me. Sometimes, when I'm struggling to find my form, I feel his hand guiding mine. I…' – her voice cracked – '…I didn't want him to go. I wish … I wish…' She shook her head and burst into tears, dropping her face into her hands.

Luke sat silent for a moment, giving her time to express her emotion. Then he shifted over to her side and put an arm around her shoulder. Lisa let her head fall to his chest, and they stayed there without words, until Lisa was able to talk again.

She straightened herself up, wiped away her tears with the back of her hand and shook her head. 'Fucking waste,' she exclaimed.

Luke nodded in agreement, and brought the discussion back to the present. 'So, how does this other guy fit in? The one who died at Parson Street?'

Lisa sniffed and composed herself. 'I genuinely have no idea. I have no idea who the guy is or why he wrote my name.'

'I guess he could have been a fan of your work,' Luke postulated.

'But … the death. It's way too coincidental.'

'Not if it was intentional. Last I heard was the police thought it was an accident, but if it was suicide, then he could have just been a copy-cat. Odd thing to copy, granted, but it would explain the coincidence.'

'I agree. It was intentional. But what if it wasn't a suicide.'

'Murder?'

'Maybe?'

'Then…' He paused to consider what this might mean. 'Then, someone's trying to send a message.'

'Exactly,' Lisa said. 'That's what I'm worried about.'

At this point, Lisa's phone rang, and it made them both jump. Lisa pulled out her phone to see a call from her dad. The Lisa of old would have declined it petulantly. But those behaviours had long since faded; washed away with the dye in her hair.

'Hi Dad,' she said in greeting as she answered the call. 'What's happening? … Really, why? … Oh, okay … Umm, well, I'm with friends … Yeah … Yeah … Not for a couple of hours, I guess … Okay, yes, see you later.'

Her voice had held strong, but the concern was etched on her face, her eyes falling to the floor in front of her.

'What's up?' Luke asked.

She raised her eyes to meet his. 'That cop again. He's at my house. Wants to speak to me.' She swallowed hard.

'Did your dad say what about?'

Lisa shook her head. 'I said I wouldn't be back for a while, so hopefully he won't hang around.'

'Lisa, you have to come clean,' Luke implored her. 'You

have to tell him everything you know.'

'What, about my *illegal* after-dark activities?'

'Well, you'll get in worse trouble if they find out afterwards. And, to be honest, I think they have bigger fish to fry right now. No offence.'

She pulled a sulky face like a child being told to eat her greens.

'Anyway, that's not the point,' Luke continued. 'The point is that I'm concerned about what all this means for you. It's a bit freaky. These deaths. Your name. Don't you think?'

She chose to ignore the question. 'You're concerned. Ah, how sweet,' she teased.

He narrowed his eyes and shook his head playfully, then stood up.

'Come on,' he said, reaching out a hand. 'Let's get out of here. I'll walk you home.'

Lisa took his hand, and he pulled her to her feet.

She didn't let go straight away.

Fifty

Raymond sat and watched patiently. He'd grown used to that. Waiting. But the context was much different now than it had been only weeks before. So much had changed. He thought back to his last day in that previous role, on that quest; sitting with the skater-boy, Spiky, who had provided the key to unlock the final door on Raymond's quest.

'The thing is,' Raymond had said to the boy, 'you know that's not true. And *I* know that's not true. But, as of now, *they* don't know that's not true.' He nodded to the lads larking about on the other side of the skatepark. 'Now, I'm more than happy for this to remain our little secret; for you to continue to tell your tall stories about the big bad thugs that beat you up; so long as you don't spin *me* any further lies.' He looked at Spiky, and with a much more direct tone of voice said, 'Tell me what you know about Gioco.'

Spiky looked at Raymond dubiously. 'What is it you think you know?' the boy challenged.

'I'll tell you what I know,' Raymond said confidently in return. 'I know that Gioco is a girl. A *school*girl.'

Spiky puffed the long fringe of hair from his face and glanced nervously over at the other kids. They were paying him no attention.

'Okay,' he sighed. 'Stays between us.'

'Between us,' Raymond agreed with a nod.

'It was about six months ago. There was this Gioco piece

on a wall near me. Poncey, y'know. All arty 'n' shit.' This
was the appraisal of an out-and-out tagger. 'I thought it had
been there long enough. So when I was out doing my thing,
I put my name over it. Next day, I came to look at it, and it
had been touched up.'

'Touched up?'

'Painted over to restore the original piece. Like my tag
was never there.'

'So I guess you weren't happy with that?'

'Well, it's not like I was gonna cry or anything. It's like
ten seconds work to put it back.'

'And you did?'

'Of course. Then a couple of days later it was gone
again.'

'So you did it again?'

'Well, that was the plan, of course. I went back that
night. But just as I was shaking up my can this figure
appeared.'

'The girl?'

'Yes.'

'And what did she look like?'

'I couldn't tell. She had a hoodie on and a scarf up round
her face. But I could tell it was a girl, from what she was
wearing. And when she spoke, of course.'

'What did she say?'

'She asked if I could stop painting over her pieces. But
it wasn't like an aggressive tone, or even an arrogant one. It
was like … well … genuine. Like … sad almost. And
then…' The boy hesitated.

'Then what?' urged Raymond.

'Then … she walked over to me. Placed a hand over my eyes so I wouldn't see her face when she pulled down her scarf. Then kissed me.'

'Kissed you?'

'On the cheek. Like a … thank you in advance, I guess.'

'And you fell for that?' Raymond shook his head in a combination of pity and mild disgust.

'Fell for what?'

'Never mind.' Raymond was old and jaded by years of such displays of passive-aggressive manipulation. Girls exploiting their sexuality at ever younger ages. It angered him. But he forced a smile. Couldn't risk embarrassing the kid. Couldn't lose him now. 'Carry on,' he urged.

'It was a few weeks later that I made the link.'

'Link?'

'I heard about this girl at school, couple of years above. She was into graffiti, had this blog about it. Just the arty farty legit stuff of course. But doesn't mean she doesn't walk on the dark side too.'

'And you think this girl at your school is Gioco?'

'Dunno, for sure, but reckon. I asked around about her. Found out she went off the rails a few years ago when her mum died. Felt a bit sorry for her. That's why I let the spat slide. So when the guys asked what happened with the feud, I just said a few guys had scared me off.'

Spiky shrugged sheepishly.

'Your secret is safe with me,' Raymond said. He slapped the sketchbook on his lap shut and put it in his bag.

'Why are you so keen to find out anyway?' the boy enquired.

Raymond stood up. 'Just a fan of her work,' he said and shuffled off, not even asking for the girl's name. He had enough information to find that out now.

He had all he needed.

After that meeting, he knew it was time.

He didn't go back to pick up his other possessions – the necessities of a homeless man. The sketchbook in his bag was all that he needed.

He didn't go back to the amphitheatre.

He didn't say goodbye to his friends on the street.

Instead, he headed out of town. First, to a patch of wasteland where he recovered a small box, buried under some rocks. Inside the box was a credit card, a phone and a single key. He put the items in his pockets and the empty box in his bag. Then he walked a bit further. He reached a quiet suburban lane flanked by grand detached properties. He pressed a button on the key he had recovered and the lights of a white Lexus SUV flashed twice.

He climbed into the car, took a moment to breathe in the leathery odour, then drove home.

That was three months ago.

Fifty-one

Quaye sat at his desk, sucking his teeth, knowing what he had to do but not quite prepared to do it. Something was gnawing away at the back of his mind.

When Wilcox arrived, she paused at the door; could tell something was up from looking at him.

'Got the results from the lab,' he said esoterically. At times like these he longed for the days of printed reports in manila folders. Dropping them on someone's desk made for much weightier an impact than forwarding an email.

'What results?'

'The fingerprints on the spray-can. I know whose they are.'

'Whose?'

'Lisa Peake's.'

'Lisa, the schoolgirl, Lisa?' she said with a degree of surprise.

Quaye nodded and filled her in on the events of the previous evening; of the assumed alter ego of the mild-mannered schoolgirl. Wilcox dumped herself in her chair, facing him. Quaye watched her doing the same as he had done, running this new fact through her mind, assimilating it with all the others. From her response, he knew she'd arrived at the same conclusion as he had. The only one there could be right now.

'Well, we have to pick her up,' she stated matter-of-factly.

'I guess we do,' he agreed. He shrugged off his hesitancy and stood up. 'Let's go.' There was nothing else to say.

When Lisa's dad answered the door, he didn't seem surprised to see them.

'Thanks for coming so soon,' he said with a tone of anxious urgency.

'You were expecting us?' Quaye asked.

'I called you guys about Lisa.'

'What about Lisa?'

'She's missing. She wasn't here when I got up this morning.' His voice was starting to crack.

Quaye and Wilcox exchanged questioning glances.

'Can we come in?'

Lisa's dad led them in off the doorstep. 'I've called her,' he said before they'd even assembled in the kitchen. 'But she's not answering. I know she was a bit of a tearaway a few years back. But she's not like that anymore. She wouldn't do this now.' The panic in his voice was evident.

Quaye figured Wilcox was on the same page as him: questioning Lisa's motives. Was she running? It couldn't possibly be because they were on to her. How would she know?

Whatever the truth, the first task was still the same.

Find her.

'Okay, Mr Peake, don't worry. My colleague here will take some details, whilst I get things moving. What's her mobile number?'

As soon as Quaye was in possession of Lisa's number he

stepped out of the house and started making calls. Lisa was seventeen, just on the cusp of someone the state still cared about. It allowed for greater resources to be mobilised in finding her. As well as ordering a trace on Lisa's phone, he spoke to his Super to approve more bodies should they be required. During the conversation, a marked cop car arrived, responding to the original call from Lisa's dad. Quaye raised a hand to hold back the two uniformed officers until he'd finished on the phone, and then filled them in on the developing situation.

Moments later Wilcox had been relieved of her post with the stricken father and was in the car with Quaye skidding out of the quiet residential cul de sac.

'Where we going?' she asked.

'Here,' he said as he threw Wilcox his phone, 'keep an eye on location updates. Last pings of her phone have her heading west out of Bristol at speed.'

'She's on a train,' Wilcox concluded, studying the route.

'Indeed. Back in your world,' Quaye said, alluding to Wilcox's substantive post at the Transport Police.

Wilcox looked up the train timetable on her own phone. 'Looks like she's on the Weston train. Next stop is Yatton in eight minutes.' Without being prompted, she made a call. 'Get the Weston train held at Yatton,' she said with firm authority. 'Get some officers there and don't let anyone off. Make sure the doors remain locked.' She then went on to explain who they were looking for and that she would get a photo sent over.

'Well done,' affirmed Quaye.

They hit traffic on the single carriageway roads out of

town. Quaye called into action the siren and the grill-lights
of his unmarked car. Other vehicles on the road began to
pull over haphazardly to let them pass.

They were about halfway to their destination when an
incoming call was received. Wilcox wasn't aware of it. It
wasn't destined for either of the devices in her hands. It was
to Quaye's *other* phone: on vibrate, in his pocket. His heart
leapt into his throat. He didn't want this now. He didn't
want it ever, but he was particularly indisposed at this
moment. He swore and slammed the steering wheel with the
palm of his hand.

Wilcox snapped around to face him. 'What's up?'

Quaye threw a glance at her, but didn't speak; just shook
his head at the uneasiness of the situation. Briefly, he
considered not answering the call, not wanting to reveal to
Wilcox his second phone: an obvious burner, a talisman of
wrongdoing. But the consequences of not answering could
be a lot worse.

He awkwardly dug the buzzing device out of his trouser
pocket, swerving between a learner driver and an oncoming
4x4 as he did so, and pushed it to his ear. He said nothing,
just listened.

He steered the car around a corner with his left hand and
suddenly found himself bearing down on the back of a slow-
moving vehicle, without enough room to pass. He hit the
brakes.

'Second,' he shouted to Wilcox nodding to the gear stick
as he dipped the clutch. Wilcox obliged, and Quaye
accelerated around the car in front as soon as a gap appeared
in the oncoming traffic.

A few seconds later he hung up the phone.

'Trouble?' Wilcox enquired.

'You could say that,' he replied. 'You're going to have to go it alone.'

'Really?'

'Yeah. This is your guys' jurisdiction anyway.' He pulled in sharply to a siding. 'You know what to do. Bring her back.'

'Will do,' she confirmed as she hopped out of the car and ran around to the driver's side. 'What about you?'

'I'll hitch a lift,' he said with a shrug. 'Good luck.'

Wilcox jumped in and sped off.

Quaye watched her go, briefly reflecting on what had just taken place; concluding he was probably being prematurely paranoid. Wilcox didn't know how his department functioned, wouldn't be aware of what operations might require a covert phone. With everything else going on, he was sure it would pass without comment.

It was time to move.

He started walking briskly back toward town, and brought up an app to request a pick-up from a nearby pseudo-cab. Five minutes later he was climbing into a random person's car and exchanging pleasantries. The driver was a hipster-styled guy in his late twenties. Big ginger beard and red trousers. Quaye showed the man his badge.

'Need to get to the centre sharpish. No heroics, but if you happen to breach the odd speed limit I'll be looking the other way.'

The man nodded with a nervous smile and set off. A

short way into their trip, he slowed up and took a right off the main road.

'Traffic looks bad up ahead,' he said, nodding to the sat nav suckered to the windscreen. 'Gonna cut across to the A38.'

Quaye acknowledged the update without comment, busy considering his predicament, gazing absently at the scenery moving past. The call had been from Myco, or a proxy thereof. His one-sided conversation hadn't told him much, only to be in the centre pronto – something big was going down, and they could use a friendly detective. Or, more accurately, a puppet detective.

This didn't fit the regular pattern. His call-ups were rare, and usually way out of town. These guys were insidious, but smart; didn't want to compromise a valuable asset, unless there was no other option.

This must be major. Whatever it was.

Quaye felt sick. At some point he was going to be put in a position where he had to make an impossible decision. He knew that. He knew it could be imminent. And he wasn't looking forward to it.

Moments later Quaye was still staring out of the window. Only now the scenery was no longer passing by. What had begun as slow progress had ceased to be progress of any kind, and it was becoming apparent that this wasn't going to change anytime soon; that this was more than everyday rush-hour traffic. Even on the outskirts of town, still several miles from the centre, the roads were gridlocked. Bristol's road network was notoriously only ever a hair's breadth from capacity. A minor incident on the wrong street and the whole thing could shut down.

This had now happened.

Quaye realised the hopelessness of his current mode of transport. He bid farewell to his driver, got out and started walking.

And then he stopped walking.

He was stuck between two worlds. Literally half-way between the required destinations of his two personas, unable to reach either.

He was standing on a road he'd only ever driven down before – until a few days ago. Two lanes, part of a one-way system that ran in a triangle at the south-western corner of Bristol. A pinch point for traffic filtering into the city from different directions. He was very familiar with it as a driver. But as a pedestrian, he saw it from a different perspective. And he'd never realised, until the other day, that this particular part of the road was actually a bridge over a railway line. The very bridge that Tobias Milner had fallen from. Only he was on the other side, looking at the track disappearing out of town.

Quaye felt rooted to the spot. Torn between his two worlds, as if waiting for a sign. And right on cue, Wilcox called.

He answered.

'She's not here,' Wilcox announced bluntly, regarding her search for Lisa.

'Not there?' Quaye repeated.

'We searched every carriage of the train. She wasn't on it. But her phone is still in the vicinity.'

Quaye processed this information.

Wilcox continued, 'So, either she dropped it or she wanted us to think she was going somewhere she wasn't.'

'Or … somebody else did?'

'True, or somebody else–' Wilcox stopped talking as she was interrupted by someone speaking to her. After a moment she returned to the conversation with Quaye.

'We found the phone,' she announced. 'In the trash. Carriage E.'

'Sounds deliberate then. Nice phone? Well used?'

'Reasonably. On both counts.'

'Like it's actually the property of a seventeen-year-old girl?'

'Yes.'

'Then it wasn't Lisa who put it there. She wouldn't have put her own phone in the bin. She'd have bought a cheap throw-away and put her SIM in it.'

'I guess, yes.'

'So something else is at play here.'

'I agree. So what now?' Wilcox asked.

It was a valid question.

Quaye fell silent for a moment as he allowed the facts of the case to ricochet through his mind.

Ryan Penrose: bipolar, graffiti artist, bullied out of his job by Tobias Milner.

Lisa Peake: collaborator, friend, fourteen at the time.

Ryan's last artwork: the name Lisa would go on to use as her own.

Ryan's death: suicide.

Milner's death: mimicked Ryan's, *not* suicide, foul play, died at the nozzle of a poisoned spray-can with Lisa's fingerprints on it.

Gretchen: escort, hired by the silver-haired Philistine, lured Milner to his end.

Those were the facts.

Then came the inevitable uncertainties.

Motive? Revenge for Ryan's death? Seemed plausible, which put Lisa squarely in the frame, even before her prints were found on the weapon. But on her own? It seemed unlikely she would have the skills or resources to rig the can. Was Philistine an accomplice? Who was he?

After running through all of this internally, he re-iterated it out loud for Wilcox, in the hope it would bring greater clarity.

'And now we have one more question,' Wilcox added. 'Why was Lisa's phone found in a trash can on the eight twenty-six to Weston-Super-Mare?'

'Indeed. Well, whatever, the imperative is still to find her. Hold on a tick.' Quaye took his phone away from his ear and studied it for a while. Then got back to Wilcox. 'So the tracking report for her phone had her at Temple Meads station at about three a.m. Then it went off-grid until this morning. What might a girl be doing hanging around in the vicinity of a train station at three a.m.?'

'What might a graffiti artist be doing sneaking around town in the middle of the night?' Wilcox elaborated with a note of sarcasm. 'Can't imagine.'

'Fair point,' Quaye conceded. Lisa as the graffiti artist was still an image that hadn't fully solidified in his mind yet. He spent a moment to allow it to bed in further, let it jar up against other recent memories.

Then it came to him. A connection was made. His first formal introduction to this world of graffiti, by Alice, was itself at Temple Meads station; looking up at that shell of a building imposing its presence over the platform.

'The sorting office,' he blurted. 'We need to get someone there.' His mind raced for a moment. 'I'll call you back,' he announced sharply, and jabbed at his phone.

As soon as he'd hung up he realised the implausibility of what he had just suggested about getting someone there. Who? With the majority of the city's emergency services dealing with a major incident in the city centre and the Transport Police ten miles down the line, he knew the response time to check out a Quaye-hunch was tending towards infinity.

It could only be him, but he had to be elsewhere.

The dichotomy of his roles was tangible – and irreconcilable. He could only be one. And he had to be it *now*.

From somewhere a sense of clarity descended upon him, and suddenly he no longer felt conflicted.

When he was looking for missing persons early in his career, people used to believe he had a special insight, an instinct, because of what had happened to him as a child – going missing himself. He never really felt he had. But an urge was driving him now that reminded him of those days. Even though Lisa was very probably involved in a murder, a sense of urgency was creeping over him, prickling at the back of his neck.

This was a girl. Young. Missing.

He thought of his first case. He thought of Beanie

MacAskill, the missing girl of two decades before – in the news again only that morning. Maybe this was what had rekindled his instincts.

Either way, it was clear. This was where his priorities lay.

Find the girl.

Quaye spun around. The traffic was at a standstill. Nothing was moving. Some vehicles were attempting audacious curb-mounting manoeuvres to turn around. Many of which had not fully succeeded, only serving to further block the flow of traffic. Some drivers had just resigned themselves to their fate and were standing around their cars catching some rays.

Nothing was going anywhere fast. Or indeed, at all.

How was someone standing over a railway line going to get to a train station? What possible method of locomotion could exist for such a journey? He berated himself silently and turned on his heels to look up the track. As if to punish his stupidity, he could see a train heading his way right now. The problem was that access to Parson Street station was from the next bridge down the line, which, although could be seen from his vantage point, was a brisk five-minute walk away, at least.

He started to run.

As fast as he could.

First, he dodged the haphazard array of cars and irate drivers to cross the road, then raced down the pavement on the other side. He could no longer see the train line, there were buildings in the way. He just kept running.

He came up against the side of a small white van,

stranded across his path, and refrained from Dukes-of-Hazzarding across its bonnet, opting instead for the safer strategy of circumnavigation. On the other side he was faced with an old lady, surrounded by a pack of small dogs, maypoling around her chaotically. Rather than attempt to hopscotch his way through the tangle of long leads, he gave the errant canines a wide berth by detouring into the stationary traffic and then back onto the pavement.

After ducking some half-erected scaffolding and hurdling some trash piled up against an overflowing dumpster, he was finally clear of obstacles.

He rounded the right-hand corner at the end of the road which took him onto the next bridge over the line. He could see the platform again, to his right. The train was already there facing him. The conductor had just gotten back on and locked the doors. By the time Quaye was at the top of the steps to the platform, the train had started to pull away.

The steps were narrow and seemed to slope awkwardly forward. He remembered them from last time. Half-way down they almost got him, but he managed to catch himself and remain on two feet.

At the bottom, he used the handrail to swing himself around and propel himself in the same direction as the train that was now coming up alongside him. He got as close to the train as he dared and held his badge up in hope that the driver would be able to see what it was.

'Stop the train!' he shouted.

The train was accelerating slowly enough that Quaye was able to keep pace with it for a short while, continuing to shout and frantically glance through the window. He thought he saw the driver catch his eye, but couldn't read the expression. Quaye was still at full pace when the platform ran out, and he crashed off the end onto the stony siding, the clattering of wheels on rails only inches from his flailing limbs.

He lay on the ground for a while, cursing himself, assessing his injuries, until he became aware of a high-pitched screeching.

Brakes.

The train was slowing down.

Quaye picked himself up, dusted himself off and jogged to the front carriage. By the time he was there, the door to the driver's cabin was open. The driver was a large black lady with dreads.

'Detective Quaye,' he puffed. 'I need to get to Temple Meads fast.'

'Well, hell, what a stroke of luck,' she exclaimed with a broad grin, then leaned down with an outstretched arm and plucked him off the ground as if he were a child. She got back to her position, and they were moving again.

'No stopping at Bedminster, if you don't mind,' he urged.

'No problem sonny,' she said. 'I don't very often get involved in police chases,' she beamed.

The train manager appeared in the cabin and was informed of the situation, which was then relayed to the passengers.

'Ladies and gentlemen, due to … exceptional circumstances … this service will not be stopping at Bedminster station. I repeat, this service will not be stopping at Bedminster station. We apologise for any inconvenience caused. Thank you.'

Seven minutes later, the train came to a halt at Temple Meads. The driver insisted on giving Quaye a hug, to which he had no choice but to oblige, before he thanked her and dropped down to the platform. He disappeared down the steps to the underground concourse and ran to the far end, popping out on Platform 15, bustling with morning commuters.

He looked up at the building before him. It had been gutted. No windows. No interior. Just walls and floors. He couldn't see anything, not that he would really expect to. But his gut told him he had to get inside.

He looked both ways briefly then leapt down onto the tracks, to gasps from onlookers, and quickly crossed the two lines in front of him. The next obstacle was a brick wall, which he scaled immediately. The ground the other side was lower, a drop of around a story and a half. He balanced on the wall, looking both ways to determine his next move. The building was at least twenty feet away at its closest point. Way too far to jump. A little further along from where he was standing were the remnants of a structure that had fitted between the wall he was on and the main building. Nothing was left but a metal framework, including the narrow apex of a roof that was just below the height he was standing. He ran along the wall to it.

On closer inspection, the apex didn't look too sturdy. Moreover, he knew he didn't have the skill to balance on it for any length of time; knew that if he tried to walk it, he wouldn't make it to the other side. The only option was to run, taking it in as few bounds as possible.

Although he couldn't divine the source, his sense of urgency was growing stronger, and he set off without further consideration. His first step was firm enough. By the third, nearing the middle, the beam dipped alarmingly under his weight. But he was committed now.

He held his balance for the next two steps, but then, still a good ten feet from the wall, his weight was starting to list to the left. His arms flailed, and it was all he could do to plant two more quick steps before leaping forward.

The window in the wall he was aiming for was not only glassless but frameless, leaving him smooth brickwork to grasp for. He reached out and got his fingers over the inside lip of the windowsill. His body came crashing into the wall below, his feet instinctively scrabbling for purchase. One found the metal A-frame of the missing roof below. It was enough to stop him falling, and with one concentrated effort, he propelled himself in through the window, tumbling onto the grimy floor the other side.

For the first time since he'd started running, he took a moment to ponder what he was doing as he lay on his back in the dust. Following a hunch certainly. Into what he wasn't sure. With the rest of the police force engaged in more pressing matters, he knew he couldn't justify back-up for a fool's errand like this. But protocol dictated he call-in his position, and for once he agreed with the protocol. He pulled out his phone and punched in a text to Wilcox, knowing he could convey meaning to her in far fewer words than calling dispatch. Then he sat up and took a look around.

He knew pretty much what to expect, from the view from the platform opposite. Nothing. The whole building had been stripped back to brick. Furnishings, fittings, electrics, partition walls – all removed. The floor was about the size of two tennis courts, and nothing impeded his view from one side to the other, besides regularly spaced support pillars. He knew anything he might find of interest would be further up, out of sight.

There were two sets of stairs, in opposite corners. He chose to head to the ones at the back. He was conscious that he'd already caused quite a commotion amongst people on the platform and didn't want to draw any more attention. So he kept low and got out of sight quickly. As he reached the quieter side of the building he grew aware of the noise his hard-soled shoes were making as his footsteps echoed about the empty space. He quickly dispensed with them and continued on his way, able to up his pace yet maintain his stealth.

The steps up to the next level were slick and grimy. He ascended them slowly, pausing before the top to see if he could make out any sounds before cautiously raising his head above floor level and doing a quick three-sixty. All clear. He made his way up and conducted a more thorough survey of his surroundings. Still nothing to report.

The story was the same for the next level, and self-doubt began to seep in. He questioned himself. What was he expecting to find exactly? He wasn't sure. But he was here now, and there was no point in turning back.

He took the next flight of steps. And as soon as he caught sight of what awaited on the next level, all doubt was washed away in an instant.

Graffiti. Lots of it.

He stepped up and spun around. Almost every surface was adorned with paint marks. The levels below had had some too, sporadically, but this was different. It was fresh and repetitive, almost manically so in places. And, as well as pictorial and abstract images, that same name, over and over. There was also an old cabinet, full of spray-cans and other artist supplies.

Without a doubt, this was Lisa's base. His hunch had been vindicated. If he found nothing else, this was a trip worthwhile.

He looked up the next flight of steps. The final flight. He could see sky above. This was the roof. If he was going to find anyone, this was where they were going to be.

He placed a shoeless foot on the first step and began his ascent.

Fifty-two

It was 4 a.m. Lisa couldn't sleep. The visit from the detective the previous evening was playing on her mind. She decided to take a trip onto the streets. Usually, she would head out earlier than this, as it would be light in a couple of hours. But as long as she was back before her dad expected her down for breakfast, it would be fine. She took her usual route, out of the window, across the garage roof, along the garden wall and down into the back alley.

She had an old BMX stashed behind a wall nearby so that she could get to and from town more quickly at night. She didn't have anything planned on this occasion – was just going to head to her cache of supplies and practice some shapes on the walls.

She made her way to the top floor – *her* floor – of the old postal sorting office, and set to work spray-painting the back wall. She had nothing particular in mind, just started with large sweeping arcs, enjoying the therapeutic motions.

It was a short while later when the voice came.

'Hi Lisa,' it said.

Lisa spun around and exhaled a short uncontrolled breath that came out as a stunted scream. She backed herself against the wall instinctively.

'Who the fuck are you?'

Her heart was racing and her breaths were fast. She could make out a figure but not much else. The only light was from a camping lamp that she'd hung up above where she was working. The figure stepped forward and allowed the dim light to pool upon him.

He was a man who looked to be in his late fifties, but distinguished looking and athletic in build. He was dressed in dark clothes including gloved hands that were down by his side. He raised his palms slowly to face Lisa in a calming gesture.

'First things first,' he said. 'Reach into your pocket, take out your mobile phone, and slide it over to me.'

'Why?'

'*Why*?' The man paused a moment before continuing. 'Because I asked nicely, didn't I? And because if you do as I ask, then everything will be fine.'

Lisa froze for a moment, in panicked deliberation. The man was standing between her and her only exit, and he was at least twice her size. Making a run for it was not an option. Not at this point anyway. She had no choice but to comply.

She plucked her phone out of her pocket, placed it on the ground and shoved it in the man's direction. It skittered across the cracked concrete and came to a stop under the man's foot. He stooped to pick it up without taking his eyes off Lisa. Then he took out the battery and the SIM, and put all the pieces in his inside pocket.

'Now, upstairs,' the man ordered with a sideways nod of his head.

Lisa didn't move immediately but realised she had no option; realised that not making this man agitated was her best and only strategy.

The man led the way to the stairwell, then stood such as

to block the route down, indicating for her to go on up. She knew this flight of steps would take her to the roof. She didn't go up there very often – there weren't many walls.

It was still half-light, but when she emerged she could make out what looked like a makeshift table and chairs.

'Go on,' urged the voice from behind.

As she got closer, she could make out the construction more clearly. An old drum barrel with a sheet of plywood made the table. On one side was a cracked plastic chair with metal legs, on the other a wooden crate.

'Best I could do from down there,' the man said. He was referring to the overgrown waste ground that lay at the bottom of the building.

Lisa half-turned to the man.

'Sit,' he said, gesturing to the crate, which was on the far side of the table. Once again it was clear he wanted to keep himself between Lisa and the way out.

She did as she was told. The man sat opposite.

From a bag that was already beside his chair, the man pulled out a bottle of red wine and two glasses. Lisa's mind was doing summersaults.

What the hell is going on?

He poured two glasses and encouraged her to join him in trying it. She took a swig, but only after he'd done so first. This seemed to please the man, who smiled at her unnervingly.

'You don't know who I am, do you?'

Lisa shook her head.

'My name is Raymond.' That was all he said for a moment, whilst he seemingly revelled in Lisa's confusion and unease. 'Raymond Penrose.' He held up his glass in salutation and took a large sip.

Lisa's mind worked quickly on the new knowledge. 'You're Ryan's dad?'

The man nodded.

Then he produced something else from his bag and placed it on the table. It was a black book. *Ryan's* black book. The one she had bought for him, all that time ago. She felt a sharp pang of sadness.

'You'll be familiar with this,' Raymond said as he began to turn the pages.

Lisa didn't respond, trying as hard as she could to not let tears well in her eyes – to show weakness. She watched the pages silently as the leaves fluttered past one-by-one. Images she had not seen for a long time. Images that were personal. That were hers and Ryan's. Eventually, she couldn't bear it any longer. She snapped her gaze up to her tormentor, who wore a subtle mischievous grin.

'What do you want from me?' she asked.

Raymond seemingly ignored the question. He stopped turning the pages and started to talk with a faraway detachment. 'A few months ago, I came back to Bristol with a single objective. I was determined. Driven by the resentment of a grieving parent. It's a powerful force. But my goal was much harder to achieve than I had anticipated. I was getting nowhere. It started to feel like a fool's errand. So I tried to put it behind me. Tried to be someone else. Not the business man, the divorcee, the father of a son who committed suicide. I wanted to leave that behind. And at the same time I wanted to understand how Ryan had lived those

last few months. So that's when I decided. To become
homeless. To live on the streets. Experience the existence
of a … nobody. But it didn't help. Didn't help to escape the
anger. It still raged inside me. Still felt like there was
unfinished business. And then I realised, that being on the
street was the perfect way to fulfil my original purpose. To
identify who *this* was.' He pointed to the name Gioco in the
book. 'Who *you* were.' He locked steely eyes with Lisa.

'But what do you *want* from me?' She repeated the
question more firmly this time.

And this time there came an answer. 'I want you to
know what you did,' he said calmly, not rising to the
hostility. 'You and that vile bully, Milner.'

At the mention of that name all trace of sadness and
anger in Lisa was cast aside to be replaced by different
emotions.

Horror.

Fear.

'Milner? You killed him.' It was obvious to her now.

Raymond cocked his head. 'Well, that's a matter of
perspective.'

Lisa frowned. 'How can it be a matter of perspective?'

'How can it *not* be? *Everything* is a matter of
perspective.' He took a sip of his wine and licked his lips
before placing the glass back on the table methodically. 'Let
me tell you the facts. Tobias Milner fell to his death due to
one of his spray-cans being spiked with anaesthetic. That
spray-can has your fingerprints on it, and came from the
same batch of cans as some of those in your cache
downstairs. Milner bullied a vulnerable young man, Ryan,

out of his job and towards his suicide. And you Lisa, are a former collaborator of Ryan's.' He prodded the sketchbook with his finger, open on a page resplendent with Ryan's drawings of her artist moniker, Gioco. '*More* than a collaborators.'

Raymond turned a few more pages in the book to reveal a picture Lisa hadn't seen before. It was a sketch of her. One Ryan must have completed from memory. Around her neck in the drawing was a subtle heart pendant. The sight of the delicate drawing made her gut wrench. Her own face looking back at her, like a message from Ryan's pencil tip, cast between worlds. A moist film glossed over her eyes which welled into a tear as she closed them shut.

Raymond continued, seemingly enjoying the torment he was inflicting. 'There will be only one conclusion to draw, when Ryan's former partner is found to have taken her own life; her body found at the base of this building clutching his sketchbook.' He raised a hand to cover his mouth, play acting that he'd let slip a big secret. 'Oops,' he said to accompany the action, then smiled wickedly.

As if she hadn't expected it before, with those words of confirmation the terrifying reality of her predicament came crashing down on her like an emotional landslide. Her stomach sank, her heart raced, the blood drained from her face. Her fight-or-flight response threatened to overwhelm her. It was all she could do to quell it to a mere twitch and darting eye, surveying for possible escape routes again, as if more might have magically appeared since the last time.

Raymond noticed her unrest. This was the point he finally decided to produce a weapon. He placed the gun calmly on the table in front of him.

'You won't get very far,' he said.

Lisa looked her captor in the eye. 'But my alternative is being pushed off this roof?'

The man didn't respond to this, just maintained his possessed half-smile.

'All this for an alibi?' Lisa probed, finding it hard to subdue her infuriation.

'An alibi? No, no, no. You are as deserving of your fate every bit as much as the man you killed.' He emphasised the last statement. The lie he was trying to convince the world of – maybe even himself too.

'What?' Lisa shook her head in a mixture of exasperation and fear. 'What is it you think I've done to be so deserving of this?'

It was time to turn the pages of the sketchbook once more, like it was a chronicle of Ryan's state of mind. Beyond the sketch of Lisa, the images got darker and more abstract. Images that could be interpreted as a fresh schism in the creator's mind. In his heart.

Lisa looked up at Ryan's father. 'You think I'm responsible,' she stated coldly. 'Think I'm culpable of Ryan's decline. Of his suicide.' She shook her head. In disgust this time. 'Jesus!' She was not accustomed to not being in control, and she was done with it. She stood up, tipping over the crate she'd been sitting on.

Her accuser went for the gun. Lay his hand on it, but didn't pick it up.

'You never did understand him.' She said this looking right into the man's eyes, and for the first time, the conceited smirk was gone.

'How would you know?' he blasted, anger edging into his voice.

'Because I was there for him. And I allowed him to be what he wanted to be, for the first time in his life.'

'You were there for him,' he repeated back. 'And then you were not. Then you were gone.' He tapped the pages of the sketchbook furiously.

'You don't know the first thing about…' She broke off and turned away. As she paced, frustration bubbled up inside her and came out as tears. She turned back and could no longer keep her voice below a shout. 'What did you want me to do? I was a fourteen-year-old schoolgirl, and he was a twenty-two-year-old bipolar graffiti artist. Did you want me to marry him? Be his carer? What?' She took confident strides back toward Raymond. 'My dad was sick. He almost died. I had other priorities. But you wouldn't know that because all you know is interpreted from this damned book.'

Lisa reached for the book and started flicking pages.

'Don't touch that,' Raymond insisted, grabbing the gun on the table with both hands and pointing it at her.

She didn't heed his warning, driven as she was by a wave of frustration that came rushing back after these years. Finally, she came to the page she knew would be there. Those dark pages hadn't tallied with her last impression of Ryan's state of mind. He'd left her a note, in their little hidey-hole. Near the end of his time. It didn't mention his intention. He would've known she'd try to find him, to stop him. But when she'd re-read it in retrospect the finalism was evident.

But, crucially, he wasn't sad. He'd found his peace. With her and with the world. And that's what she'd taken with her. Clearly, Ryan didn't feel his dad deserved the same comfort. And maybe if that man wasn't pointing a gun at her right now, Lisa could almost feel sorry for him.

'You know what you're doing? You're trying to find people to blame. Trying to deflect responsibility from the one person who really is culpable. Yourself.'

'What are you talking about? I tried to keep him away from the very thing that ultimately killed him. This!' He pointed to the artwork with the barrel of his gun. 'Living on the streets. Meeting girls like you. Getting stupid romantic ideas in his head.'

'You think graffiti killed him?' She threw her arms out agitatedly. She tried to find more words, but they wouldn't come. She turned away in frustration, walked to the very edge of the building and looked down. A dark sensation crept over her, and she twirled around quickly.

Raymond hadn't moved.

Lisa inhaled a few deep breaths and took a few steps back towards the man.

'There isn't a day that passes that I don't wish things could have been different.' She spoke in softer tones now. 'Wish that I could've been there and changed his mind. But do you know the one piece of comfort I take from his final act?' She paused and swallowed hard to keep her emotions in check, just for a moment more. 'It was *his* choice. For once in his life, he felt able to take control, without anyone telling him he had to be different. You knew his condition.

You knew how low his lows could be. How enduring and destructive. The truth is, this time, when he reached the top of that shitty roller-coaster he was on, he just didn't want to go down the other side. Not again. Not anymore.'

'The top? You think he was at the top? After you discarded him?'

'I *know* he was.' She couldn't stop crying now. Thinking of his face. But she didn't care. Not anymore. 'You think a few dark pictures in that book meant he had sunk into depression. But he hadn't. And you know how I know?' She wiped tears from her eyes with her sleeve. 'Because there *were* pictures. When he was in his dark place, there was nothing.' She sucked in a deep breath. Collected herself. 'Those pictures were just a product of everyday sadness. Like the rest of us feel from time-to-time. *Temporary* sadness, which he moved beyond. One thing I can assure you of, his last decision – however terrible it seems to us, however difficult to comprehend – was one made in happiness.' She took a step closer. 'You were just too blind to see.'

'See? See what? I wasn't there.' His voice was cracking now, too.

'You didn't need to be.' She picked up the book, turned it around and held it out at arm's length. It was showing the very last sketch Ryan ever made.

'What do you see?' Lisa challenged.

'A bridge. The bridge he jumped from.'

Lisa shook her head. She knew he could see the towers and the suspension cables that hung between them in a smooth arc. But he was missing what they were symbolising. The symmetrical curve of those cables, turning up at the ends.

Not just a bridge.

A smile.

And in the clouds, a face.

Eventually, the grieving father saw it.

'It's Ryan,' he said barely audibly, and then broke down into a sob.

Fifty-three

Lisa opened her eyes and took a sharp, paralysing intake of breath at the sight she was confronted with: a shear drop down the side of a building. Her head was fuzzy, disorientated. She couldn't remember the events that had led to her current predicament. Her instinct was to hold herself frozen like a statue, not dare to move even a muscle, should it cause her to topple forwards. After a while she summoned the courage to turn her head just a little. She could see blue. Splattered on her shoulder and arm. It triggered a foggy memory. There had been paint, spray paint.

Then nothing. Black.

It didn't make sense.

She turned her head a little more. Her arms and legs were bound to a chair. The front legs of the chair were on the low wall at the perimeter of the roof. The back legs were on the crate she had been sitting on before. The crate was slightly higher than the wall, such that the chair sloped forward, only a little but terrifyingly all the same.

Each of her limbs were bound to each of the chair's legs independently; cable ties around her ankles and thin rope around her wrists, with padding beneath each. Her movement was almost entirely restricted, limited to her head, hands and feet.

Then came the voice. A voice she was all too familiar

with.

'You're awake,' it said, with a jocular lilt.

Raymond was sat a little way along from where Lisa was tied up, his back against the wall of a higher part of the building. Lisa said nothing; the inevitability of her situation growing increasingly inescapable.

'Things had taken a little longer than anticipated,' Raymond announced. 'So I had to nip out to run some errands. Put your phone on a train out of here. Just in case anyone is looking for you now the sun's up.' He paused for a beat. 'I don't know, though, Lisa. Would anyone be looking for you? Does anyone care?'

Fuck you, Lisa thought, but she wasn't brave enough to say it out loud. As futile as it was to not provoke him now.

She started to contemplate death. Not everyone had the luxury of notice for their own demise. *How honoured*, she thought, being bitterly ironic within her own inner monologue. Strange things came to her mind. Little things. Loose ends that would never be tied. A blog post she'd never finish writing. A missed call she'd never return. That damn jar of pesto she kept forgetting to throw out, and would never get to tell her dad not to eat. It was always so hard to tell how long pesto had been open – it was already green.

She realised, at some level, these stupid little trivialities were bouncing around her mind to mask the other things, the big things – to keep her from breaking.

'Oh don't go quiet on me, Lisa,' that voice came again. 'Where's the fun in that?'

Lisa despised the fact that he was enjoying this, even

more than she despised the man himself.

'Let me help you out,' he continued. 'This is where you're supposed to ask: *why are you doing this*?' He changed his tone for this last phrase, to mimic Lisa asking the question. Then responded to himself. 'Well, I'm glad you asked.'

But then nothing more came.

Lisa found the man's silence even more unnerving than his speaking. She steeled herself to glance sideways at him. He was staring into the distance. His chipper veneer seemed to have faded.

After a while he began to speak with a solemn tone. 'People handle loss in different ways,' he said. 'Some people turn to religion, delude themselves that there is some supernatural decision maker, some reason for everything, some *meaning* to everything – even the bad things.' He nodded to himself contemplatively. 'I chose the other end of the scale – nihilism. Because if you're brave enough to accept the facts, the evidence, then that's where enlightenment is truly to be found. Where there is *no* meaning. It's the only position that makes sense. People are just not very good at accepting it. That's why so many go for the God option.' He snorted a little at the preposterousness of it. Then turned to Lisa with a grave expression. 'But you have to choose one path or the other, Lisa. If you want to stop the hurt. Everyone else, everyone in between, is just swilling about in the pain of their own everyday tragedies; not delusional enough to believe in a grander purpose for their suffering, or cynical enough to accept that there is none.' He stood and started to pace.

'You see, nothing really *matters*. That's the point.' He grew animated, throwing his arms in the air. 'Whatever we do. Anything we can possibly achieve doesn't even register on a universal scale. In space, our entire planet is not even a speck. In time, our entire history, not even a blip.' His tone transitioned from the philosophical to a kind of mild disgust. 'And all these worthy people trying to save the planet. Save it from what? It was here long before we were and it'll be here long after we're gone. The only reason people want to halt climate change is to save their beachfront holiday homes from slipping into the sea. The only reason people want to protect endangered species, is so they can continue chasing them around with telescopic lenses. All motivations are selfish in the end.' He sat down again and locked piercing eyes with Lisa. 'And none of it *matters*.' He emphasised the word like it was a ridiculous concept. 'If I push you off this building – it doesn't matter.'

Finally, Lisa chose to speak. 'Then why bother?' she said flatly.

'Fun?' her tormentor replied with a shrug, suggesting he wasn't really sure. 'Anyway,' he waved his hand dismissively, 'it's time for this to be over.' He stood, walked right up close to Lisa. 'I guess you're wondering how this works? Because, obviously, I can't push you off in the chair. That wouldn't really support the suicide angle. So, it's a two stage thing. First, I'll snip the ties around your ankles.' He produced a small pair of wire cutters from his pocket. 'I've used padding here so as not to leave any marks on your skin that might rouse the suspicions a pathologist.' The man seemed to take pride in explaining the details –

proving he'd thought of everything. Like he was his own omnipotent being in his solitary nihilistic universe. 'Now,' he continued, 'you'll notice your arms are tied with rope. Importantly though, the knots I've used are Highwayman's Hitches. Do you know what one of those is?' he asked condescendingly. 'Did they teach you that one at Girl Guides? Hmm?'

Lisa didn't dignify the question with a response.

Raymond leaned in toward Lisa – putting his ear near her lips. Not too near – he wasn't stupid – but near enough for her to be able to smell his breath. It smelt like evil.

Raymond continued with his murder tutorial. 'The Highwayman's Hitch is a quick-release knot; a tug on the loose end and it will untie. And I've anchored these ends to the floor behind you. So when I push the chair, they will come undone, leaving you to fall freely to the ground. And the chair itself is tethered so it won't follow you all the way down.' He made a diving gesture with his hand. 'And that's it,' he concluded. 'All Clear?'

It was clear. Terrifyingly clear. And however much Lisa hated to admit it, he was right. She was one of those people in the middle. She desperately wished she could suddenly believe in a God or in the pointlessness of existence – one or the other – just to make these last few moments bearable. But she couldn't. Neither seemed remotely intuitive.

'Oh, I almost forgot,' Raymond announced. 'The drawing.' He pulled a sheet of paper from his inside pocket and held it up for Lisa to see. It was Ryan's sketch of her. 'To seal the connection,' the man added.

He folded the drawing and placed it between Lisa's

fingers. She gripped it. Strangely, she found some comfort in it.

Then she watched as Raymond took his wire cutters and snipped away the cable ties around her ankles. This was it. She knew she could delay the process, stall for time, but to what end? To prolong the suffering? How could a few more moments make a difference?

But then, that's how life is programmed. When the gazelle is finally felled, a pack of cheetahs at its throat, it still thrashes. There is no way out, but it still tries; still grasps for those last few seconds of existence. Waiting for a miracle maybe? A miracle to repel the impending nihilism?

Lisa wasn't dead yet. The jaws were at her throat, but she was still breathing. And whilst she was breathing she was fighting. Meaning or no meaning. Whether it mattered in the grand scheme of things or not.

'What about the tattoo?' she asked esoterically.

'What?'

'The tattoo Ryan designed for me. Don't you want to see it in the flesh? His last work of art ever to be rendered on a surface?'

'You're lying. You're not even old enough to get a tattoo.'

'You think that would stop me?'

'So, where is it?'

'That would be telling.' Lisa raised a mischievous eyebrow. 'It's, umm, fairly intimate.'

'Hey, I'm not a pervert you stupid little girl.'

The suggestion seemed to anger him a little. Lisa had

obviously struck a seam of morality in what otherwise appeared to be an endless pit of malevolence.

'So what if you are a pervert?' She threw his existential reasoning back at him. 'It doesn't *matter*.'

He shook his head, took a couple of paces away and then back again. 'I know what you're up to,' he accused. 'I'm not an idiot.' He placed his hands on the back of the chair. 'Okay, stop talking. This is happening.'

For what it was worth, Lisa had earned a few more seconds of life. The miracle hadn't come. She felt pressure on her back as the man behind her started to push. She wanted to scream, to yell out *stop*, but nothing would come. Nothing would *help*.

And then, there was another voice.

Further away.

Loud.

'Mr. Widdecombe, I presume,' it said. It came from behind them.

Raymond whirled around and whipped the gun out of his waistband.

Fifty-four

When Quaye had emerged from the stairwell onto the rooftop he could tell he was almost too late. Maybe he *was* too late. He was too far away to intervene. The situation was too volatile to rush in. He had to act quickly to prevent what was about to occur. His only option in the first instance was to distract the perpetrator – and then work it out from there.

'Who are you?' Raymond snarled, making several aggressive steps toward Quaye with his gun outstretched.

'DI Quaye,' he said. 'And you are Raymond Penrose. Formally PC Widdecombe, yes?' Quaye didn't have a gun. The only weapon he could wield was knowledge. It was the only way he could assert his authority, such as it was. 'You used to hunt down the graffiti artists, way back when. Until you got caught up in something bigger and had to take witness protection.'

'I don't care what you *know*,' Raymond hissed. 'You've made a mistake in being here.'

'Why's that?'

Quaye tried to take a step forward but his adversary shut it down.

'Don't move another inch,' he said with dark menace, shaking the tip of his gun agitatedly.

Quaye held firm. Neither man spoke for a moment, weighing up the options, playing out the scenarios. Usually, in such a situation, Quaye could draw confidence from the fact that most people wielding a gun don't actually want to use it, don't want to kill anyone, especially a cop. And with that comes a narrow window of opportunity; to offer another way out, an alternative path.

But on summing up the moving pieces of this puzzle, Quaye realised there was no alternative path. There was only one route for the aggressor to take.

Kill the cop.

Leave the gun.

A second death to pin on the girl.

That was the only way out.

And Quaye could tell the man in front of him had just come to the same conclusion.

The gunman's eyes narrowed. The arm straightened. The trigger finger flexed.

The bullet was about to fire.

But the crash came just in time.

Raymond spun around to see Lisa on her back on the floor, still bound to her chair. He swore loudly and returned to face Quaye who was now charging him. But the distance was too great. The gun fired. The bullet pierced Quaye's chest. He hit the deck like a sack of bones. He wasn't going to move again.

In those moments, when her captor had been distracted by the policeman, Lisa realised that now her legs were free she could use her toes to tip herself over backwards. She was several feet above the ground and it was going to hurt like hell, but she had to override her instincts and go through with it. It was her only option. She pushed down with her toes, and when she began to tip over, she rolled her head forward as much as she could to minimise its impact with the hard surface. When the impact came there was no pain. Adrenaline had flushed it from her system. She knew what she had to do next. She used her weight and her free legs to roll the chair over. The ends of the quick-release knots were anchored to the ground. As she moved, one came taut enough to pop open. She heard a gunshot. Then caught sight of the man who had fired it come running back towards her. She jumped to her feet, her other arm coming free as she did so. Just as her tormenter was bearing down on her she swung the chair around, threw it at him, and ran. Not towards the exit. She knew she'd never make it that far. Nearby, on the roof, was a small outbuilding, one storey high. She launched herself at it, scrabbled for purchase, found the top and hauled herself up. Her pursuer gave chase. Didn't shoot. He needed her dead in a different way than by gunshot. He didn't have the agility or skill to climb the wall unaided. Lisa knew it wouldn't hold him back for long. He had apparatus to assist his ascent. But she had the territorial upper hand for a moment at least. Like a fort on a hilltop. She ducked out of sight and took a breath. She had only seconds to make a call. She could stay and wait, try to fend off her pursuer's assault with a boot to the head; or she could take the offensive.

The decision was an easy one. She'd played the victim too long. Both on this roof and in life. She refused to play the victim anymore.

She stood. Her aggressor was dragging the chair he'd been sitting on earlier in the direction of her castle. But when he saw her, he stopped and locked eyes with her. That next moment felt like an eternity. Until the man raised his gun slowly.

This was it.

Lisa took several step backs, readied herself, then ran. Fast. At the edge of her platform she launched herself high into the air. From this height hitting the deck would hurt. She needed flesh to break her fall. It did. Her target didn't have time to avoid her approach. She came crashing down on top of him, her full weight on his chest. It winded him enough that his grip on the gun loosened. Lisa prised it from his fingers, then brought its hilt smashing into the side of his face with a sickening crack and spewing of blood. She did it once more. Then she stood up and kicked him a dozen times in the abdomen. She couldn't bring herself to pull the trigger but she wasn't going to take her eye off him. She would kill him if she had too. She would have liked to have secured him – tied him up with the rope that had recently bound her – but there was no time.

A man was dying.

She rushed to the policeman, lying in a large pool of blood. Last time she had been a first responder she'd been unprepared. This time she was not. She'd taken every first aid course going after the incident with her dad. Unfortunately, gunshot wounds had rarely featured on the syllabus, but she figured the principles would be the same.

She assessed the patient quickly. There was a faint pulse. There was life in his eyes, but only just.

'Stay with me,' she urged. 'It's going to be okay.' She sounded confident of this fact, though she wasn't so sure.

The bullet had entered just above the heart and below the shoulder. There was no way of securing a tourniquet.

'I'm going to have to apply some pressure,' she informed. 'It's gonna hurt.'

Without hesitation, she put her right knee against the entry wound and put all her weight onto it. The policeman rasped. But rasping was good. It was a sign of life. Lisa couldn't tell whether there was also an exit wound, but pinning his shoulder to the floor would hopefully close that one off too if needed.

Lisa had positioned herself such that she was facing her assailant, who was still lying motionless where she'd left him. She had used her knee to apply the pressure because she knew she could hold it for longer, but also to keep her hands free for what she had to do next. She patted down her patient's pockets, found a phone and dialled emergency services. It rang.

It rang.

It kept ringing.

'Jesus, 999 aren't picking up!' she exclaimed in exasperation. 'What the fuck is going on?'

She needed to call someone. *Anyone*. But the phone was locked with a PIN.

'What's the PIN?' she ask the detective with shrill urgency.

The detective's lower lip moved almost imperceptibly, but that was clearly as much as he could manage. His eyes widened with the pain of the effort, then fell shut as he gave up.

'No, no, no,' Lisa shouted. 'Open your eyes.'

His eyelids raised heavily, reluctantly.

'Okay, okay, we got this. You can blink. Blink to tell me the right number, when I say it, okay? One at a time.' She started to count and held her fingers up to reinforce the digits. 'One … two … three … four–'

There was a slow blink. She couldn't tell, was it three or four?

'Shit, which one. Four?' No movement. 'Three.' Slow blink.

She counted slower next time. And repeated the process until she had four digits. She hammered the number into the device. It unlocked. The last call in the register was from a PC Wilcox. That sounded good. She called it back. It was answered quickly.

'Quaye? Where are you?' came the voice at the other end.

'He's hurt badly. He's been shot.'

'Who's this?' Wilcox asked.

'Lisa.'

'Lisa? Okay, where are you?'

'On the roof of the old sorting office, at Temple Meads station. I need someone here quick.' Her voice was starting to crack. 'And 999 aren't answering.'

'I know. There's a major incident in town. All emergency responders are attending that. But Lisa, try to stay calm and hang tight. I'm with the Transport Police and we are on our way back now. We're on the train. We'll be twenty minutes.'

'Twenty minutes is too long.' Lisa was holding back a sob now, as she felt the life of the man beneath her ebbing away. 'And I don't need police. I need a *fucking ambulance.*'

'Okay, okay–'

Lisa hung up; looked into the policemen's eyes. She took a deep breath but couldn't stop the tears from tumbling over her cheeks. He was still here, but for how much longer? His eyes flickered occasionally. She watched. Helpless. But then she thought. Was it a flicker? Or was it a movement? A conscious movement. Was there a pattern? Each movement of the eyes seemed to be down and to the right, like the man was trying to communicate something. She looked down, but didn't know what she was looking for. She saw nothing to begin with, but then just made out the slight movement of the detective's index finger beside his leg. What was the significance?

It dawned on her. The pocket.

Lisa reached inside and found another phone. A cheaper one. It was locked with a PIN too. She tried the same one as before. It worked. She quickly analysed the phone. There were no contacts in its address book, and only one incoming call in the register.

She called it back. What else could she do?

A man answered.

She talked.

Fifty-five

When Wilcox arrived she found a girl hugging her knees, back up against a wall. There was blue paint up her arm and on the side of her face. Her hands and lower legs were covered in blood. There was no-one else; only the signs of where someone might have been: a large pool of blood near the girl and a smaller one further away.

'Lisa?' Wilcox asked as she approached the girl cautiously, flanked by four other officers. A nod was the only response as the girl stared at the stained ground in front of her. 'Where's DI Quaye, Lisa?'

'They took him,' Lisa said almost inaudibly.

'Who did?'

'The men.'

'What men?'

Lisa just shrugged. 'They took him,' she repeated. 'And the other one.'

'Other one?'

Lisa nodded. 'The bad man.'

The girl unfolded the blood-stained piece of paper she was clutching in her hand and studied it for a moment, and then started to cry.

She didn't say anymore.

Fifty-six

When Quaye awoke, he was in a bed, but he wasn't in a hospital. The ceiling above him was high and gloomy. The walls of his room were fashioned from semi-opaque plastic sheets hanging from a metal frame. Through the sheets he could see little other than the impression of a dark cavernous space. A warehouse maybe. He took a moment to reflect on his own condition. He didn't feel anything other than numbness. And he couldn't move. A machine beside him chirped softly – beating out the rhythm of his own existence. He lay awake for a long while.

Nothing happened.

He drifted in and out of sleep. Fractured dreams invaded his mind.

After a period of time Quaye could not gauge, he awoke to the sounds of footsteps echoing. Distantly at first, then growing louder. A figure appeared, silhouetted behind the sheeting. The soft chirping accelerated a little. The figure emerged, dressed in white, and approached his bed; its face covered by a mask. In his hazy state Quaye could not determine conclusively whether the person was a man or a woman, but he thought it was woman. Was she familiar, or was his mind playing tricks on him? Either way, it didn't matter. She raised a syringe, flicked it with an index finger and depressed the plunger a little, sending a jet of liquid into the air. Then the contents of the syringe was administered

to the back of Quaye's hand.
    Everything faded to black.

Fifty-seven

The next time Quaye awoke he was in a hospital. A real hospital. This time he was more lucid. There was only one person at his side. A girl with blonde hair. He did his best to smile at her and she beamed the most magnificent smile back, its warmth almost tangible as it fell upon him. He looked into the girl's eyes. Eyes he would never forget. Eyes that had kept him in this world when he teetered so near the precipice.

He was weak, but nothing was going to stop him moving his hand, just enough to rest his finger-tips on the girl's arm.

'Thank you,' he said breathlessly.

'No, thank *you*, you silly old fool,' Lisa replied light-heartedly. 'You know, you could have gotten yourself killed,' she added with a strong note of sarcasm.

Quaye laughed inside.

He did not know how he had made it to the hospital, though later he would learn that his body had been found in an alleyway, two days after he had gone missing. He figured the authorities would know by now that his saviours had been summoned by Lisa, on a phone found in his own pocket. He would have some explaining to do. But at least he was alive to do the explaining.

Before that time came, he was happy just to sleep. Just to *be*.

Lisa stood to leave. 'There are some other people who

will be pleased to know you're awake,' she said. 'I told them I'd give them a call when you came round.'

She smiled that glowing smile and Quaye bathed in its recuperating qualities. But then the girl's soft features hardened as a stony expression swept across her face. There was a reason Lisa had sat sentinel by his bed. There was something she had to tell him. Before he spoke to anyone else. So that he would know.

Lisa looked at Quaye with intense eyes, then spoke. 'The man on the phone told me not to say anything,' she said. 'So I didn't.' She paused for a moment. She looked conflicted. 'I thought that was best.'

Quaye nodded.

Good girl, he thought. *Good girl.*

He had survived. So had his deceit.

Now to make it count.

Learn More

www.pauljnewell.com

author@pauljnewell.com

@pajone

facebook.com/pajone